DARK
BLUE
RISING

TERI TERRY

DARK BLUE RISING

Book 1 of The Circle Trilogy

Hodder
Children's
Books

HODDER CHILDREN'S BOOKS

First published in Great Britain in 2020 by Hodder & Stoughton

1 3 5 7 9 10 8 6 4 2

Text copyright © Teri Terry, 2020

The moral rights of the author have been asserted.

A CIP catalogue record for this book
is available from the British Library.

ISBN 978 1 444 95710 5

Typeset in Bembo by Initial Typesetting Services, Edinburgh
Printed and bound in Great Britain by Clays Ltd, Elcograf S.p.A

The paper and board used in this book
are made from wood from responsible sources.

Hodder Children's Books
An imprint of
Hachette Children's Group
Part of Hodder & Stoughton
Carmelite House
50 Victoria Embankment
London, EC4Y 0DZ

An Hachette UK Company
www.hachette.co.uk

www.hachettechildrens.co.uk

Make no mistake: what faces us all is an unprecedented emergency.
Our actions must be judged within this context.

Seraphina Rose
Chief Scientific Advisor
The Circle

It is human to doubt; it is human to hope.
Justification is all too easy if you lose one or the other.

Cassandra Penn
Elder and Seer
The Circle

1

I breathe the sea.

Eyes closed, I draw air in oh-so-slowly until the wave I follow reaches its peak on the beach. As the water falls back I relax, release the air I was holding inside, drawing it out until the next wave begins its return. In a ritual of controlled breathing and rising tide the rhythm is so perfect I almost lose connection with my body and float away, asleep, on the water instead.

But part of me is still watchful, still aware. All I hear is the music of the sea, but is there a small change in the way the air moves on my skin, some disturbance nearby?

I open my eyes. Warm brown ones are looking back into mine from above. I smile, stretch, sit up.

'I thought you were asleep,' Jago says.

'I was, nearly. And I thought you couldn't come today?'

'Made an excuse and got away early.'

'To see me?'

He grins and those dimples in his cheeks appear like magic. 'Yes, to see you.'

He sits next to me on the damp sand, close, but not quite touching my bare arm with his. 'I couldn't wait to tell you something.'

'What's that?'

'You wouldn't tell me, but I found out your name. I saw you

1

leaving the library yesterday; the librarian said your name is Tabitha.'

Guilt stirs inside me. The only library I can get to from here is the mobile one in Boscastle, and it's only there for a short time every four weeks; I couldn't sit in it and read. To let me borrow books she said she had to know my name, and I wanted to read them so much that I told her the true one even though I knew I shouldn't. And now Jago knows it, too.

'That *is* your name, isn't it? Tabitha?'

'She said she wouldn't tell, not so long as I brought the books back when I should.'

'It's not her fault. I kind of tricked her, made her think I already knew what it was, and then she said it.'

'Oh.' I raise my eyes to his, trying to think what I should say, but there is nothing I can do when looking in those eyes but tell the truth. 'Yes, I'm Tabitha – Tabby, really. But don't tell anyone.'

His eyes crinkle in the corners. 'OK, Tabby Cat, how about this: I won't tell a soul if you give me your number?'

My number? I'm confused for a moment, then think I get what he means. 'Do you mean, my phone number? I haven't got one.'

'You don't have a mobile?' His eyes open wider with surprise.

'No.'

'Landline, then.'

I shake my head.

'Is that no, you won't tell me, or no, you haven't got one?'

'Haven't got one.'

He looks both amazed and doubtful, like not having any sort

of phone to be traced and reached by is so unbelievable that I must be lying.

'It's the truth,' I say. 'We don't have anything like that. But I can meet you here again tomorrow afternoon?'

'What if something happens and you can't come? Take my number just in case.'

I shake my head, unable to think of anything that could happen that would stop me from being here tomorrow. This whole feeling of having a friend of my own, someone who smiles to see me, talks to me and wants to meet up every day, is all so new; I couldn't stay away. But still he insists. When I tell him I don't have anything to write it down on he says the numbers over and over again until I can repeat them back without fault. Will I ever call him? Would I dare?

The sun is pulling further across the sky. Cate will be back from her second cleaning job soon, and if I'm not there when she gets back and she asks where I've been and what I've been doing – well. What would I say? Talking to an outsider like this breaks so many rules. If she found out, that'd be the end of it.

'I have to go,' I say, and reach across the sand for my trainers. But when I look up again his smile is gone, his eyes focused beyond me. There are footsteps, voices. Laughter.

I turn and there are four of them walking towards us – three boys and a girl – gawping like they've found something unpleasant washed up by the tide. Another two boys hang back behind them.

We scramble to our feet.

'Honestly, Jago. How could you sink that low?' the girl says.

Hard eyes flash with anger, disdain, and something else. Is she jealous?

'This is none of your business,' Jago says.

'Who is she?' one of the boys says, looking at me up and down in a way I don't like.

'Nobody,' another of them answers. 'She's from one of those caravans parked up the hill. They'll be asked to move on soon.'

'They should get the push, shouldn't they? Dad says property values will fall if they stay.'

They laugh. Jago doesn't stand up for me; he says nothing. Maybe he didn't know that's where I live, and now that he does, he'll disappear. I thought Jago was my friend, that I could trust him, but townies are all the same, aren't they? Even though he seemed different, he's still one of them.

Cate's voice is in my head. *Don't react to stupidity, Tabby. Ignore them.* And I listen for once, turn, start walking away – across the sand towards the steep, stone steps that wind up the cliff to the coastal path.

Footsteps follow behind me.

'She's kind of cute.'

'Don't get too close, you might catch something.'

'We could give her a good wash first, maybe?'

There's an edge to their voices, beyond their mocking. Where is Jago? Why didn't he say anything else to them, or come with me now? Even as I wonder these things there is certainty in what I must do:

Run.

When I reach the steps I try to ignore the sharp pain of jagged rock on bare feet, but it drives home my mistake. I'm not a good

4

runner; I should have turned to the sea instead. They'd not have followed and, even if they did, could never swim as fast as me.

I get to the top and dash for the path to the road.

Another step, two, three – and then one of them grabs my arm from behind, yanks me around to face him.

'Let me go!' I say, and add a bunch of words Cate wouldn't like to hear, wouldn't like to think I even know, but he twists my arm around my back.

'Such filth. We need to wash out your mouth,' one of the other boys says, having caught up now, along with the rest of them, except for Jago and the two that were behind. I'm struggling and then one of them has a bottle in his hand and twists my head back, and now I'm coughing, choking, on something vile – some spirit – while they laugh.

I twist and elbow the one holding me, hard, in the stomach. He falls to the ground.

The girl grabs my hair. Furious now, I swing out with my fist, catch her full on the side of her face, and push her back into the other two.

Again: *Run*. Not even feeling my feet any more with adrenalin and fear, as fast as I can up to the end of the path to the road, and then –

Headlights—

Brakes, screaming—

I'm hit hard, and fly through the air.

2

'She came out of nowhere. It's not my fault.' A disembodied voice penetrates the blackness.

Hands are touching me and I open my eyes, try to struggle, but with movement comes *pain* like I've never felt before, and now I'm crying.

'Keep still,' a woman says, and I try to focus on her, her voice, instead of the pain. 'It's all right, we're paramedics. We'll look after you. What's your name?'

'Tabby,' I manage to say, gasping it out before remembering I shouldn't.

'Where does it hurt, Tabby?'

'Everywhere,' I say, then try to focus – my left arm burns like it's on fire, my head is pounding. 'My arm. My head.'

They're strapping something to my neck and my back.

'We have to lift you.' There's someone else here now, a man, on the other side. There is movement and agony explodes in my arm; I cry out.

'Smell that?' he says to her. 'Probably drunk.'

'No!' I say, wanting to protest. The taste of it is still there and my stomach twists with nausea.

'Hush,' the woman says. 'It doesn't matter.'

The ambulance is bright inside and I close my eyes. Siren on, we lurch up the bumpy road and I cry out again.

There's a pinprick in my arm. 'That should help, love,' she says. 'Now, what is the rest of your name? Where are your parents?'

Don't tell strangers about us, Cate always says. But if I don't, how will she find me?

I don't know what to say, so I keep my eyes closed and say nothing.

Bright lights are strange, fractured – moving oddly as I'm wheeled down a corridor, and I feel as if I'm floating like I did by the sea. Is this a hospital? I've never been in one before.

There are voices. They're talking about me?

A woman – not the paramedic, a different one – comes closer. 'Hi. Tabby, is it? Who's your mum, sweetie?'

'Cate,' I say, answering without meaning to, again, and the fear rushes back. *Never give our names. Never.* I've broken this rule so many times now. What will happen?

'What is her surname?'

But I'm too scared to answer and don't say anything else.

'We're just going to take some blood and do some X-rays,' another cheerful voice says. Then there's a sharp prick again, in my right arm. There's a tube put there. Bright red fills it, and then another.

I'm moved again on the trolley and close my eyes.

Time shifts. There's someone cleaning a cut on my foot; it stings. She's talking to someone else about my feet while she works, wondering why they haven't been *seen to*. What does she mean? I'm self-conscious and tuck my feet away when she's done.

7

Then I'm half sitting up in a bed, watching a man wrap wet strips around my arm. He's chattering on about what he's doing, says that it's a temporary plaster cast, that I'll have to come back for a permanent one once the swelling has gone down.

Finally he says, 'There. All done, Tabby. It takes a few days to dry completely so take care with it.' My arm is propped up on pillows, and he's saying it needs to be kept elevated with my hand higher than my elbow, and to wiggle my fingers now and then to make sure it's not got too tight from swelling.

Then there are voices beyond us, and one of them I know. Cate is here? And I'm both relieved to see her when she comes in and scared it was my giving her name that brought her. This place, it's official, part of the government. We shouldn't be here.

'Tabby! What's wrong? What are you doing to her?'

'I'm sorry,' I whisper.

'She's been hit by a car,' the man says. 'She's got a broken arm – a clean break, should knit no problems – a mild concussion, and a few minor scrapes and cuts on her feet.'

Another woman has followed Cate. 'You're Tabby's mother?' Cate nods. 'We need some details. If you can come with me for a moment?'

They want to know things about me? *Trouble.*

'What do you need? Why?' Cate says.

'Just the usual – name, address, and so on – and we need to find her previous records. There's an anomaly in her bloods—'

I cry out like I'm in terrible pain and Cate turns away from them, comes to me. 'Oh, baby. Can you give us a moment alone? Please.'

'Of course.' They step away, go around a curtain.

Cate's hand touches my cheek, she kisses my forehead, and I want her arms around me but she pulls away and peers through the curtain on the other side. 'We've got to get out of here. Do you think you can walk?' she says, voice low.

'I don't know,' I say, and I'm scared if I move that the pain will be as bad as it was before. I try to sit up and my head spins. 'I'm dizzy. They gave me a shot of something.'

She helps me sit up all the way. It's awkward with my left arm out of action, and I stare at it: the bone inside there is broken? To think of it makes me feel sick.

'It wasn't my fault,' I say.

'Tell me later.'

I swing my still bare feet over the side of the trolley bed. She helps me put my weight forward and stand; my head does a massive spin and I almost fall over. I test my bandaged foot and it's sore but OK. I look about for my shoes, but they're not here. I must have dropped them when I was running.

'I'll help you,' Cate says. 'Quick, now.'

Her arm goes around me and I lean on her. We go through the curtain on the opposite side from where the others went, around another bed. The patient in it, an old woman, looks at us with eyebrows raised but doesn't say anything.

We move around a few more curtained beds to a door, then a hallway.

My steps become surer and we go faster until we've reached the front doors of the hospital. Cate turns her head, nudges me to do the same – away from some CCTV cameras. Then we're stepping outside into darkness. It's night? I've been here longer than I thought.

We walk across the car park to our car. She has just finished helping me get in when a police car goes past. It stops by the hospital entrance. Fear lurches inside of me: did they come for us?

Cate swears under her breath as she gets in. 'Too close,' she says, and reverses out of the spot.

'What would have happened if we were still there when they came?'

'Don't worry; we weren't. Anyhow, they might have nothing to do with us.' But I can tell from the way she says the words that she doesn't believe it.

'What now?' I ask, though I know. This is what always happens, isn't it? Though not usually with a hospital and broken arm thrown in. *Or a Jago.* Pain and confusion make me push any thought of him away for now.

'It's time to go,' she says. 'We've been here far too long when somebody recognises you and comes to tell me what happened – though in this case, that was helpful. Lucky the car had a full charge today.' She's driving carefully at the speed limit as we leave the car park. At the roundabout, she turns left, starts going faster.

'What about our caravan – are we going back for it?'

'It's been slowing us down, don't you think?'

I sigh. The shot must be wearing off; the pain is starting to come back in my head, my arm is throbbing.

'Can we stay in Cornwall? Or at least somewhere near the sea?'

'We'll see. Try to get some sleep, Tabby.'

Despite the fear, pain and movement of the car – or maybe

because of it, too – I start to disconnect. Random thoughts and images flit in and out of my awareness.

Why can't we stay? Not just here, but anywhere?

Because they'd come for us. The police. Just like Cate always said – and tonight, there they were. She was right.

Faces. The first paramedic, she was kind. The cheerful one at the hospital with the needle. The man who put this cast on my arm.

Don't get too close to strangers; they're dangerous. Cate's warnings sound in my head even though she isn't saying a word, as if something I've heard often enough becomes so much a part of me that the echoes will always be there.

Maybe she was right about Jago. But the paramedics, the doctors and nurses in the hospital; they were helping me, weren't they?

But they stole from me. Bright red tubes of blood, taken from my arm without permission.

An anomaly? What's that?

They won't find any previous records on me – there aren't any – but they have part of me: they still have my blood.

My books and notebooks – in our caravan. Gone. Seashells I've collected; some smooth pieces of wood. Nothing else there matters much, but still, it was mine, and now it isn't.

Later we're on a motorway, and then I'm gripped by another sort of pain. It's not physical; it hurts far more. We're heading away from the sea. I can feel it getting further and further away, and with every turn of the wheels of our car, part of me is dying.

Sun . . . sea . . . earth . . . sky . . .

Sun . . . sea . . . earth . . . sky . . .

The words, chanted by many voices — past, present, future — drum through my blood:

Sun . . . sea . . . earth . . . sky . . .

3

Part of me is awake while the rest is caught in a dream. I want to get completely lost in the unreal, the imagined, not come back to here and now. I hurt.

The harder I try to stay asleep the more I wake up, until finally I give up and open my eyes. The car has stopped and Cate is gone.

We're parked next to a rundown building, doors with numbers on them along the side and windows between. A hotel?

There are footsteps and Cate is back now. She unlocks the car, comes to my side and opens the door.

'We're staying here?' I say.

'Just for tonight. Let me help you.'

It's awkward with the broken arm being on the same side as the door. I swing my feet out first and gasp; everything aches. I guess getting hit by a car can do that. I shuffle forwards on the seat and Cate leans around me to take my right hand. I manage to shift my weight forward enough to stand.

Even though it's warm, I'm shivering. Cate helps me to a nearby door.

Inside, there are two small double beds, a door that must go to the loo. She helps me to the nearest bed, sits me down.

'I'll just be a sec,' she says, and goes back out through the door. When she returns she's got a suitcase in one hand and a few bags in the other. 'I grabbed some things. Just in case,' she says, but finding out I'd been taken to a hospital wasn't really in the *just-in-case* category: we both knew we'd have to run.

She unzips the case and I smile when I see the blue cover of one of my notebooks on top of some of our clothes – it's a special favourite. Cate made it for me for my fifteenth birthday last year, from thick recycled paper; she copied Hokusai's painting *The Great Wave* on the cover, and wrote *Tabby's Notebook* on the spine with a calligraphy pen. I love it so much I haven't been able to bring myself to write in it yet.

'Thank you for bringing that,' I say.

'I didn't think to bring spare shoes,' Cate says. 'We'll get you some soon. Do you want anything to eat?'

I shake my head, then wince at the movement. 'I just want to sleep some more.'

'OK.' She helps ease me down, under the covers, and gently props my arm up on spare pillows. The mattress is lumpy but it's better than sleeping in the car.

I close my eyes.

'You are not alone,' Cate says, and starts to sing, a song without words; it's a healing song. Her hands lightly touch my arm, my head, while she sings, and warmth slowly grows inside me in response.

I wonder what they'd make of this in the hospital?

It wasn't that many years ago that I started to realise how different we were to those around us, even to the name that I call her – *Cate*, not Mum. When I asked her about this, she explained: we are mother and daughter, sister and sister, daughter and mother, best friends. No matter what labels we use, we are all things to each other, and she was right to say this. We may look different on the outside – my long hair is dark, eyes grey-green; she is my opposite, blonde and blue-eyed – but like the night needs the day and the day needs the night to make each who they are, we two are one. Our hearts beat together as if we were under the same skin.

There is growing warmth, there is Cate's voice, there is sleep – for the other part of me this time, that was awake in the car. The part that stays awake now is the wild half of me; it doesn't use words. It keeps vigil as Cate sings, and I begin to heal.

4

Hunger pulls me from my dream. I start to stretch but am stopped short by the cast on my arm – it feels strange, alien, to have something attached that isn't part of me. At least the pain is less than last night.

'Good morning. Tea?' Cate says, and holds out a cup.

'Yes, please.'

As I sit up and she passes it to me, my stomach rumbles so loud that she can hear it, too, and we both laugh. 'Appetite back?' she says.

'I'm *starving*.'

'A good sign.'

She's already dressed and reaches into a hessian shopping bag; she must have gone out while I slept. There is orange juice, some fruit, nuts – she's even managed to find some vegan sandwiches. We make quick work of much of it, and I can see Cate glancing at her watch, out the window. She wants to go and that makes me hurry. Does she think the police could find us here?

After a quick sink wash with Cate's help to keep my cast dry, we get ready to go. Cate has us wear different-coloured T-shirts to yesterday; she puts my hair up and a scarf on hers. She's making us look different, I realise, and that makes me even more nervous than I was before. I hurry as we gather our things, though I'm not much help with only one arm. We head out the door.

'Where's our car?'

'I sold it,' Cate replies. 'But this one is ours, now.' She walks towards an old car, a nondescript grey under the dirt and rust. My eyes widen: did she sell our car in case anybody knew what it looked like and told the authorities?

I carefully get in while Cate puts our stuff on the back seat. I loved that car and I know Cate did, too, and being electric, the carbon cost was so much less. I helped pick it out – the bright blue, my favourite colour – and had just washed and polished it a few days ago. It's just so not *fair*. This one is way too old to run on anything but fossil fuels, and it doesn't look like it has been washed for years.

When Cate starts the engine, the roar it makes seems deafening but is probably just like most cars that aren't electric. She pulls out on to the road, and soon we've left this little town behind and are on the M6, trailing poisonous exhaust fumes all the way.

'I know this car isn't right for us,' Cate says, 'but it is a compromise we need to make for now, so we can go far and fast; we can't do that if we have to keep stopping to charge.'

'Where are we going?'

'A quick stop in the Lakes, then we'll see.'

I stare out as the motorway rushes by. The pull of the sea ebbs and flows as the motorway's distance from it changes over time, like an itch, deep inside. One I can't scratch.

'Are you going to tell me what happened yesterday?' Cate says.

I sigh, uncomfortable, but needing to talk, too. 'Do you want me to?'

'Only if you do.' She glances at me sideways. 'There was a boy named Jago who came and found me, told me where you were. He knew your name.'

I bite my lip.

'He had a lovely, gentle soul; I could feel it, and I could see why you trusted him. But you have to be careful, Tabby. Even someone who doesn't mean to could be used by the authorities to set a trap.'

'I know. I'm sorry.'

'It's hard to ever completely know outsiders, what they are capable of. They're not the same as us.'

They're not, are they? I understand this teaching better than I have before, in a deeper, more personal way. Jago didn't stand up for me, didn't say anything, didn't even try to help. Maybe he found out what happened to me and felt guilty, and that is why he went to find Cate and tell her where I was.

'Jago is a perfect example,' Cate says. 'He didn't seem like the sort to fight, but he obviously had been.'

'What do you mean?'

'He had bruises and cuts around his eye, his cheek. A split lip.'

I stare at Cate, shocked. It couldn't have been long after I got taken to the hospital that Jago went to find her. What happened to him in between? There were two boys hanging back when the others came up to us; they weren't there later when I was chased. Was it those two boys that Jago fought with? Maybe he didn't help me because he *couldn't*. Was I so intent on running away that I didn't see he was the one who needed help?

'Was Jago all right?'

'Time will heal him quicker than it will you. Are you ready to tell me about him now?' Cate says.

'Yes,' I say, and pause. 'You know I've been going to the beach in the afternoons when you were cleaning.'

'Yes. At Tintagel?'

'To start with. But then I found one off the coastal path – Bossiney Cove. It's a bit of a hike down so it's really quiet. Anyhow, I met Jago there a few weeks ago. He tried to talk to me. I walked away the first time.'

'And then?'

And then: I tell her everything that happened, remembering at the same time. I'd been feeling a little lost, alone, drawn to go to the sea to find something I needed without knowing what it was. Instead of soothing me like it usually did, being there made the longing worse, but I couldn't stay away.

Then Jago was there. As if I'd called him – someone from another world.

I'd walked away from him that first time, then later wished I hadn't, that he'd come back.

And he did; the next day. This time I stayed, listened to him – until his voice and the music of the sea were sounds that went together.

Then I started to speak to him, too. It was easy even though he was so different. When I wouldn't talk about myself he told me stories about him, his life. His mum and dad, two sisters. Where they lived and what they did, and things they squabbled about at home, like his little sister always taking his phone to play games. And he thought it was boring but it wasn't to me: it was a glimpse into another way to live.

'When did you give him your name?'

'I didn't.' Time for another confession. 'I told the librarian in Boscastle my name, to borrow books; he said she told him.'

'I see.' Cate sighs now. 'So, it wasn't just a boy with dreamy eyes; it was someone else, too. That's even more dangerous, Tabby. Your name at a library may only seem a slim wedge into their world, but it is one that could grow and take you away for ever.'

Tears well up in my eyes. 'I'm sorry. I never thought—'

'Please, Tabby, in future, *think*. Now tell me the rest about Jago.'

'We started to meet every day at the same place on the beach, late afternoon, when he was finished school and you were cleaning. He wasn't supposed to come yesterday; it was his sister's birthday, he said. But he came anyway.'

'And how did this lead to you being hit by a car?'

I tell her everything – the others, what they said. What happened when they chased me. I can see her hands tightening on the steering wheel as I talk.

'I'm so sorry this happened to you, Tabby.'

'It's not your fault.'

'Isn't it? Maybe I should have prepared you better. People can be wicked. But you did well to get away; running in front of a car not so much. How are you feeling?'

Miserable about Jago: maybe both trusting him too much at first and then not enough. Guilty, too, like I have failed Cate by not taking better care of myself. But I know that isn't what she means right now. 'I'm OK. My arm is throbbing a bit; they said it might swell more. My foot is sore and I've got a headache.'

'Poor baby. I'm glad it wasn't any worse.'

Having talked about Jago to Cate and remembering how I'd felt when we met has got me thinking. Maybe the wonder of finding a friend in Jago wasn't all about *him* – it was the place, too. The sea. The beach, and finding my own space on it. Thinking about how the beach – and Jago, too – are getting further away with every mile hurts me inside.

'Where are we going?' I ask her again.

'We'll see,' she says, giving the same answer as before, but this time I don't leave it alone.

'Where is *we'll see*?'

'Well, that depends.'

'On?'

'I've got to find a job; other things that may or may not happen.'

I sigh, first annoyed and then angry – not at Cate, but at *everything*: the world, the way we live in it. Talking to Jago and hearing about his family made me think that maybe staying in one place wouldn't be so bad. They didn't sound like they were trapped in their lives by the authorities; he made it sound like they could do what they like – or, at least, they thought they could – and isn't that kind of the same thing?

The police don't come for them, though, like they do for us. Is that because they do what is expected of them? Then, like Cate has said many times before, they aren't truly free: it's an illusion of freedom if you always take the path that is laid down before you.

But would that be so bad if you didn't know it?

'I don't want to go somewhere else; I liked it *there*,' I say, voice

21

low, my anger giving way and leaving loss and pain behind. Despite what happened yesterday, I really did. I'd almost felt like I *belonged* to the place or it belonged to me.

'I know you did, Tabby, and I'm sorry. But once you'd been to that hospital they wouldn't have left us alone. We had to go.'

With a shiver I see in my mind the police car that had gone past us to the hospital doors, and I know she's right. But that doesn't make it any easier.

Tiredness settles around me once again, and I close my eyes. It's being hurt, beginning to heal; these things make me need more sleep. One part drifts away while the other keeps watch, and the miles slip past us as I dream of Jago and the sea.

5

They appear at first as hills in the distance, then mountains that grow bigger and slowly surround us. As we go further, the endless dead and parched lands we'd driven through in the drought-stricken Midlands are a memory. The lush green surroundings of the Lake District make my spirits rise, but it's not just the change in landscape: it feels like a place I know, one I've been to before. I soak up the unfamiliar coming-home-feeling, the greenness and beauty of the spring.

After a while we turn on to a narrow road that winds around a lake, and hungry for water – even fresh, not salt – my eyes drink it in. Now I'm sure: I recognise where we are. But we *don't* return to places; at least, we never have before.

'We've been here, haven't we?' I say.

'Yes.' There is a note of surprise in Cate's voice. 'It was many years ago – you were only small. Do you remember?'

'Yes.' There's a warm feeling inside me to be coming back to something from my past – to know I was happy here a long time ago. I can feel it. 'Are we going to stay?'

'No, we can't. This is a brief visit only. There's something I need to collect before we move on.'

We wind around another lake, then climb higher, through trees. Finally, she turns off down a lane that is more a track than a road, and as we bump up and down I wonder if the car will hold together.

We stop at a house masked by trees. A secret, hidden place. There are solar panels on the roof and along the most open side of the house – the roof slants down to the ground in a way that says it was built for this purpose.

'Wait a moment,' Cate says. She opens her door and gets out of the car. Two massive dogs bound towards her, barking.

'Hold,' a voice says – a man. The dogs stop, still bristling and intent on her. The man steps out around the side of the building. He's got a shotgun in his hands pointed at Cate, but then he lowers it.

'Could it be? Is that really Catelyn?' he says.

'It's good to see you, Eli.'

He shakes his head like he can't believe his eyes, then says something else to the dogs who now sit and wag their tails while the man hugs Cate. She says a few words to him that I can't hear, and he turns to the car.

'This can't be Tabby.' He opens the door, sees the cast on my arm. 'Been in the wars, have you?' I'm staring at him and trying to remember. He had a beard then, I think. I was scared of both this place and him at first, but then we were friends. He used to carry me around on his shoulders?

Smiling, I get out of the car, moving more easily than yesterday. He hugs me too, careful of my arm, and introduces me to his dogs: Bear and Max. They're like giant, bouncy puppies now we've been introduced, and I'm remembering another dog, gentle but bigger than me. Gem?

'They're Gemma's boys,' he says. I remembered her name right, and that makes me happy. 'Can the two of you stay?'

'Just tonight,' Cate says.

Later I'm cosy on the sofa, snuggled up against Bear with Max by my feet: lucky it's a big sofa. There's a fire in the grate and I'm drifting towards sleep. Cate and Eli are at the kitchen table behind me, candles casting their shadows on the walls. They've been talking about politics, mostly. Eli thinks the world is going wrong, that when the dust settles it'll be up to people like him, who know how to survive and protect themselves, to carry on. He asks us to stay and I know what Cate will say, but I wonder if I'd even want to? This is lovely for a while, here, with his dogs. But there's no one else, no one my own age. Since I've met Jago I'm starting to see how important that is.

Anyhow, what would be the point of surviving if you're all alone?

6

Kneeling down, I bury my face in Bear's fur while Max licks my ears. Maybe we don't actually need *people*.

I wait in the car while Cate and Eli say a goodbye of their own. They must be close to hug like that, after so many years. She's got another small bag over her shoulder now – is that what we came here for? When she gets to the car she opens our case on the back seat, puts the bag inside and zips it up again.

Cate doesn't look back as we drive away, but I do; Eli is watching and I wave just before he's lost from sight.

There was something in his eyes when he looked at her last night that made me wonder, and now that we're alone I can ask. 'Was Eli your boyfriend?'

'I guess you could say that. It was a long time ago,' she says.

'You said not to trust men, but didn't you trust him if he was your boyfriend?'

There's a quirk to her lips as she drives. 'I understood him, and I trusted him to be the way I knew him to be. That's not the same as complete trust. There are things I wouldn't tell him. Did you remember Eli?'

'A little. And his other dog, Gem. Can we get a dog?'

'I don't think that would be fair on a dog. We move around too much.'

And I know she's right, but something aches inside of me – for a house, a dog, staying in one place.

For a life I've never had.

Hours later we stop at a service station. We find some canvas shoes that fit well enough, and it's a relief to not be hobbling around barefoot any more.

Cate goes to buy supplies; I'm looking at the papers in a newsagent. Half of the headlines scream about the last of the ice packs melting, drowning islands and islanders, the death of the great coral reef in Australia. The others condemn the effect of climate strikes on the economy, and say things like, *Keep Climers Out* – that's what they have started to call climate refugees. But they are just people, like us, whose land is drowned or dead in drought; all they want is a safe place to live. If everyone says *keep out* then where can they go?

And what about us, Cate and me? Are we like Climers that nobody wants? That boy on the beach said we'd have been asked to move on soon, and he was probably right.

'You're being quiet,' Cate says when we get back to the car. 'Does your arm hurt?'

'A little.' I shrug. It does, but I hadn't been thinking about it.

We get in and I squirm sideways to grab the seat belt with my right hand.

'Leave it for a moment,' she says, and she doesn't put her seat belt on or start the car either. Instead she takes my right hand in both of hers, and as if she heard my unspoken thoughts so many miles ago, she answers them now.

'I'm sorry, Tabby. Things are getting harder for you, aren't they? But you know as well as I do: if we don't stay off the grid and keep moving around, the authorities will find us. The system has slots for people and we don't fit into them, do we? They'd take you away from me, make you wear a uniform, go to school, stand up and sit down when bells ring. It's like prison.' Her hand touches my cheek. 'You do understand, don't you?'

I nod, scared to even think of being taken away from Cate. We belong together. No boy, beach or fantasy of a house and dog could ever be more important than us being with each other, and being free.

'Say it, for me. Please,' Cate says, and worry lines crease between her eyes, on her cheeks.

'I understand.'

She smiles. 'Good girl. I love you, Tabby. No matter what happens, always know that I love you.'

No matter what happens . . . like what? What could happen? My throat catches in an odd way, and I move closer to her. Her arm goes around me.

'I love you too, Cate,' I whisper into her hair.

Daughter, mother.

Sister, sister.

Mother, daughter.

Best friends.

Everything.

Always.

7

We get to Manchester. There's a place she knows, Cate says, where she might get some work for tips. She doesn't want me to go with her. It's a club.

I wait in the car, radio on, but no matter how many times I channel surf I can't find a song I like and soon turn it off. I get out of the car and then into the back seat. I unzip our case and find my notebook with *The Great Wave* on the cover. But I'm not ready yet to dip into its blank pages and mark them for ever; I haven't decided what it is *for*. Everyone and everything needs a purpose to not be wasted.

Yet . . . there is one thing it could be: a place for memories. Things I write down because I don't want to lose them.

I open the notebook, but instead of the first page, I go to the last. I hesitate, then before I can change my mind, quickly write down a sequence of numbers: the ones Jago had me repeat back to him. I can put it out of my mind now; I don't have to decide to call him, or not, or worry that if later on I decide I want to I'll have forgotten his number. It's here if I need it.

I close the notebook again and open the case to put it away, but as I do, I see the bag – the one Cate tucked away inside it when we left Eli's. I wonder what's in it? I'm curious, but hesitate. She didn't say not to look in it, did she?

I take it out. It's heavy for its size, something lumpy inside. I undo the zip.

It's full of little felt bags and boxes – all with jewellery inside. Really expensive-looking sparkly stuff. I hold a heavy gold bracelet in my hands, a thick bangle with blue and green stones set in it. The gold is shaped like waves and the colours of the stones make me think of the sea. It's so pretty. There are also earrings, a watch – it doesn't have the right time – several necklaces and rings. All amazing, but the bracelet is my favourite.

Why did Eli have all this? Was it something he'd kept for Cate, or was it his and he gave it to her?

I slip the bracelet on my wrist, hold it this way then that to look at it against my skin.

Suddenly nervous in case anyone walking past sees the jewellery, I check the car doors are locked and look around. I see Cate at the end of the road, walking this way. Feeling guilty, I quickly put everything back as it was. I'm sitting there with the notebook in my hands when she gets to the car, as if to say this is why I'm in the back seat.

I get out. 'How'd it go?'

'I got the job.' She doesn't look that happy about it. 'It'll do for a while. And now we need a place to stay tonight.'

Later, I'm in bed, Cate is on a sofa across the room – I can tell by the way she's breathing that she's asleep. This place is even worse than the place we stayed after we left the hospital. Cate put a chair under the doorknob, as if she wasn't that sure of where we are, either.

My arm is throbbing and itchy under the cast, and I grip my

left hand tightly in my right, as if squeezing it hard enough will make me stop feeling the need to scratch the arm above it.

My right wrist is the one that wore that shiny thing a few short hours ago. There was something about that bracelet, something I can't begin to explain. It was like it *spoke* to me, and I yearn to hold it, to wear it again.

It isn't just because it was a pretty thing – though it was, not like anything I've seen before. It was *more*.

Arms are around me, holding me close. Thud-thud *beats where my head rests against her. A hand brushes hair from my face, and I reach out to touch what is around her wrist.*

It's shiny; the colours sparkle like the sea. My eyes close but I see it still, a circle of fire that spins in my dreams.

8

'I didn't think you'd ever wake up.' Cate is there, watching me, tea in her hands, when I open my eyes.

'Are you all right?' she says. 'You're pale.' She gets up and places a hand on my forehead, concern in her eyes.

'I've got a headache,' I admit. 'I had trouble getting to sleep.'

She's there next to me, close. Warm. Her hands rub my temples, her voice soothing as she gently sings the pain away.

I look up at her and smile. 'Thank you. I feel much better now.'

'Good. We've got to go do some things.'

'Are we checking out?'

'Yes. Come on, time to get up.'

A bit later when I come out of the bathroom Cate has that bag in her hands from the case.

'There's something I want to show you,' she says. She unzips it, spills it out on the bed. One by one the contents of each velvet bag and box flash and sparkle – even more beautiful than I remember. And now is the time I should tell her what I did, but I don't, and I don't know why.

Instead I ask her what I wondered yesterday: 'What is all this stuff? Did Eli give it to you?'

'No. A long while ago I asked him to keep it for me for a

rainy day, and the sun may be shining just now but it's rainy enough. I thought we could use some of it to get a better place to stay for a while.'

Cate starts going through it all, sorting what to sell. She picks up the bracelet and holds it out to me. I hesitate. 'Go on,' she says, and I take it into my hand.

The cool weight of it against my skin makes me shiver and not from being cold. Touching it gives me a strange double feeling of holding it *now* and *then*, and I don't mean yesterday in the car. In my dream it felt different – warmer, bigger – or was it that my hand was smaller? If so, it was a long time ago.

'Are you all right, Tabby?'

'Yes. I mean, I don't know; I think so. There's just something about this bracelet.'

'Do you like it?'

'It's beautiful.'

'Try it on.'

I hesitate, then slip it over my right wrist like I did yesterday, hold it up to the sunlight at the window. The blue and green stones seem to hold and reflect the light like they did in my dream. A smile takes over my face.

I take off the bracelet, hold it up to give it back to Cate. She shakes her head and closes my fingers around it with her hands. 'It's yours.'

'Really?'

'Really. We can sell some of the other stuff.'

'Are you sure?'

'Keep it. Wear it. It's a pretty thing for a pretty girl like you,' she says, and I smile at the unusual compliment. Not that Cate never compliments me, but I don't think she's ever called me pretty before. She says people are too worried about their looks and not enough about their thoughts.

There's a question inside of me as I look back at the jewellery on the bed: *Where is all of this from?* I almost say it out loud, but I'm looking at the bracelet, and all I say to Cate is, 'Thank you.'

9

It turns out that selling jewellery is easy, if you know where to go. Cate has me stay close and tells me to keep the bracelet out of view under my sleeve, as we visit one pawn shop, then another. The secret, she says, is to only show one thing in each shop, and to look around first and see which piece they're most likely to be interested in. If they see multiple pieces of jewellery they'll want a deal for the lot and never pay as much.

She changes her name and story in each one. When they ask for ID and she says it was stolen, or left at home, or lost in a fire, they don't believe her – even I can see that – and the price they are willing to pay comes down. But we still have made enough money to make Cate happy within a few hours.

We have a quick lunch in a vegan café. Cate has newspapers spread out, circling ads for rooms to let. There's a payphone nearby. She makes calls; some she crosses out straight away and a few we go to see. One we drive up to and so don't like the look of the building that we don't even stop. Another she dismisses as the landlady is too curious.

'Third time lucky?' Cate says, as she pulls in front of the next one.

She knocks on the door of the bungalow and we wait; no one comes. We're about to give up but finally the door opens. A white-haired woman peers out.

'Yes?' she says.

'Hello, Mrs Fulton? I'm Alison Smith,' Cate says. 'This is my daughter, Jenny. I called about the room to rent?'

She comes out. 'It's around here,' she says, and we go down the side of the house, through a gate. In the back garden is a granny flat, separate from the house.

She unlocks the door. 'It's one room. The sofa opens out,' she says. There's a small fridge, an electric hot plate on top of it, and a bathroom with the world's smallest shower, but it's all spotlessly clean. 'No parties, no overnight guests.' She glances at me. 'There's a high school up the road.'

'Jenny is home schooled,' Cate says. There's a pause and Mrs Fulton doesn't react or say anything else – she passes the curiosity test.

'Maybe it's too small for two of you?' she says – exactly what I was thinking. Even our caravan had more space.

'It could work,' Cate says.

Mrs Fulton is looking doubtful. 'Do you have any references?'

Cate reaches into a pocket, takes out some notes. 'First and last month's rent. Cash in hand?'

The sight of the money seals the deal.

Soon after that, Cate has to leave for her five p.m. shift. By the time the door closes behind her and I hear the car start on the drive I'm already feeling bored and claustrophobic – like I can't breathe.

She's left some money and the usual admonishments: don't do anything to be noticed, keep myself to myself, be in by dark.

I head out for a walk.

Our road of bungalows gives way to high narrow terraces.

36

I wander, find a street with restaurants, shops. I walk and walk and there is more of the same. It's a city, I know this is what they're like – we've stayed in them before – but even though I know the way back, the longer I walk the more lost I feel.

I find a few old SF novels I haven't read in a second-hand shop and head back to our place. I can't call it home – at least, not yet.

It's gone midnight when I finally make up the sofa and lie down in the dark. Cate said she'd be late; I don't know how late. There's traffic noise, both near and distant; voices from next door; barking dogs behind and a loud TV from our landlady. I try to block it all out and remember the sound of the sea, to breathe in and out with imagined waves.

That last day, lying on the beach, feeling the scratchy damp sand against my skin. The taste of salt on my lips and the tang of sea air in my mouth and throat as I breathed in slowly.

Then I opened my eyes, and there he was: Jago.

I sigh. I'd thought he abandoned me, didn't care what happened to me – but with what Cate said about him being in a fight, I'm not sure. I know I can never see him again, but it still feels so important to know what really happened.

I never even got to say goodbye. Somehow that is the worst thing of all.

10

The next day when Cate leaves for work, all that stretches in front of me is another long evening on my own, and another pointless walk because there is nothing else to fill the time.

Though there could be something different to do; something *very* different, in fact. I've tucked my *Great Wave* notebook in my bag, with its guilty secret hidden on the back page. I haven't decided yet whether I should call Jago – well, that's not quite true, I know I shouldn't – but will I, anyway?

I watch out for payphones; there aren't many around. Pretty much everyone has a mobile phone tucked in their pocket, so why would they need one?

Everybody but us.

I walk faster and faster, as if trying to run away from the decision. But is it really such a big deal? One phone call, that's all. Find out what happened and say goodbye. I won't tell him why we left, where we went or where we are now. What could be wrong about that?

After walking past a likely payphone – one that is on its own, pulled back from where people walk – for what feels like the millionth time, I've had enough. I need to either do it now or forget it for ever.

My heart is hammering in my chest when I go up to it and read the instructions. Money in, numbers. I make a mistake with shaking hands and have to start again.

It rings: once, twice, the third ring is cut off.

'Hello?' It's a girl – one of Jago's sisters?

'Uh, hi. Is Jago there?'

I hear her hollering. 'Jago? It's another *girl*.' I almost hang up when she says that, but hesitate, and now it's too late: I hear him pick up.

'Hello?' he says, and now he's connected to me again even though he's so far away. 'Hello?' he says again.

'Hi,' I finally say into the silence.

'Who is it? Is that Tabby?'

'Um yes, it's me.'

'Where are you?'

'Doesn't matter. I just wanted to say . . .' What did I want to say? Now that he's there, listening, I'm struggling to find the words, but somehow make myself force them out. 'Well, sorry we took off without saying goodbye. Thanks for telling Cate where I was. She said you looked like you'd been in a fight?'

'It was nothing, not compared to what happened to you. Are you all right?'

'You mean from being hit by the car? My arm is broken; I had a headache, but it's mostly gone now. Besides that, I'm fine. But Cate said you were hurt, too?'

'Nothing major – just those other two idiots stopped me from following you. By the time I got away and up to the road, someone who saw what happened told me. You were gone in an ambulance by then.'

I let out a breath I hadn't even realised I was holding. He

would have followed; they stopped him. Relief floods through me.

'Where are you, Tabby? People have been looking for you – the police. They came to talk to me.'

'They did *what*? I'm so sorry.' I say, shocked. They must know we left, so why would they bother Jago?

'They're trying to find you, to make sure you're OK. Where are you? Tell me, Tabby. Please?'

I stay silent, trying to take it in. So, the police didn't give up when we weren't at the hospital when they got there. They're still looking for us.

'Tabby, where are you? You can trust me.'

'I . . . I do,' I say, and as I say it I know I mean it. But I can't tell him where we are, and he won't understand. He couldn't even begin to understand how things are for us when his life is so different. And I don't know how to say that to him, or even if I should.

'Tabby?'

I panic and hang up the phone, leaving his question unanswered.

I lean back, breathing in city air so fast that I feel dizzy.

It's like Cate has always said: once the authorities get their hooks into you, they won't rest until they track you down. And it's all my fault. They want to lock us up, take me away from Cate . . .

Though Jago said the police wanted to make sure I'm OK. That doesn't make sense. Why would police do that? If they cared in any way about me being *OK*, they'd just leave us alone.

They must have been lying; trying to manipulate Jago. They

made him worried about me so that he'd tell them where I am if he finds out. But he doesn't know; he can never know.

I can never call him again.

Waves of sadness grip me now, and I'm blinking, hard. Cars go past and people walk on the pavement nearby, but I'm as alone as if none of them were in sight. I sink on to a bench and let the tears fall; everyone just keeps walking. No one seems to notice, or if they do, they pretend that they don't.

Sirens sound in the distance. At first they don't really register, but when they start to get louder, I tense up and wipe at my face, ready to run. Then the sound fades away again.

Get a grip, Tabby. No one knows where we are, do they? We're hours away from where we were – anyone looking for Cate and Tabby in Cornwall isn't going to find Alison and Jenny in Manchester.

I walk back to our place, fast, trying not to flinch whenever there are distant sirens. None get as close as they did earlier, but it feels like they're circling around me, drawing in, bit by bit.

When I get there I lock the door tight and turn off the lights.

11

'Try these ones,' Cate says, and holds up some decent jeans in my size hidden in the middle of the charity shop rack.

I take them through to the changing room: they're a good fit. This shop is amazing. Not only is it restricted to ethical products and fabrics, it's more trendy-vintage than second hand. I'm trying to be happy that she'd had such good tips this weekend that we're splashing out for some new stuff, but it's hard when I couldn't sleep. I couldn't stop thinking about Jago, the police and agonising about what to say to Cate, but my lips wouldn't unseal and come up with any words this morning.

We go to a bookshop next, since the ones I had got left in our caravan. Jago was talking about exams – GCSEs, he said – and I look at the GCSE study guides. They're *so* boring, full of boxes to tick. Why would everyone want to learn the same things as everybody else when there is so much in the world to choose from? Instead I seek out things that interest me: marine biology, human anatomy and physiology – I want to learn about how broken bones heal, blood.

There's a big hardback, the sort that is all photos, of underwater life. I'm holding it and stroking the cover, then start to put it back on the shelf – it costs a mint – but Cate picks it up with the others and goes to pay.

We get back in the car and head for our place. The whole time I'm watching the traffic, looking in the mirrors.

This is crazy; they've no way to find us here. I try to relax but can't and keep scanning around us.

When we're about to turn left to our road, my stomach constricts in a knot. There are police cars – two of them. I grab Cate's arm. 'Look,' I say. They're pulled in front of the bungalow where we stay.

'Well spotted,' she says, then shakes her head. 'How could they have found us here? Maybe it has nothing to do with us.' But she doesn't take our turn, and instead drives to a back street some distance away. She parks, then finds a scarf in the bag of stuff that we'd bought. She wraps it around her hair, puts her sunglasses on. 'I'll check it out. Wait here,' she says.

'Let me come with you.'

'No way. With that arm in a cast you're too easy to spot.'

'What if you don't come back?'

'I will.'

'But what if you don't?'

'I *will*. I promise.'

She heads off and, stomach churning, I'm tempted to follow behind despite what she said. I'm caught in indecision and then it's too late. She's out of sight.

I glance at the clock in the car: it's twenty past twelve. How far did we drive from there? Maybe it's a ten- or fifteen-minute walk each way. I watch the minutes count down, one after another. By the time it is one, my nerves are in overdrive.

Is she all right? What will I do if she doesn't come back?

When Cate finally appears in the distance I almost cry.

She walks briskly to our car, then gets in the driver's seat.

'You were gone for ages!' I say, blinking hard.

'I'm sorry. Were you worried? I told you I'd be back.' She takes my hand and gives it a squeeze. 'I went a roundabout way in case anyone saw where I was going.'

'And? What happened?'

She smiles. 'It looks like we're off on another adventure. Just you and me.'

She pulls out on to the road.

'Why?'

'The police were at the house, talking to Mrs Fulton.'

'Maybe she's got parking tickets. Or it's the tax department – they're after her for taking rent cash in hand. Or maybe she's been shoplifting or something. You don't know it has anything to do with us,' I say, but I don't believe my own words, and my voice doesn't sound right even to me.

'Tabby? Something's wrong. What is it?'

I sigh.

'Tell me,' Cate says, and I don't want to – she's going to be upset – but there's no real choice.

'Well, I kind of called Jago.'

'Tabby! You didn't. Where?'

'From a payphone. Anyhow, he said police were looking for us in Cornwall.'

'When was this?'

'Last night.'

'Did you tell him where you were?'

'Of course not!'

She's silent for a moment, concentrating on negotiating

44

heavy traffic, getting us as far away from the police as she can.

'Cate, is us having to leave my fault?'

'It could just be a coincidence – or not. Please, Tabby, don't call him again, or call anybody, without checking if it's OK with me first. Promise?'

I don't understand how me calling Jago on a payphone last night can have anything to do with police being at our place this afternoon. But what if it does?

'I won't, I promise,' I say. And even though I already knew I should never call him again, saying the words out loud drives the loss further home.

Goodbye, Jago, I whisper inside.

12

Hours pass slowly on the motorway. We've been heading south, but apart from that I don't think even Cate knows where we are going. Finally we stop at a services. Killing time while Cate gets supplies, I go to the newsagent and look at magazines.

A man with a newspaper in his hands walks over. He's looking at the paper in his hands, then at me.

'This looks a lot like you,' he says.

'What does?'

He turns the paper around. On the front cover, headlines scream, 'Missing Girl Spotted in Manchester'. There are two slightly blurred photos underneath – it's *me*.

In one, I'm facing away from the camera, standing at the payphone and talking to Jago; in the other, I'm facing forward. I'd just hung up the phone and was standing there, lost in feeling sorry for myself.

But how? Oh. There was a bank nearby. Did it have CCTV? Of course it did. Cate would never make a mistake like that.

'It's not me,' I say.

'So, this girl just happens to have a broken arm, too. And is wearing the same jacket you are?'

'What a coincidence,' I say, my voice sounding false. I turn away from him and dash for the door.

Cate is in M&S with a half full basket over her arm when I find her. She must see it on my face. 'What's wrong?' she says.

I pull her to the newspapers at the front; she sees the images. Her eyes widen. 'Get in the car,' she says.

'But why—'

She presses the keys in my hand. 'Go. Now.'

I walk quickly to the car, forcing myself not to run so I don't attract attention. Is that woman looking at me? Those two men?

Cate follows a few agonising minutes later, chucks a bag on the back seat and starts the car.

There are distant sirens, getting closer. We follow the exit to the roundabout just as a police car leaves it to go into the services. Did the man in the newsagent call them? I'm scared, and don't understand why I was on the front page of the paper like that.

'Cate? Why did it say I'm missing? Do they mean because we disappeared from the hospital in Cornwall?'

'Probably,' is all she says. She's concentrating on merging back on to the motorway, on going fast, switching lanes to get around other cars, even on the inside. There are sirens in the distance, getting closer. She takes the next exit.

'Cate? I'm scared. What's happening?'

'Don't worry. You'll be fine, I promise.'

We're on minor roads now. She turns frequently, heads down a country lane. The sun is starting to set. She pulls off the road and stops behind a barn – it looks half wrecked, like it'd topple over with a good push.

'Let's see if we can hunker down here for the night,' she says. 'Wait a sec.'

She gets out. She pulls on the barn door; it's half off its hinges. She looks inside, then goes in. A moment later she comes out and pulls the doors open wider, gets back in the car and drives it in.

'Let's have a picnic in the barn. Not the most balanced of meals; I wasn't finished shopping when you found me.' She gets back out of the car, shuts the barn doors again and takes the bag from the back seat.

'Cate?' I get out of the car now too and grab her hand, make her turn to look at me. 'What's going on? Tell me. Please.'

Her eyes are wide, a bit unfocused, and I'm even more scared now. Cate is always calm, collected; she always knows what to say and do in every situation.

'It's too soon; you're not ready,' she says.

'Ready for what? Cate?'

Slowly her breathing evens, her eyes focus on mine. She reaches out, cups my face in her hands.

'Promise me, Tabby, that you will always think for yourself. Don't believe what you are told.' Her words are fierce, and I'm shaken even more.

'Cate?'

'Promise me!'

'I promise. Of course I will.'

She pulls me towards her and I lean against her, her arms around me. 'It'll be all right,' she says. 'Things always go the way they are meant to in the end. You'll see.'

I don't believe her.

Somehow I fall asleep, or at least part of me does, and slip into wordless nightmares. Later they ease to something else: Cate is

48

there, in my dream. She holds me in her arms and whispers secrets, but it isn't just her voice – there are many voices, a chorus that rises and falls. It is, at once, both soothing and terrifying: things that must be and could be in a circle of loss and pain held within her arms.

The other part of me listens, keeps watch – seconds, minutes, hours – until finally it shouts inside my head to wake up. I open my eyes, confused, stiff; I'm still on the back seat of the car.

It's day. Light glints through cracks in the wooden barn walls. Every part of me is alert now, listening, focusing on sounds outside the barn. Are there footsteps?

I reach between the front seats and push at Cate's shoulder. 'Wake up,' I hiss. 'I think someone's coming.'

She sits up. The light increases; someone is opening the barn door, stepping through.

'Catelyn Green?' a voice calls out, loud in the stillness. But that isn't our surname.

Cate reaches between the seats to grab my hand in hers. 'Listen to me, Tabby. Beware The Circle!'

'The what? What's happening?'

They're at the car now, opening the front doors, pulling Cate out. Her hand is ripped out of mine.

'Tabby, I love you!' she says and now one of them is at my door too, but I've already started to get out, to go to Cate.

'Let her go!' I say, but he holds me by the shoulders so I can't get away, and I'm struggling, pushing at him as much as I can with one arm in a cast. Two of them have Cate – they're in uniform, I see now. They're police. She's being marched between them out the barn doors and she's going, not struggling. Her shoulders are slumped.

49

She twists to look back at me. *I'm sorry*, she mouths. And I'm struggling still, but held fast as they go out through the barn doors and disappear.

13

'I understand that you must be confused and scared. I'm here to help you, but I can't help you if you won't talk to me.'

I ignore her, this woman – Sophie, she said her name is Sophie. After Cate was taken away they put me in a police car, brought me to this government place in London. They said I'm not under arrest but won't let me go. They brought Sophie in when I refused to speak to the police, but why should I talk to someone who tells me nothing but lies? She said she's a social worker but she's still one of *them* – part of the government. My head is tilted forward so my hair almost hides my face.

'I know my colleagues have already told you that the woman you knew as Cate Seymour isn't your mother. That you went missing from your parents when you were three years old. Your mother is here now. She's very anxious to see you. She's waiting for us to give the OK.'

I look up this time. 'Cate?' I say, feeling *hope*, despite everything, that they've realised this is all some stupid mistake, and we'll go off together like we always do.

She shakes her head. 'I know this must be so hard for you to accept. Your parents are Simone and Alistair Heath; it's Simone who is here. Tabitha was actually your middle name and your first name is Holly.'

I turn away.

'I know Cate must have lied to you your whole life, so why should you believe anything that I say? I've brought some things to show you that may help.'

She opens a file and takes out a newspaper clipping. 'Look. This is from over thirteen years ago.' She points at the date. She holds it out and I glance at it through my hair, but don't take it.

'I'll read the headline to you. "Three-year-old girl kidnapped by nanny." Look, there are photos. There's one of Catelyn Green – your nanny, as she was then – and another of you.'

I keep my eyes down, staring at the edge of the table.

'There's some more photos here, too.' She reaches to the file, takes one out. 'This is you with your real mum. The one waiting to see you now. And here is another one of the both of you and your dad, too. See? He's on his way now and should be here soon.'

Don't believe everything you're told, Cate said – and I don't. I *can't*. This is crazy.

'It's not me,' I say. 'You've got us mixed up with somebody else.' The lengths they'd go to, to put us in a box – a prison, whatever else they call it – are unbelievable.

'If you're so sure it's not you, what harm is there in looking at these things? I'll leave you alone for a while and then come back. Do you need a drink or anything?'

I shake my head. She gets up from the table, goes to the door. Knocks on it once and it opens from outside and she steps through.

This is all so . . . It's just . . . insane. I get up and stick out my tongue at the mirror on the wall behind Sophie's chair. I bet it's a two-way mirror and they're watching me right now. I won't give them the satisfaction of doing what they want me to do.

I go to the table and pick up the second photograph she showed me – some people I don't know holding a small child. What is that supposed to prove? It could be *anyone*. I turn back to the mirror and slowly, deliberately, crumple it up in my hands, then throw it at the mirror.

I pick up the other photo to do the same, but stop short when I look at it. It's a woman with long, wavy, dark hair, a laughing toddler on her knee. She has a hand curved around the child – and there on her wrist – a bracelet.

A gold bracelet shaped like waves, set with coloured stones. They're blue and green.

I look at the bracelet on my wrist, then back to the photo.

They're just the same.

Maybe there is more than one bracelet like this one? There could be *hundreds* – thousands! – of them. Just because I've never seen one like it before doesn't mean anything.

But if – just for a moment – I assume the one in the photo and the bracelet I'm wearing are one and the same, what does that mean?

This woman whose child was stolen had the bracelet. Cate had a bag of jewellery – for a rainy day, she said – stashed with Eli. And inside the bag was the same bracelet.

She said we'd stayed with Eli before when I was small, that she'd left the jewellery with him then. Was I small like in this photograph?

I'd remembered Eli and where he lives; I also remembered that I'd been scared staying there to start with.

Could Cate have taken me away from my parents and hid out with Eli, until the search died down?

No. *No way.*

Everything in the world has gone nuts. Completely crazy, like Eli said it would that time. None of this can be real; I have to figure things out for myself.

Maybe if I read this newspaper article, I'll spot the flaws – the ones that show I can't be this missing kid.

I sit down at the table, stomach clenching. Resolved to read it but afraid to do so.

Just look at it, then. I force my eyes up. The newspaper cutting is there, upside down so the words are still a mystery, but . . . the photo, the one Sophie said is of the missing girl's nanny? She's younger and her hair is shorter, but there's no mistaking her, even upside down: it's Cate.

Cate, with her fair hair that is nothing like mine.

I don't . . . I can't. This can't be . . .

My hand is shaking. I reach out and pull the paper towards me. I turn it the right way around and try to read. At first the words keep going in and out of focus and won't register, but bit by bit the gist of it starts to get through:

A missing child.

Heartbroken parents.

The child's nanny went missing at the same time and is wanted for questioning.

A large reward offered.

And . . . *and.* Jewellery was taken from the parents' home, too – including a distinctive, one-of-a-kind bracelet. And there it is again, in another photo. My bracelet.

If it's true that it is one-of-a-kind . . . this must be the same one. Stolen along with a child.

I reach again for the photo of the mother and child. Search the mother's face, the way she looks at her daughter and not at the camera, then focus on her long dark wavy hair, so like mine.

The child's face holds no clues: she's too young for there to be any resemblance I can see, either to this woman or to me.

Is it me?

How can this be?

Cate? What have you done?

Much of what comes next is a blur.

I'm crying, wrapped around myself on the floor.

Sophie comes back in; there's a hand on my shoulder.

Voices.

Time passes.

I'm put on a stretcher. More paramedics?

Another ambulance ride.

So much started with the first one. Back then, everything was set – not just my arm. I understood the world, or at least my corner of it, and that was enough.

But now?

There are more voices, asking me things, but I can't answer. I'm locked inside myself.

There's a pinprick in my arm, and gradually, everything eases.

I'm so tired. Someone is tucking me into bed. Cate?

Then everything goes black.

14

I wake slowly, not sure where I am but somehow knowing I don't want to be there. I reach back for sleep, still half in a vague dream, one where I'm swimming – holding my breath, underwater – trying to get away from something, or to something, but I don't know what it is. The more I try to go back to the dream to find out, the more sleep edges away. I'm holding my breath for real without realising and then, when I finally gasp for air, I'm awake.

I sit up and stare around me. I'm in a narrow bed with metal sides – a hospital bed? There isn't a curtain around it like the last time, and it is the only one in the room. I'm alone.

My thoughts feel dull and sluggish. I struggle to remember where I am, how I got here, then panic rushes through me as it starts to come back.

I can't process what has happened. Cate – taken away – she isn't my mother? How can that be when everything inside me screams that it is wrong?

Think, Tabby. What do I *know* with absolute certainty to be true?

The authorities separated us and took me away from Cate, just like she always said would happen if they ever caught us. They're trying to put me in one of their boxes, make me like everybody else: here you go, Tabby – two parents you never knew you had; a fixed place to live where the state can keep an eye on you, change you, indoctrinate you. And how best to make that happen? Lie. Lie and say that Cate isn't my mother and make up this whole crazy story. They saw my bracelet and mocked up a fake news article – easy enough to do. *None of this can be real.*

I have to get out of here. Cate will escape wherever she is being held, I know she will. I have to do the same.

But how will we find each other?

Cate will find me, somehow – if there is any way she can get to me, she will. I know it.

I'm getting out of here *now*.

I swing my feet down off the side of the bed and stand, feeling a bit woozy, much like how I felt the last time I escaped from a hospital. But this time I'm in a shapeless gown with a draught; it's open at the back. And my wrist . . . It's not there. The bracelet is gone. The last thing Cate gave me, and it's gone.

I feel a pang of loss to leave without it. But it's just a thing, something they twisted and used to try to make me believe their lies.

I walk carefully to the door, raise my hand to the knob.

It won't turn. It's locked.

It's too late; I'm already in a cage.

Fear and then anger burn in my blood. I want to punch and kick at the door and it is all I can do to stop from hurling myself at it. To get away I have to be smarter than that – smarter than *them*.

I rest my forehead against the door, close my eyes. Concentrate on breathing, on slowing the mad rate of my heart. I'm going to have to play their game, at least for a while. It's going to be hard. I've never been any good at hiding my feelings, but somehow, I'll do it.

There is a faint regular noise from outside the door – footsteps? They're getting closer and fear lurches in my gut.

They pause, then there is the clunk of a lock. I stand back from the door as the handle turns. A woman looks in. She's wearing hospital kind of stuff and a fixed, bright smile.

'Good morning, Tabby. Up I see. How are you feeling?'

'I – I don't know. Why was I locked in?'

'You were a bit hysterical last night, I'm afraid. Now. Would you like something to eat?'

She says she is a nurse and that her name is Priya. She jollies me along, through breakfast, into a shower. Into another horrible hospital gown but this time there's a dressing gown, too. Then she takes me for blood tests, an X-ray of my broken arm. She doesn't ask me questions and I go along, saying nothing, while everything is whirling around in my head. Every moment I'm here the more I feel trapped. They could keep me here for ever; they could do anything to me, and who would know?

After the X-ray, my cast is changed. This time it isn't plaster, it's fibreglass – and I get to pick the colour, so it's blue. They say my arm is healing well, faster than usual, and they seem surprised.

I'm taken back to my room, told to rest until I see yet another doctor in a few hours. I hear the click of the lock as I'm left alone, trapped within four walls that are too close together. I want – *need* – sun in the sky above me, fresh air. The sea to hide within. Panic is rising inside me again no matter how I fight it.

The door was locked, Priya said earlier, because I was hysterical. Does this mean if I keep my cool – or, at least, pretend to – and go along with what they want, the door will be unlocked at some point?

But I wasn't being hysterical now and the door was still locked. Maybe just going along isn't enough: I need to hide my fear, to convince them that I believe everything they say, that I'll do whatever they ask. Then, when they let down their guard, I'll have my chance.

15

'Hello, Tabby? I'm Dr Rasheed. Please, sit down.'

She smiles and I make myself smile back, sit on the chair she gestures towards. The room is bright with posters of animals and cartoon characters; there are toys all around, and a play mat on the floor. I'm concentrating on breathing evenly, keeping calm. Somehow the childish things in the room make it easier. I focus on a teddy bear and try to pretend he is the only one I have to convince.

'Sorry, it's not really age-appropriate for you in here, is it? I usually talk to younger children.'

I shrug. 'Doesn't matter.'

'Let me tell you a little about myself. I'm a clinical psychologist. I work with patients at this hospital, and one of the things I do is help them come to terms with difficult issues in their lives. I'd like to talk to you for a while, see how you are feeling and if there is anything we can do to help you. Is that OK?'

I nod. Swallow and scramble to think of something to say. 'Yes. Thank you.'

'How are you today, Tabby?'

'Tired.'

'Ah. I know it's been a difficult few days.' Her face is concerned, eyes sympathetic. But she is watchful, too; I need to be careful. 'But what I mean is more how you are feeling?'

And I don't know what to say. 'How do you think I'm feeling?' I can hear the annoyance in my voice and try to pull it back. 'I *am* tired – that is how I feel right now.'

'OK. How about a more specific question. How do you feel about Catelyn Green?'

I love her. I miss her.

But I'm supposed to believe she kidnapped me. 'I'm confused. I don't understand why she did what she did.'

And she's nodding, writing something down.

She looks up from her notes 'What did she do?' she says.

'Don't you know?'

'Well, I know what I've been told in a report. I want to hear what you know about it.'

'Oh. Sophie told me Cate took me from my parents when I was three years old.'

'Do you believe what she said?'

It's time to lie. And there is silence, too much of it, while I try to come up with what to say. I wrap my right arm around me under the cast on the left and go back to what I felt yesterday.

'I didn't believe Sophie. But then I looked at the photos she left, and there was this bracelet in them – I don't know what's happened to it, I was wearing it yesterday?'

'They've probably got it somewhere safe for you. Do you want me to check?'

I nod, and she makes a note.

'Anyhow, the woman in the photo was wearing the same bracelet. And in the newspaper clipping it said it went missing when the child did and that it's one of a kind, and there was a photo of the nanny who they thought took her and a bunch of jewellery. And it was Cate.' My stomach is clenching and I'm feeling sick, remembering how I felt yesterday, how they almost made me believe their lies.

'And?'

'Cate must have done it. Stolen me. I don't remember, but that must be what happened.' Lies, lies, all lies, to match their own. I keep my eyes downcast, afraid if she looks into them she'll see.

'How do you feel about meeting your parents? Going to live with them?'

Now I look up at her. 'I . . . I don't know. Do I have to?'

'They're very anxious to see you. But you can stay here until you are ready.'

Here, where doors are locked and eyes watch me closely like hers are now.

I swallow. 'I want to meet them.'

'Are you sure, Tabby? I know you were very upset last night. Is there anything else you want to ask, to talk about?'

I shake my head. 'When can I meet them?'

She's looking back at me, concern in her eyes. Head tilted to one side as if she's considering what I said and is unsure of it. 'Soon.'

As we carry on, the questions seem endless but become easier to answer. She wants to know about places we lived, what Cate did, if I ever went to school. Stuff about what it was like living with Cate. If I was happy.

And I was. The more I talk about Cate the harder it is to hide how much I miss her.

And then she asks a question again that she asked earlier: 'How do you feel about Cate?'

'I told you before.'

She nods, saying nothing, wanting more, but I am tired, so tired now, and don't want to keep playing along even though I know I should.

'Tabby, it's OK that you have feelings for Cate. As far as you knew, she's been your family for a long time.' Her voice is gentle. 'Do you want to talk about her?'

'No.'

'All right. We're nearly done for today. Let's get back to recent times. Tell me about the day that you broke your arm.'

'I ran out in front of a car; it hit me. They took me to the hospital.' That makes me remember something else. 'They said there was an anomaly – is that the word? – in my blood?'

She looks in her file. 'Yes. That's part of the reason they were taking blood samples this morning. I think the haematology department are a little overexcited.'

'Is something wrong?'

'From what I understand, not wrong, just different. It's how they worked out who you were at the other hospital when you broke your arm. When the hospital searched for information to help explain your blood test results, it came up that a girl your age with the same blood anomaly was registered as missing.'

'Is that why the police came?'

'I believe so. But you'd already left when they got there.'

Too close, Cate had said then, and she was right. *My fault.* Everything, it's all my fault.

'How did they find us?' I ask, and I can see she's hesitating, which means she knows, doesn't she? She knows but isn't sure what to say. 'Please tell me.'

'There was someone you called?'

'Jago,' I say, dismayed, even though I'd guessed as much.

'He told the police that you called and then hung up suddenly; he was worried about you. They traced the call to a payphone in Manchester, then checked CCTV in the area at the time.'

'I saw those photos in the paper.'

'They decided to go public with the images to try to find you.'

'And there was this guy at the services who recognised me.'

'Yes, someone called, but the police missed you again.'

'How did they find us in the barn?'

'Some walkers saw the car being put into the barn. The next morning the story about you and the make of the car and so on was on the TV news; they made the connection and called the police.'

'It's been on TV about me, too? Does everybody know who I am?' I'm horrified. If I get away how can I escape that? Even if I change my clothes, my hair, this cast on my arm will mark me out wherever I go. There's a sinking feeling inside when I realise: I'm going to have to wait until the cast is taken off to do anything.

'It'll be all right. People have short memories, and as a minor your identity and where you live are protected.'

I stare at her, not reassured. It's been so ingrained into me by Cate to never leave traces or images of ourselves behind that I'm feeling sick at the thought of being all over the news, but I can't tell Dr Rasheed that. Instead I go back to where we were. 'So, what is this blood thing I've got?'

She looks at her file again. 'They're not sure. They'll want to do some more investigations, I think.'

I shake my head. 'I don't want to be tested on any more. When can I meet my parents?'

I'm told in my room after dinner that I'll be meeting with my so-called parents the next morning: Dr Rasheed must have believed me at least enough to make that happen.

I'm surprised when I'm also told that my parents agreed with me about not having more tests done here, that they said they'll take me to their own doctor when I'm home.

Home?

Not my home, at least not for long. Once this cast is off my arm I'm gone.

16

The night is full of uneasy dreams, the sort you can't quite remember but which still leave feelings of dread behind. The next morning I'm even more tired than I was the day before. Cate used to say dreams like that were a warning, one to listen to. I ache with missing her at the same time as trying to shake off my misgivings. I need my wits about me today.

After I shower, the door is unlocked with breakfast. I'm still picking at the hospital's barely edible idea of how to feed a vegan when it opens again a while later.

'Hi, Tabby.' It's Sophie.

'Hi.'

'Sorry, I didn't mean to disturb your breakfast.'

I shake my head. 'You haven't. I'm done.'

She comes in, sits on the chair next to where I'm perched on the side of the bed.

'I'm sorry about the other day. About how upset you were. Dr Rasheed bit my ear off, and she was right.'

'Right about what?'

'It was too much to confront you like that with the truth all at once,' she says, and she's looking at me and her eyes – and her words – feel so genuine that it is on the tip of my tongue to tell her that it's OK, because I've realised I was wrong to believe any of it. *Be careful*, I remind myself.

'It wasn't your fault. I mean, it is what it is.'

'Maybe, but it should have been handled more gently, so I'm sorry about that.'

'It's all right.'

'I've got to know your parents a little over the last days. Are there any questions you have before you meet them?'

I should be curious, I remind myself. 'I don't know where to start,' I say, while my mind searches for something to ask. 'What do they do?'

'Well, let's see. You mum – she's lovely, by the way – was a lawyer years ago, but hasn't worked since you were a baby. Your dad is vice president of a big company. They live in Dorset – nice place.'

'You've been?'

'Of course. We're checking everything is good for you.'

'Oh.'

'Look, are you sure you're ready for this meeting with your parents today? It isn't too late to delay it.'

I shake my head. 'Let's do it.'

Not much later Sophie is waiting with me and a few others, men in suits. They're introduced as someone from the police, the other one is my so-called parents' lawyer. Why do they need one? The room we're in isn't small, but it's like the walls are closing in on me.

This is surreal – as if I'm living inside a crime novel. No, it's a movie. I have to remember that; they'll all be acting and so must I.

I long for Cate, to be with her; I've never been apart from

her before for more than a matter of hours, and I feel like something essential is missing – as if there isn't enough oxygen in the air. I want to find her and for us to go off together like we always do – disappear from these people, their boxes, forms and rules.

But for that to happen, first I must pretend.

'Tabby? It'll be all right,' Sophie says, the same thing Cate said to me a few days ago. But look what happened then?

There's a knock on the door.

'Are you ready now, Tabby?' Sophie says.

Not even close, but not for the reasons she might think. My traitor tongue is dry, so stuck to the roof of my mouth that I can't say a word.

Sophie opens the door; the two of them step into the room, with Dr Rasheed following behind.

The woman isn't very tall; my five-foot eight is probably inches taller than she is. Her dark hair is still long, like in the photo; there are some white streaks in it now. She's trembling; the man next to her has a hand on her arm as if holding her back. Sophie and the other two have got up, not leaving – Sophie said they wouldn't – just kind of getting out of the way, along with Dr Rasheed.

They come closer and sit on two chairs already set across from mine. My knees are drawn up in front of me with my right arm hugging them against me, the left arm in its cast behind them – keeping my legs and arms up like a barrier.

'Holly?' she says. 'I mean, Tabby. They said you go by Tabby. Oh.' She half chokes on her words and looks up at her husband next to her. They look mismatched – he's so much taller and all angles where she is round and soft – yet I can see the bond between them in the way she looks at him.

'This must be so hard for you, Tabby,' he says. 'Dr Rasheed said you were having trouble accepting that we are your parents, that you were stolen from us by Cate.' There is barely controlled anger behind his last words and I make myself not react to it. And Dr Rasheed said that? My acting hasn't been good enough then, at least not with her. He shakes his head. 'None of this is your fault. We're just so happy you're OK.'

The emotions the two of them are radiating feel so strong, so real; that and the trouble I feel breathing are making me dizzy. *Don't forget: they're acting*, I remind myself. But I can't stop my eyes from clenching shut – as if that can make them go away. I hear movement, then a hand touches my arm – lightly – and then it's gone before I can react.

'I used to read to you,' she says. 'Stories every night. You were such a happy baby! Always laughing. We've been so sad without you.' The pain in her voice sounds so genuine that it makes me open my eyes to look at her.

I untangle my arms and legs and put my feet on the floor, so I can pull up my sleeve. I hold out my wrist with the bracelet; they'd given it back to me on our way to this meeting.

'This is yours. Isn't it?' I say, wanting to push, to test. All she's done and said so far could have been practised again and again. How will she respond to something I say, unrehearsed? 'I saw it in the photo.'

She's on her knees next to my chair now. 'Yes. Your dad had it made for me – a present when you were born. After so long I didn't think I'd see it again. Or you.'

I start to take it off, to give it to her, but she shakes her head. 'It's yours, Tabby.'

I'm looking at her eyes, at the tears streaking her face, and can see no trace of dishonesty. For a moment I'm knocked off balance. I give myself a mental slap: *don't fall for it, Tabby.* Something hardens inside, sickened by how good she is at lying; how good they all are. *This* is what I must learn.

Now her husband gets up from his chair and stands next to her; he puts a hand on her shoulder, and then one on mine. I flinch – I can't stop myself – and he takes it away. Pain crosses his face.

'It's OK, Tabby,' he says. 'We know this is going to take some time. All that matters now is that we've found you again.'

As if she is some sort of mind reader and knows that things have gone as far as I can handle right now, Dr Rasheed comes nearer. Her calm voice is saying something but I'm not listening, not really – not to the meaning, just the tone.

Instead I'm focusing on making my face hide what I really feel: revulsion at their lies.

17

I'm brought back to see Dr Rasheed that afternoon.

'We need to make this difficult transition as manageable for you as we can,' she says. 'Everything in your life has changed. Are you ready to go to live with parents you don't remember?'

'It's going to happen anyhow, so let's get it over with,' I say. She's watching, waiting for me to say more and I'm trying to think what she needs to hear for her to let me leave this place of locked doors – to go to a place I can escape.

And then . . . What then? Where will I go?

No. I can't think about that now. Trust in Cate: that we'll find each other. The rest will fall into place.

It has to.

'Tabby? Tell me what you're thinking.'

I can't.

'Look. Maybe it's like a plaster,' I say. 'Pull it off fast, not slow – it's easier in the long run.'

'Or maybe the plaster can't be pulled off yet, not until it heals more underneath. I am here to help you: what is happening under that plaster?' She half pulls a face. 'I think that analogy has stretched as far as it can go. Talk to me, Tabby.'

'I think we should keep going with the plaster. If you get cut bad enough, you bleed. If it is deep enough, even with a plaster it may leave a scar. Collecting scars is just part of life.'

She tilts her head to one side. 'You are speaking in generalisations,' she says gently. 'I'm on your side in all of this, Tabby.'

'What are the sides? If you are on my side, then who is against us?'

'Well, not *against*, exactly. But your parents have missed you desperately; they're anxious to get you back with them as soon as possible. I'm here to make sure you're ready for that first.'

I'm curious and can't keep my question back. 'What if I'm never ready, what happens then?'

'Hmmm. Well, their lawyer is already making noises about hurrying this process along, and it's only been a few days. But I promise you, Tabby, your best interests are the most important thing in all of this.'

That night I'm thinking about what she said.

This controlled world I'm in now – where everyone is counted, monitored, contained, like Cate always said – is difficult for me to understand. But not absolutely *everybody* can be in on it, can they? The population is controlled precisely because they don't realise that is what is happening. They are generally led to make the choices the authorities want them to make – after all, they couldn't coerce everybody, all the time, could they? Patterns of society and expectation do much of their work.

And I think I believe Dr Rasheed – that she means what she says, that she thinks she is on my side in all of this. Sophie, too. But what do either of them know about *my* best interests? If I opened up to Dr Rasheed like she wants me too – if I told her I don't believe Cate isn't my mother and that I'm planning to run and find her the first chance I get after this cast is off my arm – they'd never let me out of this place.

I have to give Dr Rasheed enough of the kind of stuff that she wants to hear, but what exactly is that? I try to imagine who she must think I am, and what things this person would be having problems with. Can I pull it off?

I don't know, but somehow, I have to find a way.

Sun . . . sea . . . earth . . . sky

Sun . . . sea . . . earth . . . sky

Four words chanted over and over again by many voices.

Cate lies next to me on the damp sand of the earth, the whisper of the sea below us, blue skies above, the sun's warmth on our skin.

'You are not alone. The four points of our compass are always there,' Cate says. 'If you focus on them, they will help you find your way.'

Sun . . . sea . . . earth . . . sky . . .

'The four must always stay in balance,' Cate says.

I try to focus on all of them equally, though the pull of the sea is strongest. At the same time other voices whisper inside me: tell me to be strong, how to be strong, what they have endured – and there are too many voices that want to be heard. I'm getting lost in their pain.

But there is a core of strength inside of me that comes from Cate, and when I focus on her I am calm. Still. Anchored to an orderly centre in the midst of chaos.

'To lie and be believed, find the truth within the lie,' she whispers.

That is what I must do.

Sun . . . sea . . . earth . . . sky

You are not alone.

18

When I'm taken to Dr Rasheed again the next morning, I'm calm. Ready.

Before I've even completely sat down across from her, I jump in. 'Can I start? I've got something to say.'

'Of course,' Dr Rasheed says. 'Go ahead.'

'I've been thinking, and I think . . . that is, I know . . .'

'Yes, Tabby?'

'It's like this. I'm finding it hard to talk to you about stuff because it's always been just me and Cate. And she's told me as far back as I can remember not to tell personal stuff to anybody – not even my name. So it feels wrong to tell you anything when I don't really know you, but I want to try.'

She smiles. 'That's great. But it must have been difficult not being able to tell people your name or anything else. Didn't that make it hard to make friends?'

I consider. 'I didn't really have friends. We moved all the time – you know that.'

'There was that boy you called – Jago. He knew your name.'

And then he called the police; Cate was taken away from me because of him. He did this – without realising the consequences, maybe, but it's true.

But it's not fair to blame him. It only happened because I broke the rules.

'What is it, Tabby? What were you thinking just then?'

'Nothing. I – well – I think Jago was becoming a friend, but I broke the rules. That's all.'

'What were the rules? Did you have to keep away from other people?'

'Not exactly. I had a lot of freedom to come and go as I wanted. It was more to stay unnoticed, to keep to myself.'

'Why do you think Cate set these rules?'

'I never questioned it, at least not until recently. She said if the authorities found us we'd be separated.'

I trusted her, but did I always believe her? I'm uneasy, and can't think about it now.

'Did she say why you'd be separated?'

'No – at least, not exactly. But she said we didn't fit in, we weren't like everybody else, and the authorities didn't like that.'

'Did you believe her?'

'I had no reason not to. And we weren't like everybody else, so that was true.'

'What do you think now?'

I shrug. 'What she said would happen has happened. We've been separated.'

'Why do you think that is?'

'Because I was a missing person.' According to the authorities. 'And she took me.' Same again. If I finish the sentence inside my head with the bit I'm leaving out, it is somehow easier.

'Did she ever tell you anything about that?'

'No. Though after we left Manchester I asked her why I was in the newspapers as missing, if it was because we'd left that other hospital.' I'm remembering now, the way she'd answered vaguely, saying *probably*, like she didn't know. There is a twist in my stomach. She wasn't doing what I'm doing now, was she? Finding the truth within a lie to tell me? Something I remember her saying that came back in my dream last night.

No. *No way*. Cate would never lie to me. She didn't always tell me everything, any more than I always told her everything, but that's not the same thing as an out-and-out lie.

'Can we talk about your parents now?'

I nod. 'I've been thinking about that. Cate and I moved around all the time; I'm used to going to new places. It isn't as big a deal for me as you think.'

'It isn't just a new place though, is it? It's also the people you will be living with.'

'I don't know them. It's a totally weird situation, but the only way I'll get to know them is for us to spend time together. And putting it off just makes me think about it more. So, can I go?'

She's looking at me carefully. 'Tabby, are you sure that is what you really want right now?'

'Yes.' *So I can escape.*

'I'll see what I can do.'

Conditions are placed. I have to see Dr Rasheed here in London at regular intervals, and have phone calls with Sophie, too.

But it's all sorted. Tomorrow I'm going to someplace they call *home*, but to me it is just the first step to being able to run away.

And then? What then?

I shake my head, push the questions away.

I may not know how yet, but *then*, I will find Cate.

19

I'm ready early; I woke before it was light. Not wanting to risk any more weird dreams, I stayed awake, staring at the ceiling and watching the clock.

Sophie is taking me. Her car is sleek and shiny – it's not hers, it's a government one, she says – a hybrid that can run as an electric one or on fuel. When we get on the motorway I can't help but think of trips with Cate, especially the last one in that wreck of a car. And now I'm on another motorway, but this time I'm being taken to Simone and Alistair.

'You'll come in when we get there, won't you?' I say. When I first met Sophie I wouldn't even talk to her, but now she's become familiar. I don't want her to go, to leave me in a place I don't know.

'Of course,' she says. 'I'm staying for lunch.'

I'm chewing my knuckles in the car as we drive, wanting the miles to go slower.

She glances at me sideways as she drives. 'Moving to a new place can be scary.'

'It's not that – I've always moved around. But this is different.'

'Yes. It is. But you'll be fine.'

Sure I will. I glance at her satnav now and then, and the miles keep ticking down. The time of arrival gets closer and closer.

We stop at a services. Sophie is in the loo still when I come out, and for a moment I think – *run. Do it now.* Before I can think it through my feet are hurrying me towards the exit. But then I catch my image reflected in the glass doors, the cast on my arm. Do I imagine curious glances from people walking by, do they recognise me from the papers, TV?

Even if not – this is crazy. I have to wait until I can get rid of this thing on my arm. And I need money, a plan. I wander back as Sophie comes out, see her looking around – I wave, and we head back to the car.

More miles tick down, and as we get closer I wonder where we are going. How long will it be until my cast is off and I can run? Probably weeks? I'm going to have to live with them until then, and I hardly know *anything* about these people who they say are my parents.

I look at Sophie sideways, knowing I've been told things already that I haven't taken in properly, and wanting to hear them again – to distract myself if nothing else.

'Can you tell me anything else about my parents?' I say.

'Well, I told you that your mum Simone was a lawyer – still is, I guess, but hasn't worked for years now. She was fighting for environmental causes against big companies.'

'Cool.'

'And your dad, Alistair – he is kind of on the other side. He's a vice president for IU – Industria United.'

She doesn't have to tell me what kind of company it is, I know: IU are the biggest oil and gas company in the world. Their mining techniques and emissions are destroying the planet. If I thought it were true – that he really was my father – I'd be freaking out about who he is and what he does.

But since I don't believe any of it, it doesn't really matter.

'Your parents met when she was suing his company for fracking damages. They ended up falling in love and getting married. And then they had you.'

Sure they did. How could Simone do that – marry the enemy? That's crazy. It shows even more how ridiculous this family they've made up for me is.

Despite the things we've been talking about, what I've been thinking, something else begins to build inside of me. It's a sense of joy, anticipation, that doesn't fit with what is happening. It can only mean one thing.

We come over the top of a hill, and now I can see it: stretching out as far as forever is the sea.

Despite everything else, there is a rush of happiness in my blood to see it below, blue and endless.

I'm sitting forward to get closer to the view.

'Gorgeous, isn't it?' Sophie says.

'They live near the sea?'

'Yes. And now you do, too.'

We turn down a lane and the view vanishes, blocked by hedges that are a startling green after the parched land that came before. A few minutes later Sophie turns into a drive; tall black metal gates bar the way. She opens her window to push an intercom button, but before she can do so the gates start to swing open. Someone must be watching – there's a camera above. I automatically turn away from it as we drive through and they shut behind.

They live with cameras behind locked gates? There must be a way out; I'll find it. But then what I can see chases those thoughts away.

A wide sweep of intense green – lawns, flower gardens. The amount of water they must use to keep it like this is staggering. Then below us, a huge building juts out of the ground and the sea view is back behind it: the house is framed in blue.

I'm looking at the place, trying to take it in, as we go down the long drive.

'Is all of this theirs? They must be minted,' I say, then want to call the words back, embarrassed.

But Sophie just laughs. 'A bit.'

The house seems even bigger as we get closer. It's like nothing I've seen before, all straight lines in wood and glass, and there is something about the place that makes me think of Alistair, tall and angular.

Sophie pulls in, and now my panic returns in a rush.

'Are you ready?' she says.

Before I can think what to say the doors are open, and *they* – Simone and Alistair – are walking to the car.

My heart is beating too fast, my breathing is quick and shallow. I *have to* hide how I feel, I *have to* gain enough of their trust that they drop their guard and I can escape.

I get out of the car just as Simone reaches my side.

'Hi, Tabby,' she says, and the smile on her face is wide.

'Hi,' I say, trying to smile back but it feels like my face is frozen, that it'll crack if I do.

'Welcome home,' she says, and if my face is closed hers is the opposite: it's like she's full of joy and struggling not to cry at the same time. I can sense her wanting to hug me and without thinking hold out my hand to stop her from getting that close. Instead of shaking it, she tucks it over her arm and starts to walk us towards the door. Sophie hangs back, talking to Alistair.

Inside, it's like walking into the pages of a magazine. There's this huge entrance hall; the ceilings are double – maybe triple – normal height. There's a sweeping staircase but I don't look anywhere but beyond the stairs to the back of the house, at the open space with floor-to-ceiling windows. Now all I can see is the sea through the glass.

'Do you need to freshen up, go to your room? Do you want to look around first? Or are you hungry?' She starts telling me about the lunch their cook is preparing, all vegan in my honour – they have a *cook*? – and I can hear it in her voice: she's nervous. Probably scared she'll slip up, that I'll catch her out in her lies.

'Can we have a look through here first?' I say.

'Of course.' We walk towards the glass wall at the back of the house. 'I wasn't sure if you'd remember living here; you were so small.' And she shakes her head as if pushing that away, and starts going on about a party they're having tomorrow to welcome me home. A *party*? I've never been to one.

Sophie and Alistair are coming in behind us now. I turn to face them as a way to get my hand back from Simone's arm.

'Do you like the view?' he says, and I nod, move closer to the glass and the sea. There's a veranda along the house outside.

'Can we go out there?' I say.

'Of course,' he says. He touches a control pad on the wall and glass slides open.

I step outside. The sea is just there, below where we stand. A path winds down to a beach. And as I breathe in, and out, and hear the waves and savour air that tastes of the sea, the tension I'm holding inside me loosens. Just a little.

'Tabby was loving the view as we were driving in,' Sophie says.

'It's why we chose this location.' He starts talking about building the house and their architect's design. The way he speaks – he always sounds sort of weirdly polite, almost formal, though of course that is how you talk to people you don't know. I'm only half listening, still transfixed by what is below us.

'Lunch will be in twenty minutes,' Simone says. 'Tabby, shall I show you your room?'

I don't want to leave the view but turn to follow her. We walk back towards the entrance and then up that big staircase.

'I didn't think you'd want your old room, at least not as it is, but do you want to see it?' she says.

She opens a door into a childhood wonderland. Toys upon toys. A princess bed with what looks like sides that go up and down – for a child so small that they need them up so they don't fall out? The windows face the gardens at the front of the house, and I stand there, taking it in. Do they really think I'm going to believe this used to be my room? It feels so *alien*. It's a rich kid's room.

'I couldn't ever bring myself to change it, or put anything away,' she says. 'But it's a nursery, not right for a teenager. Oh. You're so grown up.' She's on the verge of tears again and I step away, back out through the door. She follows, and shows me to another door, further down the hall.

'I've put you in one of the guest rooms for now. We can redecorate, or do up the nursery. Whatever you like.' She opens

82

a door, and I stand there. It is like the poshest hotel room *ever*, but I don't care about any of that: there are floor-to-ceiling windows, and this room faces the sea.

Is that a balcony through the glass?

'Are there doors to outside up here, too?'

'Yes.' She shows me how to make them slide open by pushing a control on the wall, and we step out to the balcony.

All too soon she draws me back inside, shows me the en suite. My own bathroom? And it's bigger than most bedrooms.

'Do you like this room? Or do you want to see the one across the hall?'

Across the hall? Would that mean garden views, not sea?

'No . . . I mean, yes. I like this one. It's lovely,' I say. 'Uh, thank you.'

'Do you need to freshen up?' she says again, and I wonder what that means until her eyes move to the bathroom door and back again.

'Er, yes.'

'I'll wait for you?'

'I can find my way back down.'

'Oh. Of course.' She backs out, shuts the bedroom door behind her.

Instead of the bathroom I go back to the balcony. First I close my eyes and fill my mouth, throat and lungs slowly with the tang of salty air. I breathe out just as slow as I can, and repeat – in, out, in, out – until the mad pulse I've had since we got here has slowed to almost normal. Then I open my eyes and drink it in.

The smell and taste of the sea are as much a part of this

connection as what I can see, maybe even more. My senses join together and say, *this is mine*. It is who I am: my home.

I'm thrown off balance by my thoughts and shake my head. It's not this particular place that says *home*, it's the sea. It's the same whenever I'm near it.

I make myself go back into the room to properly check it out. It's *huge*. I mean, six people could sleep on this bed and it doesn't look big in this space. What Cate would say if she saw—

There's a twist in my gut, pain like a physical punch. *Cate. Where are you?*

I need to focus on here and now to get through this. I try to push her out of my mind, go back to checking out the room.

There's a row of doors, wardrobes, mostly empty but there are some clothes hanging inside one section. With tags attached – they're new. Are they for me? I shut the doors, not wanting to even look at them. They can't buy me with all of this.

Freshen up is a strange way to say pee if that's what she meant, but I do that too, marvelling as I wash my hands at the size of the bath, the separate shower. This bathroom is acres of shining white tiles and glass. It'll take me ages to keep it clean. I mean, it *would* if I were staying.

Another moment on the balcony, and I might be ready to face—

There's a light knock on the door. It opens; Simone peers in.

'Lunch is ready,' she says.

20

A square table has been set on the veranda downstairs. Alistair shows me to a seat. I'm between him and Simone, Sophie on the opposite side.

Another woman is here also, and she comes up to me now. 'What would you like to drink, Miss Tabby?'

Miss Tabby? I glance at Sophie.

'Soft drink or juice?' she suggests.

'Orange juice?' I say, tentatively.

The woman – who is she, the cook? – soon comes back with a tray of drinks. No one introduces her.

She puts my juice in front of me. 'Thank you,' I say, and take a sip; it practically sings *freshly squeezed*. Then she and another man come out with dainty bowls of vegetable soup, rolls, butter, and the soup smells *amazing*. It reminds me I'd been too nervous to eat anything this morning.

'Sorry. Is it OK if I just check – it's all vegan, isn't it?'

'Yes,' Simone says. 'We've stretched our cook's repertoire a little. Have you always been . . . I mean . . . Well, why?'

'As long as I can remember, and for so many reasons. Animal welfare is only part of it. Clearing forests for livestock that then strip the land and turn the grass they eat into methane all contributes to climate change.' I'm saying words that I believe, but Cate could have said it better.

Another course follows – tofu in a light spicy sauce with fancy veg – and, like the OJ set the stage, everything is the best I've ever tasted. Yet it's as if I'm noticing that on remote, almost as if I'm acknowledging it rather than experiencing anything directly. Sitting here feels so *wrong* – these people, this setting. There's no way I could ever belong to a place like this.

All the while Simone and Alistair are trying to make small talk – is that what you call it? – with Sophie, with me. Sophie does a better job at it than I do. I eat slowly, knowing that when we're done, she'll leave.

Tea and coffee come at the end, with little pieces of chocolate cake. I look at Sophie with *please don't leave me here* in my eyes.

'There are a few things we need to discuss before I go,' Sophie says. 'One thing I wanted to mention is that I think Tabby has been feeling unsure about what to call both of you.'

I look at her, surprised. I never said, but somehow she knew – maybe she noticed I avoided using their names or any labels the few times I spoke to either of them.

'Tabby?' Sophie says. 'Is that so?'

'Well, to me it's like we just met. So to say Mum and Dad would feel . . . well, strange.'

'Oh,' Simone says, a look of hurt crossing her face.

'I'm sorry,' I say. 'It's just so weird, but—'

'It's understandable,' Alistair says. 'What would you like to call us instead? Simone and Ali?'

'That'd seem a different sort of weird to me,' Simone says. 'Oh, I know: how about this? My mother – your grandmother, you'll meet her tomorrow – is from Paris. In French, Mum and Dad are *Mère* and *Père*. Could you call us that?'

There are more pretend relatives I'll have to meet – a French grandmother? I didn't think that far ahead. Maybe they've got a whole big family, and more nerves twist in my stomach to think it. The French names – *Mère* and *Père* – still sound too much like Mum and Dad, but what does it matter? I know they're not real, and they'll still be Alistair and Simone in my head.

'OK. Let's do that,' I say.

'This is perfect: you've confronted something that is a problem and solved it together,' Sophie says. 'Another thing I know you both wanted to discuss is Tabby's education.'

'Dr Rasheed told us you've never been to school before,' Ali says.

'No. I was home schooled.'

They all exchange a glance at that, but I *was*. It might not have been the way most people do things, but I learned about whatever I wanted to from books and talking to Cate, and I was always curious. I'd ask questions and if Cate didn't know, we'd find the answers together.

'We've arranged for a highly recommended tutor to come next week,' he says. 'She'll assess where you're at in the core subjects, and we'll go from there.'

'There's a very good girl's school nearby,' Simone says.

A school? Uniforms, standing up and down when bells ring. Cate said they're like prisons.

There is a slash of pain inside me. While I'm here in these beautiful surroundings, is Cate in an actual prison? I close my eyes and wish all of this away: to be with Cate, back in our caravan.

'Tabby?' Sophie says. 'Is everything all right?'

I open my eyes. Three pairs of concerned eyes look back at me, but I know they don't really want to hear what I was thinking; even if they did, it's best kept to myself.

'It's just the thought of going to school.'

'It doesn't have to be straight away, does it?' Simone says.

'We'll see,' Alistair says.

They start going on about the nearby school and I pretend to listen, but soon tune out. Is Cate in prison? If she is, how will she get out and find me? If she can't, can I go to her?

I give myself a mental shake. I need to hold on to hope, and trust in Cate. What was it that she said? Things always turn out the way they are meant to in the end. And there's no way I can believe that we aren't meant to be together.

Soon after, Sophie says goodbye, shakes their hands and I follow her out to the car.

She gives me a quick hug, and now is my chance: to ask her something without my so-called parents listening.

'Sophie, there's something I want to know. Where is Cate?'

'She is in London, waiting for her trial. She's in custody.'

'In prison?'

'A type of prison, yes,' she says, and even though I'd guessed that must be the case, I'm still shocked.

'Can I visit her?'

'I don't think they'd allow a visit from anyone involved in the case. Do you want me to check?'

I nod.

'OK. But even if it is possible, you'd need a parent or guardian to apply for a visit and accompany you.' She doesn't add, *and that'll never happen*, but we both know it. 'Look, I know this must all be overwhelming just now. But you have two parents in there who love you. Give them a chance?'

How can they love me when they don't even know me? It's all a big act, and I need to keep acting, too. 'I'll try,' I say.

She says goodbye, and I watch her car wind up the long drive to the gates. They open, and she's gone from sight.

21

When I turn to go back to the house, Simone is still there, at the door, and there's no Sophie to hide behind.

'Another delivery of clothes came while we were having lunch,' she says. 'I've had it taken to your room.' I must look puzzled. 'Oh, I didn't say, did I? I've had a bit of a guess at your size and ordered a few things. Just so you're set with things to wear the next few days. There were some in the wardrobe in your room already.'

'Thank you,' I say, feeling awkward, weirded out and just a little excited at the thought of brand-new clothes – and then annoyed at myself for feeling that way.

'If you don't like what I've chosen you can pick your own, of course,' she says. 'We'll go shopping together in London? Or you can order online. Or both.'

Alistair comes through. 'Now for the full tour of the house,' he says.

There follows a bewildering number of rooms. Trying to keep it all straight makes my head spin. There are more levels than I realised, including some underneath the main floor. A gleaming gym. Kitchens, and now I get introduced to the cook, the housekeeper. There's mention of gardeners and security, too, and alarm systems. It's easy enough to follow along, nod and even smile a bit sometimes, with Alistair telling me all about the construction of the place and the built-in technology, though I don't understand most of that. The whole place must use so much power and there's no solar or wind power sources I can see.

I can't figure Alistair out. Simone's emotions are so obvious it's like she's overacting all the time, but with him, how he feels seems locked away. The way he talks he could be giving a tour to anyone, not the long-lost daughter I'm supposed to be.

When we're finally back to the veranda overlooking the sea, I ask the question I've been holding inside. 'Is it OK if I go down to the beach?'

'Of course. I'll come with you,' Simone says.

I try to hide my reaction: I was desperate both to go there and be alone, but should I pretend I want her to come?

'Let her go by herself,' Alistair says to Simone. 'She needs a minute alone to breathe I should think.'

'Oh. Tabby, is that what you want?' she asks.

I look from one to the other, caught between what I want and not being sure which of them I should side with.

Alistair laughs. 'Just go. It's OK.'

As I go down the stairs from the veranda and start down the steep path I can hear their voices rise and fall behind me in something that is not quite an argument. Is that my fault? Is Alistair the one to side with – when the time comes, will he be more willing to let me out of sight long enough to run away?

As I get closer to the beach and can't hear them any more, the tight feeling in my chest begins to ease.

I take off my shoes. Wet sand squelches beneath my toes as I walk to the water's edge; the tide is on its way out.

At that first hospital, the nurse who bandaged my foot had

said that she wondered why my feet hadn't been *seen to*. I know my toes are different – different to Cate's or anyone else's I ever saw in flip-flops or sandals – with skin joining them together. I looked it up once: it's a birth defect, called syndactyly. Cate said it was part of me, that it showed I was special, and not to be concerned if my feet got odd looks. That didn't stop me from getting in a fight when I was about ten and some boys were making *quack, quack* noises at me, saying I must be a duck to have webbed feet.

I roll up my jeans and step into the cool water, let the waves lap at my ankles. It's June now and getting warmer all the time. It must be thirty degrees today, and I know that shouldn't make me happy, that the summers are getting longer and hotter because of climate change, but just now, in this moment, standing in the sea and soaking up the heat of the sun feels good.

No matter where I am or what has happened, the sea is the sea. The tide comes in; the tide goes out. Nothing that happens or doesn't happen to me will ever change it, and somehow that makes me feel better than I did a moment ago.

If it wasn't for this stupid cast on my arm I'd be tempted to take off my jeans and dive straight in, swim out as far as I can and then back again. But imagine the panic if they saw me do that?

Instead I walk back up the beach to where the sand is a little drier and sit down, then lie back, knees up. I slow my breathing gradually until it is in harmony with the waves.

Water sweeps in, I breathe in; it falls back, I breathe out. This perfect rhythm starts to take the knots and stress away, and I relax more completely than I have in a long time. Really since the last time I did this, at another beach – in Cornwall.

And then Jago came.

My breathing falls out of synch with the waves. Jago turned my life upside down: in a good way to start with, but then everything changed – first, when those others came to the beach, then when I called him and he told the police. Cate is in prison and I'm here with people I don't know, missing her with an ache deep inside of me, and it's all because of Jago.

Did he think I needed help, that he was doing the right thing?

Maybe, but how I feel about him now is a confused mess.

I could call him and ask why he did it. Cate banned me calling him again but it's not like I'll be found by the authorities if I do; they've already got me.

His number: what was it? I cast myself back to that other beach and my breathing steadies in synch with the sea once again.

I opened my eyes and he was there.

We spoke; he knew my name.

But his number: no matter how I try to bring it back, I can't. I wrote it in that notebook: another thing left behind. And now I can't remember.

Tears sting under my eyelids. *Everything* I've ever had has been lost: Cate. My whole life. My only friend.

All I have is the sea, and as I breathe with the waves once again I begin to ease, to release the tension inside.

But then, like that day with Jago, slowly I become aware that someone is approaching. I open my eyes.

It's Simone.

'I've brought you a towel. Do you want to come up and get dressed for dinner?'

I look at the sky; the sun has moved much further than I thought.

'I'm sorry, I must have nodded off.' I take the towel, scrub the sand off my feet and put my shoes back on.

'It's fine. You know, I used to bring you down here all the time. It looks different now; the beach was much wider when the sea was lower down – high tide was in line with those rocks.' She points out some rocks offshore, just breaking the surface now and probably completely hidden when the tide is in. 'We'd make sandcastles together, then you'd knock them down. After you were gone, I'd come here alone and stare at the sea, wondering if somewhere you were doing the same.'

Everything she says and does seems so real, so genuine. Maybe I've got some things wrong, and she isn't acting. Maybe her child *was* taken away from her, and she has been told that I am that child.

I try to imagine what that would have been like – losing a child, pining for them for so many years, then being given someone else: me. A poor trade for what she has lost – especially when I disappear, and she has to go through the pain of loss all over again.

If that is true then she is a victim in all of this, too.

She shakes her head. 'I'm sorry. That both staring at the sea thing sounds a bit fanciful.'

'No, it doesn't. And I might have been.'

We're both looking out to sea now and must see them at the same moment: Simone's hand points as the pod seems to fly out of the sea at once, silvered in the afternoon sun.

'Dolphins used to come near all the time, but I haven't seen them here for years,' she says, wonder in her voice that matches how I feel, too. Watching them, their flight a special kind of gravity-defying magic, both joy and yearning swell inside me.

They've disappeared under the waves and just when I think we won't see them again they surface as a group – even closer to shore. I long to run across the sand and dive into the waves to join them, to swim as they do.

They break the surface once again, heading back out now, and I ache to watch them go.

'It's good luck for us to see them together like this again,' Simone says. 'Do you remember how you always wanted to run into the sea and play with them?'

'That sounds about right. I've always loved dolphins.'

'But you don't remember, do you? Do you remember anything of being here at all?' she says, and I know she means of *her*, not dolphins or sandcastles. Her eyes are so open, so full of longing. But even if the child she lost was here now, she's gone for ever, isn't she? I'm not a child any more, and she wouldn't be, either.

'I'm not sure. There has always been this pull the sea has over me. I feel happy when I'm near it. Maybe that's because of living near it when I was small? I don't know.'

She nods, wanting *more*, so much. I feel sorry for her, but there is nothing else I can give her that would be anything like real.

22

Back in my room I run the bath, ease myself in, careful to keep my cast out of the way. The heat helps ease the knotted muscles I hadn't noticed I still had – neck, shoulders, back. Even my hands. I've been holding myself wrong, too tense.

I'm confused about so many things. First, I thought everyone – the police, Sophie, Dr Rasheed – were all lying. Then I realised not everyone can be in on how the population is controlled by the authorities; I started to believe Dr Rasheed and Sophie, at least. So where do Simone and Alistair fit in with all of this?

Either Simone is the best liar *ever*, or she did lose a child, and thinks that child is me. So, which is it?

I don't plan to stay here for long – once this cast is off my arm, I'll run – but if she really believes that I'm her daughter, it's cruel. It won't stop me from doing what I need to do, but somehow, I need to know.

How do I find out?

If I were really their daughter, I'd have so many questions. I'd want to know everything about them and the first years of my life. If I ask them everything I can think of, surely then I'll be able to see if this is real for them or a charade.

I get out and wrap the bathrobe from the back of the door around myself.

She said something about getting dressed for dinner and I'm

guessing she didn't mean to put back on the stuff I had on all day, and it's about all I've got otherwise. I go to the wardrobes and open the section where I'd seen stuff hanging before.

I hesitate, not sure where to begin.

Cate always let me wear what I liked – second hand, generally – but I had the final say on what I would wear, even when I was small. An unbidden memory flashes into my mind: me in a fuzzy onesie of a bunny. When I was about six I insisted on wearing it everywhere, to the point that it fell apart and even Cate couldn't mend it any more.

Cate couldn't buy me expensive things like these, but it never mattered.

A bit later I'm ready to go downstairs, but pause when I catch myself in the mirror.

These clothes – leggings and a tunic – that I picked from the endless supply Simone had bought and hung in the wardrobe are just so – well – *gorgeous*; I almost don't recognise myself. I'm not sure about some of the other stuff, but I would have picked this if I'd seen it.

And the bracelet matches the tunic – the same blues and greens.

I breathe in deep, and head downstairs.

23

'You look lovely,' Simone says. 'Dinner is a little delayed; Ali had to take a call.' There is disapproval in her voice. 'Do you want something to drink? Are you hungry? I can get some snacks brought, or—'

'I'm fine. Actually, I was wondering if there are some photos of all of us I could see?'

She beams. 'Of course.' I follow her into one of the rooms that flashed by earlier; Alistair called it a sitting room.

There's a photo on the wall of the two of them and I walk up to it for a closer look.

'This is you? Your wedding?'

'Yes.'

Alistair looks much the same now, a little older I guess, but Simone has changed. In the photo she is so beautiful, so young, too. Her face is split with a huge smile.

'When did you get married?'

She seems uncomfortable with the question; she shrugs. 'It's our twenty-fifth anniversary this summer.'

'So you were married for nine years when I was born.'

'Yes. I always wanted children; Ali did too. But it wasn't to be for a long time; you were our miracle baby.'

'Is that why you didn't have any other kids?'

She nods. 'We struggled, ended up trying IVF – in vitro

fertilisation? – and failed again and again, until they wouldn't let us try any more. But then we found the Penrose Clinic; actually, my mother did. We checked it out, had another go, and here you are.'

'The Penrose Clinic? What's that?'

'It's a private IVF clinic. They still follow their babies, like you. You're booked for a check-up there the day after tomorrow.'

'Does IVF mean like test-tube babies?'

'Some call it that. What it means to us is that you were the most wanted and loved baby there could ever be. Do you want to see some baby photos?' I nod and she pulls an album off a shelf and goes to the sofa.

I sit next to her and she opens the book. There's some other stuff first and she starts to flip past it, but I'm curious.

'What's at the beginning? Can I see?'

'Of course.' She turns back the pages. 'The first one is me, holding the pregnancy test result.' Her face is beaming; she's holding a little stick in her hands. 'That's when we first knew you were on the way.' She turns the pages.

'These next ones were us tracking my baby bump once a month all the way.' There's a series of shots of her in the same red jumper, from no tummy I can see, to a tiny bump and more and more until the red jumper is stretched right out of shape.

'Here's the first time we saw you – it's an ultrasound.'

'That looks more like a fish! With a funny big head.'

'Perfect in every way. Because of all the trouble conceiving, you were tracked more closely than is usual, so we had regular checks and ultrasounds at the clinic; here's the rest of them.'

There's a series of ultrasounds and gradually it starts to look more like a baby.

'And then it was the big day: your birthday! The seventeenth of April.'

I look at her. 'My birthday is in April? I thought it was the twenty-first of June.'

'How very odd.' She frowns. 'I suppose Cate told you another day, as part of changing who you were. Oh. I'm not supposed to talk about her.'

'Why?'

'Dr Rasheed said not to mention her. Unless you do first.'

'So, Cate was my nanny?'

She nods. 'She seemed so perfect. Afterwards we agonised over it, why we didn't realise anything was wrong. If only we had. Or if only I hadn't gone back to work, then . . .' She shakes her head. 'I never could, after you were gone. I mean, go back to work again.'

'Sophie said you were a lawyer?'

'That's right. A barrister – appearing for clients in court.'

'And how about Alistair. I mean, *Père*. Did he? Go back to work?'

She tilts her head. 'Ali suffered too, but in his own way. He threw himself into work more instead of less.'

The door opens; Alistair – Ali? – comes in.

'Ah, the photos are out, I see.'

He sits down next to me and more pages are turned. Now there are photos of a tiny baby held close in Simone's arms – and you can see it, invisible yet somehow still a tangible thing. The cord may have been cut when she was born, but it ties them together for ever. Taking this baby away from Simone has broken something inside of her.

There's no point in denying it any longer to make myself feel better. I believe her – that she's lost a child, that is, not that it is me. She's being lied to by the authorities just like I am.

I touch a finger to the baby's cheek in the photograph. *Where are you, Holly?* I whisper to myself. *Come home. She needs you.*

24

This bed is too big. I can lie in the middle and stretch out both arms and not reach the sides. It's comfy and warm and I should be asleep, but it's just *weird*. It feels wrong. I can't sleep.

We were only in Manchester a few days on that small sofa bed, Cate coming in late from work to sleep next to me. It wasn't unusual – we've stayed places before where that was the norm. Even if not, she was usually nearby. I ache with missing her, having her close, the familiar sound of her breathing.

It's these pillows – also too big – and it's like my head and neck can't get at the right angle. I push them aside and lie on my back in the dark, knees up and staring at the ceiling above. There's no light at all, not like in Manchester – there was light pollution everywhere there. Simone showed me how to lower the hidden blinds over the windows, but once she left I'd opened them again. All I can see is dark sky, stars; all I can hear is the whisper of the sea, the beating of my heart.

I'm so tired, but my mind is busy, turning things around and around. I arrived here convinced Simone and Alistair were liars, taking part in a charade to keep me here and away from Cate. But now I've accepted that they have lost a child and think it's me.

What if they're right, and they really are my parents?

No. Just *no*. That's crazy. Cate *is* my mother; I know she is, as sure as I breathe.

I can't stay still so I get up, shrug on a dressing gown. I pace back and forth at the windows, then stop, stand there in the starlight for a moment.

If there is anything I do know, it's that I need sleep – desperately. A good night and my brain will work better, everything will make some kind of sense.

To sleep, I need a smaller pillow. It's ages since they said goodnight; they're probably sound asleep. Simone showed me where her room is, across from the nursery; she said to come if I needed anything, but I don't think complaining about the size of the pillows at two a.m. was quite what she had in mind.

Hang on a minute. She said it was *her* room. Don't married people usually sleep in the same room?

Maybe I misheard her or misunderstood.

What about the nursery? The bed in there was small; there must be smaller pillows there?

I hesitate, then open my door. There are dim motion lights that come on as I walk down the hall as quietly as I can.

I open the nursery door carefully, shut it behind me and turn on the lights.

The hairs stand up on the back of my neck. It feels wrong to be in here, like I'm trespassing. Can I somehow feel the sorrow that centred on this room after Simone's child was taken from her? Or maybe it is *her*, Holly – their missing daughter. Maybe something happened to her, and she's come back to this place and not gone beyond.

I cross the room to the bed – a normal-sized twin bed, but for a three-year-old it'd have been as big as the one I've got is for me. And yes, there are two normal-sized pillows.

Part of me wants to grab one of them and back straight out of this room, but even more I want to try to get to know Holly, to find any traces she may have left behind.

I wander around the room, walking slowly, touching toys, picture books. There's a big soft toy bunny on a huge rocking chair – the bunny would be as big as a three-year-old, at least – and I'm drawn to it, to pick it up and wrap my arms around it.

I go back to Holly's bed with the bunny still in my arms, so tired I'm almost sleep walking, and sit down. Did Simone come in here after Holly was gone? Did she lie here in sadness, with her arms around this bunny like mine are now? Simone feels imprinted on this place in a way that Holly does not. It's been a long time since she was here, after all.

I try to imagine what that must have been like for Holly also – a little girl, just three years old, living here surrounded by love. Taken away from everything that she knew.

I'm hiding. She's counting out loud and I hear her but can't see her and I'm giggling still when she stops.

'Where are you, Holly? Are you in the wardrobe?' Doors open and close. 'No. Are you in the bathroom?' Another door opens and closes.

'Oh well, if no one's here, I'll have to find someone else to read a story to.' Footsteps start across the floor, tap tap tap to the door.

I jump up and shriek. 'Here! Mummy, here!' Toys fly off my bed where I'd piled them on top of me.

'Ah, there you are! OK, it's bedtime now. Who do you want to snuggle tonight?'

I point. 'Bunny!'

She gathers up my giant bunny and tucks him in next to me. I hug my arms around him but can't reach all the way.

'How much do I love you?' she says, and reaches for the book that is always there just under my bed – the first and last story of every day. She opens it and begins.

25

My eyes open wide. My heart is thumping wildly and it's a moment before I realise where I am: in the nursery, on the bed. With the bunny. I didn't mean to fall asleep, but I was so tired; I just lay down for a moment, and then . . . that dream.

The bunny was bigger than me; my arms were small.

Was it just a dream, or something more?

It *can't* be. I talked myself into it, didn't I? Trying to be Holly, imagining being her, here, in this place, with this bunny, and my unconscious mind came up with a dream.

I get up and cross to the window. It's very early morning; the sun is only just coming up. Hopefully no one else is awake – I can't face anyone until I get my thoughts straight. I put the bunny back on the chair and smooth out the bed. As I do my toe connects with something and I reach down.

A picture book – *Guess How Much I Love You?* – with a bunny on the cover.

Just where it was in the dream.

Hairs are standing up on my neck, my arms. I reach down, replace it. Walk swiftly across the room, peek out; the coast is clear.

I head back to my room, go in and shut the door. Lean against it, still shaken.

I believe there are spirits left behind when people we love

leave us. Not ghosts, exactly, but echoes of who they were stay with people or places they loved – that's what Cate said. Someone you love can never really leave you because of this.

Was that Holly, in her room, haunting my dreams?

As wild as that seems, there are only two other explanations I can come up with. One is that I made it up in my unconscious mind because of being there and thinking about Holly. But how did I dream about a book that I never knew was there until after I woke up? I don't remember seeing that book on the floor, but I was so tired, I might have and just don't remember.

Or . . . that dream *was* a memory, brought back by being in that room. Which would mean that I really am Holly.

No. That's impossible. No.

Cate is my mother: I know it. I hold on to this, like a lifeline inside me. I can't let go.

26

I'm in a deep dreamless sleep when I'm yanked awake by the part of me that listens and watches.

'Good morning, Tabby.' It's Simone?

I sit up, looking all around for her, but the door is still shut and I can't see her anywhere.

'I'm on the intercom,' she says. 'There's a phone call for you; it's Sophie. You can pick it up in your room, there's a handsfree on the dressing table?'

'Um, OK,' I say, wondering if she can hear me, and hoping I don't talk in my sleep.

There is indeed a small base with a handset on the dressing table. I push the green button. 'Hello?'

'Hi, Tabby. It's Sophie. How're things?'

'Um, OK I guess.'

'Are you settling in all right?'

'Yeah.'

'You don't sound yourself. Is anything wrong?'

'No, I'm fine. The phone – well, that is, the intercom thingy – just woke me up.'

She laughs. 'You must be settling in well to still be asleep at ten-thirty in the morning.'

Apart from being awake half the night, yes.

'There is something I need to ask you about. Was there

anything in the place where you stayed in Manchester that you want sent up to you?

My eyes open wide. 'Yes! There's a notebook. It's blue and white with a drawing of waves on the front. It says *Tabby's Notebook* on the spine.'

'Yep, got it. I'll pass that along. And how about from your caravan in Cornwall? It was impounded there. Is there anything in it that you want?'

I smile and start running through my notebooks, books, trying to think if there is anything else.

'OK, I'll see what I can do. You can always call if you think of anything else. Have you got my number?'

'I don't know. Do they have it here?'

'They do, but I'll give it to you, then you can call without asking for it if you want to. Most of the time you'll have to leave a message and I'll call back as soon as I can. But if you are having any problems or just want to talk, you can call, OK?'

I find a notepad and pen on the dressing table and write down the numbers as she says them.

'Thank you,' I say.

'That other thing you asked me about – visiting Cate. I'm sorry, Tabby. It was a no. Not until the trial is over, and then, while you are a minor, only if your parents agree.'

'When will the trial be?'

'These things take ages – months or longer, most likely. And then it depends on the result, the sentence.'

I feel numb. Months, in prison – Cate? She who loves open places, blue skies.

109

Then the *sentence*. With the authorities against her, how long will that be?

'Tabby? Are you still there?'

'Yes. I'm here.'

'Do you want to talk about this some more? Perhaps with Dr Rasheed?'

'No!' I say. I don't want her in my head. Did I say that too emphatically? 'Really, I'm fine.' *The biggest lie of all.*

'All right, but if you change your mind, give me a call, OK?'

'I will. Thanks.'

We say goodbye soon after that.

I just stand there for ages, not moving, barely breathing.

Cate is in prison. Maybe for a long time. I can't see her.

And even with all of that to deal with, my thoughts keep veering back to the dream I had, the bunny, the book: what does it mean?

No. I have to focus on here and now: on getting through each hour, each day, until I can get out of here.

But if Cate is in prison, where can I go?

No. I can't think about this any more, I *can't.*

I push it all away, visualise a door slamming inside my head. One I never want to open.

After a quick shower I find some jeans and a T-shirt that fit near enough.

It's time: I have to go downstairs and pretend. Talk normally. Not give them any reason to worry.

How?

Ask questions. Before they have a chance to ask me anything, ask them.

I find Simone and Ali in the smaller of the dining rooms, the one next to the kitchen.

'Good morning,' she says. 'Did you sleep all right?'

I give a noncommittal so-so gesture with my hand. 'Actually, if you've got some around, would it be possible to get a smaller pillow?'

'Of course.'

'How does the intercom work?' I ask Simone. 'Could you see me or hear what I said back to you?'

'No, just guessed. It's by the door. You have to go to it and push a button to answer. Did I wake you?' I nod. 'Sorry.'

'Doesn't matter. I don't usually sleep in so late.'

'When you were tiny you didn't sleep very much – at night-time, that is,' Simone says. 'You'd wake up crying at least three or four times a night until you were over a year old.'

'That must have been fun.'

'I didn't mind.'

'Yes, you did,' Ali says, and she laughs. He's got newspapers spread out over half the table and looks more chilled than he did yesterday.

'We've got a laptop and a phone that have come for you,' he says. 'You'll need the laptop for working with the tutor, and then for school, of course.'

My eyes open wider. A laptop? And a phone – he must mean a mobile phone? Of my own? 'Thank you,' I say. I'm alarmed to hear the word *school*, then remind myself: *it doesn't matter. I'll be gone before they can send me there.*

Where will I be? I bite my tongue until the thought goes away, and there is a bitter, metallic taste of blood in my mouth.

111

'I'll help you set up the phone and laptop after brunch,' Simone says.

My new phone – a smartphone – makes me feel dumb. Simone has to show me over and over again how to use it, then gets me to text her to make sure I know how.

All that is on it are her, Ali, all the numbers for the house – kitchen, housekeeping, study, security – and once I get back to my room, I put in Sophie's.

I've seen girls my age, even younger, staring at their phones endlessly, tapping away at the screens, taking selfies of themselves making weird faces with their cheeks sucked in and eyes opened unnaturally wide. Why they find it all so fascinating I don't know, but I'm guessing their contacts go beyond parents, home and a social worker.

The laptop, though, is more familiar – the way it works isn't that different to computers I've used in libraries. From somewhere they've found a desk and moved it into my room while we were having brunch – along with some smaller pillows – and I'm sat there, phone pushed to one side and laptop open.

Simone helped me set it up, and an email account, too. She forwarded stuff from the tutor to my email that I'm supposed to be reading now, but there are other things I want to do.

A search: 'Catelyn Green'. It gives a long list of hits but I hone in on one of them, and click on it. The heading is *Former Nanny Arrested*.

> *Catelyn Green, the former nanny of a family in Dorset, has been arrested on charges of kidnapping their three-year-old*

daughter over twelve years ago. The missing girl was spotted
in Manchester. An appeal for public help led to the arrest of
Ms Green and recovery of the girl, now aged sixteen.

Now another search: 'Missing Girl Manchester'. Up comes
the newspaper front page I saw at the services. I study the photos
of me from the CCTV; they aren't that clear. Without the cast
on my arm and wearing different clothes I doubt anyone would
be able to recognise me, but it still feels so weird to have my face
in the papers like that, let alone that it was on TV. At least TV
is fleeting; will these things be online for ever? Like Dr Rasheed
said, our names or where we live aren't mentioned in any of this
beyond saying Dorset, but how hard would it be to work it out?

I hesitate, then do another search: 'Holly Heath'. It comes
up with loads of stuff that doesn't look relevant. I add, 'missing',
and presto.

The article about when Holly went missing – the same as the
one Sophie showed me that freaked me out – comes up, as well
as others. I stare at the screen, shocked. I'd convinced myself it
was faked, but here it is, online.

I read through it again, feeling the same twisting panic in
my gut that I did the first time I read it.

The authorities could fake an old news article online as
easily as they gave me a copy of it via Sophie. But if I accept
that Simone and Ali did have a daughter who went missing and
that this is an actual report from back then, how do I explain
Cate's photo being in the article?

Hang on. Have Simone and Ali seen this article? Would
they recognise Cate, say she was the one who was their nanny

and disappeared with Holly, or is it just some dramatic case of mistaken identity?

One thing I do know: they photographed every possible stage and event in pregnancy, birth, and afterwards. It's inconceivable that Cate was here and not photographed with Holly, but there weren't any photos of her I saw in their endless albums.

But then there is the bracelet. Simone said Ali had it made for her, and here it is on my wrist – from Cate.

And my blood – this anomaly I'm supposed to have, the one their baby had, too. It was unusual enough that Dr Rasheed said that other doctors there were interested in it and wanted to do tests, so there can't be that many around with the same thing.

No matter how I try, I just can't make any of this make sense. I *can't*.

27

There's a low knock on my door and I shut my laptop fast.

It opens, and Simone peeks in. 'How are you getting on?'

'Um, OK.'

She comes in further. 'Can we work out what you want to wear tonight?' I must look at her blankly. 'For the party,' she reminds me.

'Oh. OK,' I say. I'd pushed that to the back of my mind, too busy thinking about other things. 'Who's coming?'

'It's just family, but this is an occasion and they like to dress for occasions. I ordered some things for you to try.'

She opens the wardrobe, takes out a half-dozen or so dresses, and they're *so* not me – they're really fancy. 'Try them on and see what you think?'

I take them one at a time into the en suite and come out again for her to see. There's an aquamarine one that she says is best on me and I like the colour, but it feels like I'm putting on somebody else's clothes, their skin.

'Honestly, it's perfect. You'll see,' she says.

'OK. It's your party.'

'No, it's yours! Your welcome home! Oh. Is this something you'd rather not do?'

She looks so stricken that I instantly shake my head. 'I'm a bit nervous, but it's all right.'

'Are you sure?'

'Yes. It's fine.'

'Everyone is anxious to see you, but we should have asked.'

'Really, it's fine.'

I hang the dress back up, and as I do I'm thinking about what I saw online before, and about there not being any photos of Cate here that I've seen.

I hesitate, unsure if I should ask – or maybe it's more that I'm afraid of the answer. 'Can I ask you something?' I say. 'I mean, I'm not sure . . . that is . . .'

'Go on. Ask me anything.'

'Well, it's about Cate. Can you tell me what she was like here? I mean, before anything happened?'

'Ooh. OK. Let's sit down for this one, shall we?' she says, and we go to the sofa. 'It's hard to talk about her without it being coloured by what happened. She caused us so much pain.'

'I get that. But I can't *not* talk about her. She was a big part of my life – even if she shouldn't have been.'

'I do understand. It might be best not to raise it with Ali, though.'

'OK,' I say, but then I let the silence stay where it is, so that it is Simone's to fill.

She swallows. 'I'll try. We got on well; I liked Cate a lot. She was fun with you, not strict, you know? Without letting you be spoiled. She had a great imagination and told stories without needing books; she'd make play houses out of cushions and sheets. You loved it. She started a few weeks before I phased back to work so we were together a lot to start with.

'I was a little jealous of her being with you all day when I was back full-time, but she even made that all right, made me feel OK about it. And you would always go to me first even after she was here. Once I was adjusted to how things were I was happy, knowing you were with someone who looked after you so well. Is there something specific you wanted to know?'

'I was wondering . . . if there are any photos of us? I mean, me and Cate?'

'There were some, but Ali couldn't stand to see any reminders of her, so I took them out of the albums.'

'I didn't see any blank spaces.'

'I had so many photos of you, I just put more of them in. Did you want to see the photos? Of you and Cate?'

'You kept them?'

'I couldn't bear to destroy any images of you, even if she was in them. Ali doesn't know I've still got them.'

'Is it OK if I do want to see them?'

'Of course. Come on, let's do it now.' She says it in a 'let's get this over with' voice.

We go to her dressing room; it's bigger than most bedrooms. There's a dressing table and in one of the drawers, underneath boxes of makeup, an envelope.

She takes it out, puts it in my hand.

I'm feeling sick and scared of what I might see. What if it really is Cate who was here, and it's all true?

My hand is shaking a little as I try to open it and Simone takes it and does it for me.

She holds out the first photograph. 'OK. So here was Cate's first day, when she first met you. You were just over a year old.'

It *is* Cate. Her hands are around a baby's middle holding her up, so the baby's feet are on Cate's knees. They are smiling at each other.

'And this one. I loved this photo of the three of us. I'd been feeling cut off, staying home for over a year. Cate became a friend. We talked about everything.'

It's a selfie: Simone and baby with Cate next to her on a sofa. Cate is laughing, and holding out the camera.

There are dozens of photos by the look of what is in her hand, the early ones mostly of Cate and me – I guess Simone was holding the camera – but after another five or six I've had enough.

'Can we stop now?' I say.

'Of course,' she says, a look of relief on her face. 'Do you want them?'

I shake my head.

'If you want to look at the rest of them another time, it's OK: just let me know. Are you all right?'

'Yes. No. I don't know.'

She hesitates, puts an arm around my shoulders and gives me a quick hug. I don't flinch or move away. It's OK, feels kind of natural this time. But now I want – *need* – to be alone.

'Is it all right if I go back to my room?'

'Of course. Get ready to come down for the party by six-thirty or so?'

I nod yes, but how will I manage a party tonight? I don't know.

Somehow I put one foot in front of the other and get back to my room.

Close the door.

Close my eyes.

Cate *was* here: the photos of her with Simone and the baby prove it. She actually was their nanny?

I just can't . . . I *can't.*

Cate loved me as I loved her. I know she did. *How* could any of this be true?

I'm missing something that will make all of this make sense; I must be. But my imagination isn't big enough to come up with anything.

28

'Tabby? This is my *mère*; your *grandmère*.'

I have never seen anyone who looked less like a grandmother. Her hair is jet black, pulled back, she's slender and as tall as me but elegant and at ease where I'm awkward and gangly.

She leans towards me, air kisses my cheeks. 'Seems fair if your name has changed that mine can, too. Don't call me *grandmère*,' she says. 'It's Elodie.' Her French accent is soft, her voice musical, and I find myself smiling back at her. She links her arm in mine. 'Now tell me: who are you, and where have you been?'

Simone starts to say something and Elodie shakes her head, makes a dismissive gesture with her hand in the air. 'I don't care what some doctor or another says to say or not to say; I won't be told how to talk to my own granddaughter.'

I shrug. 'I'm just me.'

'The perfect answer.'

'And I've kind of been everywhere – in the UK, that is.'

She claps her hands together. 'Another perfect answer! I think we will get along, *ma chérie*.'

More people arrive – aunts, uncles, cousins. It's a blur of faces and names, and I soon lose track of who most of them are. They're all dressed like they've stepped from the pages of a fashion magazine and I'm happy now that I let Simone guide me in what to wear, even though I felt ridiculous in this dress before I came down. There are friendly faces, happy ones, curious ones, even some that look less than happy to see me. It's overwhelming being the centre of so much attention.

But after a while it's like they get bored with the novelty and start talking to each other, and I listen.

'I hear climate protestors have been occupying the street and the entrance to Industria United's head office in London,' a man says, a cousin of Simone's.

'What's this?' Simone says, a note of alarm in her voice.

'It's not a problem,' Ali says. 'They can sit on the street all they like; a helicopter to the roof takes care of that.'

'Maybe it's time to listen to what they have to say,' the cousin says.

'We always listen, very carefully,' Ali says. 'It makes knowing who to bribe and who to have arrested much easier.'

There's uneasy laughter, and I'm shocked at what Ali said, dismissing climate protests like it's something to laugh at. But most of me is too caught up inside with Cate that it doesn't completely register.

Simone's face is cross also, and she walks away to the window. I'm about to follow her but a woman – Ali's sister? – is there with Simone now, and I hang back.

'Simone, darling. That girl might have dark hair, but apart from that she really doesn't look like you.' She's lowered her voice, but it's like a stage whisper: it stands out more than if she'd talked normally. 'Have they done DNA tests? I'd hate for you to be tricked after all you've been through.'

Simone's face is like stone. 'The doctors are sure.'

DNA tests? Did they? Does that mean . . . and my thoughts won't – *can't* – go there, not now.

Elodie joins them. 'Tabby looks more like me. Height skipped a generation – who knows what else?' And with that, she takes my arm again, draws me outside on to the veranda.

'It's too soon to throw the kitten amongst the sharks,' she says.

'Sharks?' I look back in through the glass doors. 'Your family?'

She laughs and sips her red wine. '*Our* family. And all the best families have at least a few, but you will be fine, as I am on your side.'

The rest of the evening is a blur. There are fancy bites of food that are called canapés, champagne and wine. I find myself with a champagne glass in my hand while Ali makes toasts to me, to family, and everyone's glasses are clinking. I try a sip and the bubbles tickle my nose.

The minutes tick slowly by, and it's all I can do to stay present enough to speak when spoken to. My mind whirls with Cate – the images in the photos play back and forth in my mind.

They prove she was here. But what that means I can't face, not now. I need to be alone.

29

PJs on, I finally get into bed with the new, smaller pillows, and pull the blankets snug around me.

I'd been counting down to when I could be alone and think, but now that I am, I don't want to.

I can still smell Elodie's perfume from when she hugged me goodbye. She's nothing like I would have imagined, but I liked her. She got me through the evening, making acid comments in my ear about someone's divorce, another's affair, another who always says the wrong thing after too much wine. Like Ali's sister – the one who asked about the DNA tests. Elodie says that's because she was hoping their children would inherit if I didn't come back.

Inherit what – an oil company? Something I'd never want.

Elodie was kind to me, but I got the impression some of the family – maybe even Simone, her own daughter – were a little afraid of her.

I've left the blinds up again tonight, but clouds have pulled in and the stars are hidden. The wind is up and must be whipping the waves below; even the sea is hard to hear over the howling wind. The coming storm echoes inside me, vibrating my bones like harp strings.

I count backwards slowly in my mind, a trick to help sleep. It doesn't work from a hundred so I begin again, this time from a thousand, but I keep losing concentration and starting over. The desperate need for sleep – a complete, bone-crushing weariness – is heavy on my body, but my mind feels like it's been prised open and can never rest again.

It's *doubt* that does this – it's corrosive, battery acid that burns, and not thinking about it won't make it go away: *the one person I always believed in, I'm not sure of any more.*

When did it start? Was it in the nursery last night, finding that picture book after my dream? Or was it the stuff I found online, and the photos of Cate that Simone had kept? Perhaps it began earlier, but I couldn't face it.

Cate said to not believe everything I'm told, to think for myself, and I'm trying, I'm really trying. I'm protesting inside that none of what they say can be true, but not really believing it any more.

The fight has gone out of me. I'm like a hot air balloon when the fire is extinguished, sinking lower and lower until it is on the ground. Empty and still.

It all really began with the bracelet.

Shiny! I have my fingers locked around it, and there is low laughter over my head.

'Let go, Holly. It's Mummy's. You'll have it one day, I promise.'

She puts down the picture book she was holding in her other hand, waggles fingers at me then tickles my tummy. I shriek and let go of her bracelet, giggling and leaning back in her arms. I look up and grab a strand of her long dark hair. Her eyes locked on mine say things I understand more than words: that I am hers, she is mine. Then she draws her arms in around me closer, leans down and kisses me

– soft lips, warm breath, a pretty smell, like flowers – and I wrap my hand around one of her fingers and hold it tight. So tight I'll never let go.

30

I stumble down the hall to the nursery and open the door. I'm not sure why I'm here, what I want – *need* – to find, but I *had* to come.

I'm shaking. That dream – was it real? Did that happen years ago, or was it from my sleep-deprived imagination?

The picture book, the one under the bed, is still there – I didn't imagine it. I pick it up, sit on the bed, holding it against me, but can't bring myself to open it. I get up and circle the room, touching things, as if the physical feel of them will make them stop being ghosts.

I run my fingertips over toys, books, ornaments. Breakable things are on higher shelves: delicate china ornaments of puppies, kittens; silver things, too – a cup and spoon – and small hands and feet.

I'm moving on but then take another look at the latter, and another. They're silver castings, I think – real representations of Holly's living hands and feet. They're so tiny, she must have been not much more than a newborn when they were done.

Two perfect hands, and . . . the feet. On each, the toes are webbed. In exactly the same way as mine. Syndactyly – duck feet – *quack, quack*. Taunts by small boys. They're not just like mine, they *are* mine, I'm sure of it.

I pick up the giant bunny, sit on the oversized rocking chair and hold it against me.

A jolt of memory runs through me, and I shudder; it isn't just in my mind but through my whole body. I am small, so small, being rocked in warm arms on this chair.

It's all true. Isn't it?

I'm . . . Holly. Simone is my mother?

But that would mean Cate stole me, that she lied to me my whole life.

That last glimpse I had of Cate: I couldn't hear but I'm sure the words she mouthed at me were, *I'm sorry*. Was that her saying she shouldn't have done it – was that a confession?

Was the real reason she had me call her Cate instead of Mum because that would have been a lie too far? Is that also why she gave me my real middle name as my name – so it was partly true? *To make lies believed, find the truth within the lie.*

Then all that stuff about being mother-daughter, sister-sister, daughter-mother, best friends, just hid a monstrous lie.

How could she do that to me? To Simone and Ali?

How could she?

Why?

I *hurt*. Something is breaking inside me; everything is wrong, so wrong. I'm crying, collapsing in on myself. Nothing will ever be right again.

How much time passes I don't know, but the door opens. There are footsteps, then a hand, a soothing voice, arms that go around me as she sits in the chair next to me. It's Simone and I don't have to open my eyes to know this – I know the feel and smell of her.

127

'Ssssh, whatever it is, it'll be all right, Tabby,' she says, and she's rocking the chair and me and this bunny, and I'm crying and can't stop.

But what she said is wrong. I shake my head. 'No . . .' I hiccup, trying to speak between sobs that grip and shake my whole body. 'Not Tabby. I'm Holly,' I manage to get out.

She kisses my cheek. Tears are streaming down hers now, too.

And she holds me, rocks me, and sings. It's not one of Cate's wordless healing songs, and I know her voice and every word:

Hush little baby.

I'm finally home.

31

By the time I've cried myself out, my eyes feel gravelly and my whole head hurts.

When I say I want to go back to bed, Simone – *Mum?* – doesn't mind. She walks there with me, and we're holding hands and it doesn't seem weird.

When we get to my room she puts the blinds down while I get into bed. The sun is just rising. She's been crying too, but her face is radiant. She's beautiful.

She kisses me on the cheek.

'Sleep as long as you want to. Come find me or text if you want anything, anything at all. All right?'

I nod, not trusting my voice, and she walks across the room. She turns and waves at the door, goes through and then she's gone.

I don't know how I feel. I don't know what to feel.

I haven't processed any of this. I need to think about it, but more than anything right now, I need sleep.

Sun . . . sea . . . earth . . . sky . . .

Cate lies next to me on the beach. We're holding hands. Knees up, the damp sand gritty under our feet. My eyes are closed, the sun's warmth on my skin, the music of the sea in my ears.

'Everything and everyone needs a purpose,' she says.

'What is mine?'

'I can't tell you. You have to find it yourself.'

'What is yours?'

She laughs. 'Looking after you, of course.' She lets go of my hand and sits up, so I do the same. Her face is sad even though she was laughing seconds ago.

'What's wrong?'

'Too many things.' She shakes her head. 'If ever you're in doubt, always remember the four points of our compass. They are the most important markers of who we are.'

We lie back down on the sand. The sun is brighter now and even when I close my eyes I can still see it, and also a phantom branching tree that seems to be above me, in the unseen sky. I know that isn't true, that it is really shadows cast by blood vessels in my eyes. My mind tries to make sense of them and so they appear to be projected out, even though they are really inside me.

Things you see aren't always what they appear to be, are they?

Sun . . . sea . . . earth . . . sky . . .

The chant is in many voices, hidden away inside me. Like the shadows.

32

It's gone midday by the time I get myself out of bed and into the shower. I stand in the cascading water for ages, first as hot as I can stand it, then as cold. By the time I come out, shivering, I feel more awake.

I should go find Simone, but now that it's hours later and I've slept, I'm feeling awkward about crying all over her last night – or this morning, or whatever it was. She was probably soggy from tears and snot. Despite having some fragments of memories from long ago, I still don't really *know* her. How do you have a normal conversation after all that?

I finally drag myself down the stairs and find her reading a book on the veranda. The sun is shining after last night's storm.

She smiles to see me.

'Hi,' I say.

'Did you get some sleep?'

'Yes. I crashed out pretty well for a while.' Before the dreams started. 'Look, I'm sorry I flipped out like that last night.'

'Come and sit down next to me?'

I do so, and she reaches across to take my hand.

'You don't have to apologise,' she says. 'It's fine. It's better than that – it was probably what you needed. There's been a lot for you to deal with. Dr Rasheed said you might have a delayed reaction to everything, to keep an eye on you in case. She didn't think you'd come to grips with everything.'

'She's like a mind reader.'

'So how are you feeling about everything now?'

Even though I have no reason to try to hide what I think or feel from her any more, I don't know what to say. Finally, I just shrug. 'I honestly don't know. It's like, after getting so upset last night, now I'm . . . empty.'

'Do you need someone else to talk to?'

'Do you mean Dr Rasheed?'

'Or someone like her. They've agreed now that you can see doctors in our clinic instead of making the trek to London.'

I process that. Another doctor, one I haven't met? 'Maybe. I don't know.'

The door to inside opens; the assistant housekeeper has a tray of sandwiches, tea.

'I asked them to bring it when you got here,' Simone says. She waves at them to put the tray down and go, and fusses with setting things out.

She gives me a mug of tea and I wrap my hands around it, soaking up the warmth into my hands. It's not cold here, in the sun, but I still feel cold inside.

'Can I ask you a question?' Simone says. I nod. 'Is it OK to call you Holly now?'

Who is Holly? I don't know her; to me, she's the lost girl, she's *other*. But to Simone, *Holly* is what she sees when she looks at me. 'I guess so. But don't be surprised if it takes me a moment to remember to answer. And can I stay Tabby generally?'

She smiles. 'That seems fair.'

'Where's Ali? I mean, *Père*?'

She hesitates. 'Look, there is something we haven't told you. We're not really . . . that is . . . not very together. He's usually in London Monday to Friday, sometimes – well, most of the time now – weekends, too.'

'Oh. But you both came to meet me together? And had that party last night?'

'Nothing would have kept Ali away when we went to see you! He's your father. He needs to be there for you.'

I digest what she's said, but don't get it, not really. They seemed really connected to me.

'Are you separated, or getting divorced?'

'Not anything like that, at least I don't think so. We're still married but have been leading mostly separate lives for a long time now. Sorry we didn't tell you before. We thought it might be a bit much to take in, with everything else.'

'Why? I mean why are things that way between the two of you?'

'With everything we went through . . .' She hesitates.

'You mean with me?'

'Well, yes. I didn't deal with it very well for a long time. Ali missed you desperately too, but he thought after some years that I should be getting on with life, like he was. But I couldn't. And gradually he started being here less and less.'

'I'm sorry.'

'It's not your fault,' she says. But it kind of is, isn't it? Or it's Cate's at least. 'We're still good friends.' She sounds wistful, and I'm thinking this isn't how she wants things.

Considering I just met my parents again it makes me feel sad for them, and for me.

As far as how I feel about Cate . . . I can't go there, not yet.

Late in the afternoon Simone says she has to make some calls, and I head down the path to the beach.

I lie on the sand, facing the sun in the sky above me. The tide is on the turn; having reached as high as it can on the shore, the sea must fall back before it can rise again. As it is now it has been and always will be – constant, reassuring –

Sun, sea, earth, sky.

The four points of our compass.

Confusion crushes me inside. Everything I know of the world is through Cate. What does any of it mean now?

I don't understand the world without her.

I'm lost.

All that stuff about keeping away from other people, not telling them anything, how the government controls people – schools being prisons – never having a home or making friends. Was any of that true, or was it all designed to keep Cate from getting arrested for kidnapping me? And I believed her; I believed everything she ever told me. I'm stupid. That's it, isn't it?

I can't control my breathing; not even the sea can soothe me.

Something is beginning to fill the void inside me – slowly, steadily. It's hot, and it burns – and it's so ferocious that it startles me when I recognise it for what it is. I'm *angry*. I'm past angry, reaching something that could never fit into one small word.

Cate did this to me. She wrecked my life; she wrecked Ali

and Simone's lives, too. What she's taken away from us we can never get back.

Why? *WHY* did she do it?

What possible reason could she have had?

But she's not here, I can't ask her, and even through all of this I still miss her. And that just makes me angrier – this time at myself.

33

That night the wind is up again. I stand on my balcony, my hair a wild thing, whipped around my face. The air feels gritty with salt and sand and stings my eyes.

I should sleep but my nerves are jangling like the wind.

I've not been paying any attention to the date – why would I, with so much happening? It wasn't until I came up to my room and looked at my phone and saw it on the screen that it hit me.

Today is the twenty-first of June. This was my birthday – not my real one, I know now – but it is the date Cate told me was my birthday, the one we always celebrated.

But I was actually sixteen on the seventeenth of April. I've missed an entire birthday. We were in Cornwall still then, Cate and I. I turned sixteen and didn't even know it.

Last year I was fifteen on this day, or so I thought. There is a pang inside me. I shouldn't do this to myself – go back to that day – but it's too late. It's there inside me and I can't make it go away.

We didn't have a lot of money for things like birthdays, but Cate made them so special. A cake she made: vegan, of course, but not like the tasteless stuff they sell in shops or cafés. This one was lemon and blueberry, and it was so delicious. And the best gifts – handmade, like my notebook.

No matter where we were staying on my birthday, no matter

how long it took, we always went to a beach for the ritual of promise: the balancing of mind, body, spirit with sun, sea, earth and sky. The sea has always had a hold on me, but Cate stressed how important it was to keep all four in harmony and not honour one above the other; the promise we make is to serve and protect all the natural things that nurture us, give us life and home.

Every birthday since I can remember we did this, and there is a sense of panic inside that I've missed doing it today and it's too late: it had to be done when the sun was in the sky. On the beach this afternoon the sun was shining fiercely like it was trying to remind me, but I was too angry at Cate to even notice. Now there is only weak moonshine above me.

But these things that always meant so much with Cate: do they even matter without her?

When I finally go in to go to bed, I close the blinds to shut out the world.

I'm wading in the sea, standing on the earth, under the sun in the sky. Cate holds my hand.

'What is a promise?' she says.

'When you say you will do something, you do it.'

She's thinking about what I said, then nods. 'I think you're old enough now to promise yourself,' she says. 'Do you remember the words?'

'Yes.'

If you close your eyes to avoid seeing what is before you, it is still there. If you close your ears to what is taught, the student fails, not the teacher. If you don't feel what is outside of you because all you do is look inside, you will always be alone.

137

We promise: to look, listen and feel with all of our senses; to protect sun, sea, earth and sky with all that we are, all that we were, and all that we may yet be.

Time shifts — to other birthdays. A kaleidoscope of promises stretches backwards in time, but time goes forwards, too.

Yet to be *is so uncertain.*

34

'Welcome to the Penrose Clinic.' The receptionist smiles and both her teeth and the polished desk gleam.

'Good morning,' Simone says. 'This is my daughter. She's booked in as Holly Heath, but she goes by her middle name now, Tabby.' I smile at her for remembering.

'Of course. Please take a seat and someone will be with you in a moment.'

The waiting room is posh, the colours muted. There's art on the walls that looks like the real deal, not just prints. This isn't the NHS experience like I've had in the last few hospitals, that's for sure. We sit down and even the chairs are comfy, too comfy for me after that endless night of dreams. My eyelids are slipping down.

'Mrs Heath?' a voice says, and I jump, open my eyes. A woman stands there.

'Yes?' Simone says.

'Dr Chang would like to speak to you while Tabby has her tests.'

Simone looks at me, hesitant. 'Are you all right on your own?'

I'm sixteen not five, is what I'm thinking, but all I say is, 'I'll be fine.' I breathe a little easier when Simone disappears through a door. She's really so very lovely, so thoughtful and considerate in every way. But she's been a bit like Velcro Mum these last few days.

Another woman in a medical sort of uniform walks out a moment later.

'Tabby? Tabby Heath?' she says.

I stand up. 'That's me.'

'Hello, it's lovely to meet you, Tabby. I'm Becky. This way please.'

I'm led to a small room; there's a desk and a few chairs.

'Could we get you to answer a few questions?' I'm handed a clipboard, a pen, and sheets of white paper with questions and places for answers. The paper is headed *Penrose Clinic*, with a symbol of a four-leaf clover printed next to the words. A four-leaf clover – asking for luck? Doesn't sound very sciencey for a medical clinic. The symbol looks familiar; maybe I saw it on some of the stuff from before I was born in the album Simone showed me.

I start on the form, answering questions about my health, medications, medical treatment. Until I got hit by a car I had none, so it doesn't take long.

When I'm done, Becky takes me to another room for a series of tests. Blood tests, first. There is a jab of pain as the needle slips into my arm; small tubes fill up with red. Then I'm taken to another room and put into a small tent, where first I sit and relax for ten minutes, and then get on a treadmill and run for all I'm worth for ten minutes. It feels good to push myself.

My broken arm is X-rayed and then I'm left to wait while the X-ray is checked.

Becky comes back in. 'We've got some good news for you,' she says. 'The cast can come off today.'

'Really? I thought they said it'd be weeks still?'

'You've healed nicely so it can come off a little early.'

Before long the cast has been cut down both sides and the two halves of it removed, the liner underneath it as well.

Becky brings a basin and warm water to wash my arm; then rubs moisturiser gently into my skin.

She checks that nothing hurts – it doesn't – and gets me to try moving my arm in different directions. Moving it a little feels like a lot, but it doesn't hurt, just feels a bit weak.

'No boxing matches for a while, all right?' she says. 'Try some gentle exercise.'

'Can I swim?'

Becky smiles. 'I was just about to suggest that. Swimming is good, but take it easy to start with. Do you have any other questions?'

'I don't think so.'

'I'll take you to see the doctor now.'

I follow her down a hall to another door. She knocks lightly and opens the door.

Inside there's a woman at a desk with files in front of her.

'Hi, Tabby? Have a seat. I'm Dr Chang. I can answer any questions you may have, and then I have a few for you.'

'Hi,' I say. 'It was great to get the cast off my arm early, but what were the other tests for?'

'We are conducting a longitudinal study – that is, one that runs for a long period of time – on Penrose babies, such as yourself. We've unfortunately missed years of data in your case.' She sounds faintly disapproving, like I've stayed away on purpose. 'Today we've been re-establishing a baseline on some key metabolic indicators.'

141

'Why? I mean, why are you doing this longitudinal study? Does this have something to do with my weird blood?'

'Weird blood?'

'At the other hospitals, they said there was an anomaly or something.'

'Your blood is absolutely fine.'

'What were they talking about then?'

'It's a bit better at carrying oxygen than most people's, that's all.'

'That's a good thing, isn't it?'

'Exactly.'

'Can I ask you about my feet?'

'Of course.'

'Can they be fixed?'

'Fixed?'

'You know, the webbed toes − syndactyly, or whatever you call it. Can you make my toes look more normal?'

'Ah, I see. Not in your case. The way the blood vessels are located means that the surgery to separate your toes isn't in your best interests.'

'Do you mean because I'd bleed too much?'

'Partly, but also sections of blood vessels would have to be moved and reattached; the surgery and risks involved are too complicated. Do your feet bother you?'

Quack, quack. Duck feet.

'You mean, do they hurt? No. But they're different, that's all.'

'Being different can be a good thing. So, how are you feeling?'

It's on the tip of my tongue to say tired, but Dr Rasheed never liked that as an answer, did she? And I'm starting to think Dr Chang is the same sort of doctor – one who wants to get into my head.

'OK, I guess.'

'Did you have a moment of personal discovery a few nights ago?'

I look at her blankly.

'I was speaking to your mum, about when she found you in the nursery?'

Did Simone tell this doctor *everything*? I'm uncomfortable and cross my arms; now that the cast is off, I can do it properly.

'Well, I got kind of upset. I remembered a few things from a long time ago, about being there when I was little.'

'That's brilliant progress, Tabby. Another question: how have you been sleeping?'

'Oh. Well, not great.' There's an understatement.

'How long has that been going on for?'

I'm about to say, since Cate was taken away – but that's not really true, is it? It was before then, too; for as long as I can remember I've had problems with sleep. It's just that it has gotten worse lately. 'A long time,' I say. 'I'm not sure when it started.'

'Have you been dreaming?'

'Doesn't everyone?'

'Some more than others.'

I shrug, uneasy. I have less reason to try to hide anything now, but I still don't like answering questions.

'Sometimes,' I say.

'What have you been dreaming about?'

'When I wake up I don't really remember them,' I lie. 'Why are you asking about my dreams?'

'Things going on in your subconscious mind often appear there. It can be a clue to any issues you are having that we should discuss. Now, what I'd like you to do before I see you again is to keep a dream diary. Get a notebook and every time you wake up – whether in the middle of the night or first thing in the morning – write down what you've been dreaming about. If you do it straight away like that you shouldn't have problems with remembering them. All right?'

'I guess so,' I say, not convinced I want to share my dreams with anybody, but curious just the same.

'Also, I'm going to give you a prescription that should help you sleep; you take one an hour before bedtime. And also some vitamins to take in the mornings.'

Soon I'm led back to the waiting area we were in when we arrived, and Simone is there, nose in a book. She looks up as I come to sit next to her.

'Your cast! They said it could come off today. How does your arm feel?'

I move it this way and that. 'I think it's OK. I mean, it feels a bit odd to move it, since I haven't been able to for a while. They said I could do some swimming?'

'Great. There's a private swimming centre that we belong to; we can go there tomorrow if you like.'

'What's with this study – long term thing that they said they're doing?'

'The longitudinal study?'

'Yeah, that.'

'It was something we agreed to when we signed up to the clinic to help us have you. It's OK, isn't it?'

'I don't know what it is. How often do I have to come here?'

'It was once a month when you were small. I'll ask.'

35

I dive in. The shock of cool water makes my head feel clear for the first time in days. I surface, look up – Simone is there, on the seats that overlook these outdoor pools. I wave, then start swimming front crawl towards the far end. I do an underwater somersault against the end of the pool to push off for the return.

The swimming centre is on the coast and has outdoor pools carved into the rock, fed by the sea. I was so happy there was more than just the chlorinated indoor option, though given the weather – dark skies and the feel of rain to come – Simone was surprised I wanted to come outside. Everyone must agree with her as I've got the pool to myself. Swimming in the sea would be even better, but I'm not sure Simone could cope with that, at least until she sees for herself that I'm fine in the water.

I switch to backstroke after a few lengths and that's when my arm starts to complain. It's been feeling OK until now, but I remember what I was told, to take it easy, so after a while I switch to sidestroke to give it a rest. My pace slows until I'm just moseying along, relishing the salt, the cool water. Moving my body through it. I have missed this *so much*.

When the rain comes it isn't just a shower. It pounds into the water with such fury that the fat drops bounce on the surface and on my skin. Half suspended in salt water and half in the rain, I feel wild, free, part of the storm. Then I glance up.

Simone is still outside, watching me, standing with her arms wrapped around her. She must be getting soaked. She waves, beckons me in.

Reluctantly I climb out of the pool and go through to the changing rooms and showers.

When we get back to the house, I find a padded envelope on my desk; *Tabby Heath* is handwritten on the front, followed by this address.

I start to open it before I remember what it must be. My stomach twists as I reach in, pull out my notebook and hold it in my hands. Handmade and painted by Cate for my birthday, with *Tabby's Notebook* on the spine. Part of me wants to hug it against myself, but more of me wants to fling it away, destroy it. The mixture of longing and anger is too much to hold inside at once.

Then I remember: Jago's phone number. It's in the back, isn't it?

I'd been unsure how I felt about him before; it was Jago calling the police that led them to Cate and me.

But maybe he did me a favour.

Before I can change my mind I grab my phone, add his number to contacts. What do I do with the notebook now? I can't bring myself to put it in the bin, but I don't want it where I'll see it all the time, either. I stash it out of sight on the empty top shelf of one of the wardrobes.

Now to send my first ever non-Simone text message.

I hesitate, not knowing what to say, then my fingers fly across the screen in a rush to get it out.

Hi Jago, this is Tabby — though sometimes I'm called Holly now. I hit send before I have time to think about it or change my mind.

Now what? Wait, I guess. I start to reach across to put it on the desk when it beeps in my hand and I almost drop it.

I look at the screen.

It's Jago; he's answered, already. *wow, hello! was hoping 2 hear from u, r u ok, where r u?*

I go to the balcony, take a photo and send it to him.

that's some view — r u in cornwall?

No — it's Dorset. Near Bournemouth.

so . . . what happened??

I stare at the screen, wondering why I got in touch. He'll just be full of questions now, ones I don't want to answer.

After a while I send this back: *Long story.* Then I switch it on to silent and put it face down on my desk so I won't be tempted to answer.

'Don't forget to take one of these,' Simone says after dinner, and holds out a small pot of pills — the ones to take before sleep.

I yawn. 'I'm not sure I need one. Having some fresh air and exercise might have done the trick.'

'The doctor said you should, so take one anyhow.'

'Fine.' She hands me a glass of water and the pills. I look at the label, thinking I'll search what they are online. That's odd: it doesn't say. They just have my name and to take one before bedtime. I'm leery of taking any sort of medicine; Cate always said not to unless you know taking it is better than not — huh. What does she know about anything, anyhow? I swallow it.

We say goodnight and I head upstairs.

In my room the lights are out, blinds open. It's a clear night; the stars and moon cast enough light to see a glint of water far below. The sea is calling me and my blood is racing – a midnight swim?

Imagine Simone's reaction. And what if that pill I took is so good at making me sleep that I'm suddenly unconscious when I'm in the water? I make myself get into bed, under the covers. I close my eyes but can still feel the pull of the sea.

Sun, sea, earth, sky . . .

I'm dreaming. I'm both in the dream and aware of what it is.

Many voices join together to tell the first story:

First there was the sun, then the earth. Billions of years ago, gases – including water vapour – escaped from the molten core of the earth to form the atmosphere. As the earth cooled the water condensed into rain, fell from the sky to form the seas.

All life came from the sea: it is First Mother.

What the sea gives it can take away.

What the sea gives it can take away.

What the sea gives IT CAN TAKE AWAY . . .

Voices are shouting – screaming – inside me and outside me and through me. I am dissolving into them, and I'm panicking—

'Tabby?' One calm voice. It's Cate? With her there is a cool safe place, a centre in the storm.

But I'm angry – furious! – at her, and try to get away, but all there is besides her is chaos.

'What is real and what is imagined?' she whispers to me and inside me at the same time. 'You decide. You must think for yourself.'

And even though I'm angry I know she is right. I find myself, my core, hold the storm of voices away. Gradually it is they who begin to dissolve instead of me.

Until I'm completely alone in the cold sea.

I dive down deep and then deeper, until I'm swimming along the ocean floor. The call to swim out, further and deeper, is strong. But when I look back to shore there is a house that stands there, and it calls to me, too. I'm caught between what I want and need, and Simone.

Cate is here; she understands.

'She needs you more for now,' she says.

Everything blurs and moves at once – the sea, beach, path, house – and then, my bed. As if I was being filmed on time lapse, I'm one place and then another in a blink.

I breathe in deep and open my eyes.

When I wake, I'm breathing fast, in and out, almost hyperventilating. I'm as soaked as if I had been in the sea – with sweat. Gross.

I shuck off my PJs and open the wardrobe to get new ones. As I'm putting them on, I remember what is on the shelf above. I can't see it, but my notebook is there.

Without even making the decision to do so, I go up on my toes and reach around the shelf blindly until my fingers connect with the book and I pull it down. I find a pen on my desk and get back into bed. I switch on the bedside lamp and begin writing, fast, every detail and feeling I can from my dream.

Not for the doctor, no: this is private, for me. There is too much going on inside me when I'm supposed to be resting. Maybe if I can make sense of it, it'll go away.

36

'Hello, Holly? Are you awake?'

I open my eyes, pulled from a twilight sort of place, one where I was half awake and half in a dream and not sure which was which.

'Holly?' a voice says again.

It's Simone on the intercom.

I get up and find it on the wall near the door, push the 'talk' button.

'Hello?'

'Could you come downstairs to Ali's study? There's someone here who needs to speak to you.'

'OK,' I say.

Her voice didn't sound like her somehow; she didn't sound right. Who is here? It's weird to say *someone* like that without saying who they are.

Feeling unsettled, I get dressed quickly and go down the stairs to Ali's study.

Ali is here with Simone. And Sophie? And another man and woman I don't know. The woman is in uniform: police uniform.

Sophie smiles, says hello, but there is *atmosphere* in this room.

'Holly, this is DCI Palmer and Constable Bopara,' Sophie says. 'They're with Scotland Yard.'

'What's wrong?'

'Why don't we all sit down?' Palmer says.

Simone comes closer now, links an arm in mine. We sit down together on the sofa. Ali stays standing.

'I'm afraid I've got some news for all of you,' Palmer says. 'It may be upsetting. It's about Catelyn Green.'

Cate? My eyes are fixed on Palmer now, and there is a cold feeling inside of me at the grave look in his.

'What's she done now?' Ali says.

He shakes his head. 'It's nothing she's done. As you know, she's been in custody, awaiting trial. This morning she was found in her cell. She'd been stabbed some time in the night; she didn't survive.'

There is a sharp hiss next to me as Simone breathes in and she grips my arm tighter.

Cate?

Stabbed?

The words are floating around in my head, refusing to connect with each other.

She's dead? Someone's killed her?

No. *No.* That can't be.

Why?

'You mean she won't go to trial for what she did to our family?' Ali says. 'How did this happen in custody?'

'The investigation is only just beginning, and it will be thorough.'

Cate. I swallow. 'She's really . . . dead?'

'I'm afraid so,' Palmer says.

'I don't think Holly needs to be subjected to any more of this,' Ali says.

'We'd like to speak to each of you in turn, if you don't mind,' Palmer says.

'Surely we're not under any sort of suspicion?' Simone says.

'We need to talk to everybody who knew Cate, knew of any reason someone might harm her,' he answers.

'Should I engage a lawyer?' Ali says.

'That is your decision. But this is just a conversation.' He turns to Sophie. 'Could you take Holly out for now?'

'Of course,' she says.

Somehow I stand and follow her out of the room.

I feel . . . numb. I can't . . . My mind won't . . . Cate?

Sophie guides me to the kitchen. She shoos out the cook and puts the kettle on.

Time must pass. There is a cup of hot tea in my hands now, but my thoughts are still going around in these circles inside of me.

I look up at Sophie, her concerned eyes. 'I've been so angry at her. And now she's gone . . . She can never tell me why she did what she did.'

'I guess not.'

'And why did Ali ask about a lawyer? Do they think my parents had something to do with it?'

'I don't think so. They probably just have to speak to anyone who might have something against Cate.'

I'm holding my feelings tight inside me. I'm afraid to let them go until I'm alone.

The last time I saw Cate, she warned me. She said, *Beware The Circle*. But what is The Circle? I don't know, but maybe somebody does.

'I need to speak to the police,' I say.

'Do you want to ask them about—'

'No. I need to tell them who might have done it.'

37

'Hi, Holly. Thanks for coming to talk to us,' Palmer says. 'We wanted to talk to you anyhow, but I understand there is something you wanted to tell us?'

'Yes. It's something Cate said, just before she got arrested. I don't know what it means, but maybe you will?'

'Go on.'

'She said to beware The Circle. And it was the way she said it – it meant something to her. Like it was a big deal that she even said it out loud.'

'The Circle?'

'Yeah.'

'She didn't say what The Circle was or if it stood for something or anything else?'

I shake my head. 'No. Does it mean anything to you?'

'Not at the moment. But thank you for telling us, and we'll look into it. Now, I know it's been a difficult day for you, but there are some questions we need to ask you. Is it OK if we do that now?'

It's coming – I can feel it. The moment when the numbness goes and I will really feel what has happened. I want – *need* – to be alone, before it does. But if I don't talk to them now they'll only come back again later, won't they?

'I guess so.'

'Was there anyone you can remember who Cate argued with, or who threatened her in any way?'

'No. I can't think of anything like that. She never really argued with anybody.'

'OK. Was she ever involved in crime that you know of?'

'You mean apart from kidnapping and theft?' Ali says.

'Let her answer.'

I shake my head again, but then think, *She's gone now. What does it matter if I tell them more?* 'Well, there's maybe a few things. Like sometimes we used different names; I don't know if that's illegal. And she told stories about where we were from that weren't true. Then when we were selling jewellery in Manchester she said things that weren't true about where it came from and why she didn't have ID.'

'Thank you, Holly. If you think of anything else, anything at all, you'll let us know, won't you? We'll leave a card.'

Soon they are leaving, saying goodbye. Ali follows them to the door and they're talking but out of sight and too far away to hear.

Sophie is still here, and Simone.

Simone's face is pale. 'Holly? Are you all right?' she says. 'Do you want to talk?'

And I'm shaking my head, standing, saying I need to be alone but not waiting to hear what else is said. I'm half running now to the door to the veranda, then down the stairs. Once I'm on the path I run full tilt down to the beach. I stop abruptly by the water's edge before I even realise why I'm here. I strip off jeans, T-shirt and run into the water in my under things until it is deep enough. I dive under the waves.

I swim underwater holding my breath, stroke after stroke, deeper and further out, and I want to keep going – to leave the land far behind. I need to surface, breathe, but something inside me is urging me on even as my body starts to falter.

I'm so caught in my own pain that it's a moment before I see her.

A dolphin swims alongside me, slowly for her, matching my pace. There are others – her pod – around us.

Then she drops to swim underneath me, a dolphin-shaped shadow, and nudges against me. Her touch is gentle for a being so much bigger than I am. She nudges again; she's pushing me up to the light.

No. I want to stay!

But this pain inside me is deeper than the sea – I can't drown it no matter how hard I try.

But *I* could drown. The pain would stop then.

My oxygen deficit is kicking in; I'm getting weaker. There will be no going back to the surface soon. Not as I am.

Cate, how could you leave me?

Part of her will always be with me, inside. And she wouldn't want this for me, would she?

My dolphin shadow nudges underneath me again, pushes me up.

Thank you.

I kick up to the light above and it takes so long to break the surface of the water that by the time I do there are spots in my vision.

I breathe in deeply. What was I doing? I'm shocked, shaken. I look around – waiting for the dolphins to break the surface – but they don't.

Did I imagine the whole thing?

Simone and Sophie will be freaking out if they saw me swim down and disappear under the surface for so long, and is there any chance that they weren't watching? I start to swim for the shore, keeping on the surface now, front crawl, watching for dolphins as I do but seeing none. I cut back and forth across to deal with currents that want to drag me out.

By the time I reach the beach I'm exhausted. Half stumbling out of the water.

Simone is there with a big towel. She wraps it around me.

'You scared me,' she says.

'Sorry. I scared me a little, too.'

Sophie is here as well; she's picked up my clothes and the three of us walk back up the path to the house together.

'Are you all right?' Sophie asks.

'You're wondering if I need locking up again, aren't you?'

'Of course not. Well, maybe a little.'

'Cate is dead. I'm not all right. Swimming is what I do to make me feel better, that's all.'

'OK. But not so far out next time, all right? Or maybe stick to a pool. And possibly stop to put on a swimsuit.'

'Sure,' I say, and head for the stairs.

'Where are you going?' Simone says.

'I need a shower.' *I need to be alone.*

Sophie is saying goodbye. After the door closes, I can hear Ali and Simone's voices rise and fall as I go up the stairs.

Bedroom door open, then shut. Bathroom door locked, closing me inside. Water on. I drop the towel, shuck off my under things and get in, and just stand there. The water is so hot it's almost scalding, but somehow I'm still cold inside.

After a while I drop to the tiled floor, pull my knees up against me, head bowed down and water pouring on my back and neck. There is a gaping hole inside of me where my anger was. Now it is filling with loss, confusion, and *pain*.

Cate, how could you leave me?

Now my hot tears finally fall, mixing in the water, a salty trickle washed away by a torrent.

38

Later I'm standing in my room in a dressing gown, looking out of the glass doors without seeing anything. There's a knock on my door.

Simone peeks in. 'Hi, Holly. Do you want to come down for dinner? It's all right if you don't.'

'Thanks. If it's OK I'll stay here.'

'I'll have something sent up. If you want anything, want to talk, even if I'm asleep, come get me.'

'Thank you,' I say, but I know I can't talk to her about this. She doesn't want to hear how I'm feeling, not right now.

Later there is another knock, and this time it's Ali. He's bringing a tray?

'Hi, Holly. Dinner delivery.'

He's awkward. He brings it into my room and I realise he's not come in it since I've been here. He puts the tray on the desk, then sits down next to it. 'Can we talk about your mother? There are some things you should know about her that you don't, and I don't think she'll tell you.' He's uneasy.

'What's that?'

'She isn't that strong, mentally.'

'What do you mean?'

'She's been treated for anxiety and depression for years. Just try to be kind to her, all right? She's your mother, not Cate.' The anger he feels against Cate is in his voice. Even with what happened to her, it always will be. And I can understand that, but have to accept how I feel, too.

'I loved Cate. I know you think I shouldn't have, but I did.'

Emotions cross Ali's face too quick to follow – a mixture of anger, hurt, and something else. 'I know you can't help how you feel, and this whole mess isn't your fault. It's Cate's.'

'You didn't know her the way I did. Despite the big stuff that she's done; you didn't.'

'OK. That's true, I guess.' I can tell how hard it is for him to say that. 'But try not to show how you feel about Cate to Simone.'

'I'll try.'

After he's gone, I pick at my dinner without noticing what it is. I don't know why I said that to Ali – that I loved Cate. I didn't need to; I could have spared him. I'll try to be more careful with Simone. I remember now that she'd asked me not to talk about Cate to Ali; now he's done the same for her. They're trying to protect each other from me, aren't they? And that they still care very much for each other is all through what they've both said.

These two people, really strangers to me, want things from me when all I want is to be with Cate. And I'm not supposed to talk about her to either of them.

You didn't know her the way I did . . . These words I said to Ali are going back and forth in my mind. I'd been angry with her, for what she'd done: taking me from my parents, changing my life – and me – the way she did. Maybe the anger was something I needed; it stopped me from hurting so much. And now that

Cate is gone, I've lost the chance to find out why she did it. Even if I was never able to speak to her directly, wouldn't she have been able to tell her story at her trial?

If there was a good reason she took me away, one that makes sense, what could it be? All I can think is that she was protecting me from something, but what? Is it this Circle she mentioned? But I don't know what that is; the police didn't, either.

And now . . . someone killed her, with a knife. Whoever they are, are they the same threat she was trying to protect me from? Am I still in danger from them?

Cate is gone. Did I come close to leaving and joining her? Did a *dolphin* actually save my life?

I didn't see them surface. Simone didn't mention them either and she would have if she'd seen them, wouldn't she? It felt so *real*, but did it really happen?

I have more questions than answers, but I can't stop myself from going over them again and again, even though I'm not getting anywhere. I'm just going around in circles.

Beware The Circle.

I'm alone in the sea, swimming ever further from the shore. There's no light from above through the water; either I'm too deep for it to reach me or it's night. I can barely see but still I'm searching. There is something – or someone – I'm trying to find. All around and through me a chorus of voices urges me on, to go further, deeper.

But the only one I want is Cate.

Cate wasn't a swimmer, not like me, so how could I find her here?

Even as I form the thought, she is with me and the other voices are silenced. She wraps her arms around me.

'Cate? I'm so sorry—'

'Hush. There's no need.'

'You don't know. I was so angry at you. I didn't believe in you.'

'That doesn't matter any more now.'

'Can't you tell me why? Why you took me from my parents?'

She doesn't answer. Instead, she begins the litany, and I join in: mother daughter, sister sister, daughter mother, best friends. You and I. All things, always.

She cocks her head to one side as if listening to something only she can hear.

'I have to go,' she says.

And I'm trying to hold her so she can't leave me, but then, like she was never there, my arms are empty.

Cate! Cate? Come back!

A bell rings.

A bell?

I open my eyes. I'm in bed, still half in my dream and not making sense of what I heard. What bell?

It rings again, next to me, on the bedside table. The screen is lit up; it's my phone.

There's a text from Jago. *hi, r u all right? i saw about cate on the news.*

I sit up, disoriented. My pyjamas are stuck to my skin with sweat that has gone cold now. I'm shivering.

I get up, pull on my dressing gown and put on the desk light. I open the laptop, and do a search for 'Catelyn Green'.

There it is, top of the list: *Nanny Kidnapper Found Dead in Cell.* Splashed out for the world to see.

There's a photo of Cate – one from before I knew her, or before I remember her, at least. She's younger, her hair is shorter, but it is *her*. My fingers reach out to touch her face on the screen.

Cate, what happened to lead you to this?

I find my notebook where I'd hidden it on the top shelf of the wardrobe. I hold it close, find my pen, then write down my dream.

Afterwards I just sit there, still holding the notebook that she made for me. I remember what she said about the sea when she gave me this gift: it's beautiful, but also wild, dangerous. It's doesn't know right or wrong, it just is. Even if you love it, you can still drown if you don't respect what it can do.

I hug it against me, stroke the cover, the binding.

Wait. At the back cover, there's a ripple in the lining, as if something is underneath.

I don't want to tear it, but I worry at the edge with a fingernail until it loosens, and I can slip a finger inside. There *is* something there. I tug at it.

A folded square of paper.

There are goosebumps on my arms, my neck. How long has this been here without me knowing?

I unfold it carefully. Inside there's a drawing: four circles in two rows of two, edges just touching. There's something about the design – it's familiar, though I can't say why – but that's not what draws my eye.

Underneath, three words are written in Cate's careful handwriting: *Beware The Circle.*

39

There's not much I remember about the next days and weeks.

I sleep. My dreams get wilder and weirder. I commit them to the pages of my notebook, then hide it away.

I swim in the mornings. In the afternoons I read books and go through endless lessons from the tutor, and almost pay attention. I should probably be at school by now, but no one has mentioned it again. It's near the end of the school year; has everyone agreed – without discussion – that next year is soon enough? I hope so.

The only time I feel truly alive is when I'm in the sea. But Simone gets so worried when I swim from the beach that there is enough of me paying attention to notice, and to remember what Ali said about her. So mostly my swimming is contained, lengths back and forth in the outdoor sea baths at the swimming centre.

Simone comes, waits and watches. Sometimes Ali comes with her, too. He's home more often than Simone said he ever was, and I sense that they are becoming closer again. Perhaps not knowing how to deal with me is doing that for them? I hope so. It may be the only thing I can give them.

No one seems to know who killed Cate, or why. I'm mourning her, but I'm not supposed to feel the way that I do. All I can do is keep it inside.

Sophie calls every few days. We talk about what I'm doing; she asks how I'm feeling. I try to say things that are real but not enough to give her a reason to wave any red flags and get me locked up in a hospital again.

Dr Chang at the Penrose Clinic wants to talk to me, too, and I've been taken there a few times. She wants to know about my dreams, if I've been writing them down.

I don't tell her that I have been, that they're getting more and more distressing to the point where I'm afraid to go to sleep. I keep taking the tablets they gave me, not sure if they're helping but afraid to stop in case the dreams get worse.

Jago texts now and then. I haven't decided to ignore him, exactly; that isn't what I want. At least, I don't think it is. But I'm mired too much in what hurts inside to be able to answer him.

Everything inside me feels out of balance, like I'm spinning, faster and faster, tilting on an axis too far to one side, and any moment now I'll lose my grip completely. Fly out of control. Crash, and then what? I don't know.

In the meantime, I sleep, I dream, and I swim.

40

'Holly? Holly Heath?'

It's a woman, one I don't know. Forty or so, standing by the side of the pool as I climb out of it. I'm exhausted after pushing myself to swim further, faster, longer. And there is this part of me still from the way I lived with Cate: I don't engage with strangers. Even if – *especially* if – they seem to know who I am.

'I've been watching you train,' she says.

'Train? I haven't been training.' I turn part way towards her, an eyebrow raised. Then walk past her and disappear into the changing rooms.

When I come out after showering and changing, and go to the café where Simone reads and waits, they are there together: Simone and the stranger.

'Holly, this is Wendy Wilson. She's a swimming coach.' Simone is smiling widely.

'Oh. Hi,' I say, still standing, hoping Simone will get up and we'll leave now.

'Take a seat,' Simone says. 'I've ordered you a tea.'

'I was just telling your mother that we are scouting for swimmers to take part in our club's training programme. Those that meet the qualifying times can compete in the British championships, and, if they do well, be selected for the next Olympics,' Wendy says.

My eyes widen. The actual *Olympics*?

She carries on, tells us about swimmers they've trained here that have done well in the UK and world competitions.

'What swimming club were you with before?' Wendy asks.

I shake my head. 'I haven't ever been in a club.'

'You haven't been coached?'

I shake my head no.

'That's – well – frankly astonishing. Your stroke work and stamina are of a level that I was sure you had been. You're a little older than we would normally begin with a swimmer, but from what I've seen – if you are interested – we can consider putting you into a fast-track training programme and see how you do.'

'Holly?' Simone says, prompting me to say something.

'I don't know. I've never competed against anyone but myself.' Wendy is nodding, smiling; she seems to like that answer. 'What is involved?'

'To begin with, some training sessions and assessments here. Early morning. If you do well there is summer swim school where it all gets very serious and competitive. Do you think you're up for it?'

A reason to swim more and more, a focus outside of myself, doing the thing I like best? Despite a sense of unease inside – one I can't label or explain, beyond my usual reserve with strangers – I find myself nodding, saying yes.

Late that night I'm pacing in my room, back and forth, along the glass wall. My lights are out and it's cloudy, the moon and stars hidden, the sea below indistinct. I can sense rather than see the rising tide – a swell building both inside and out, a twitching anticipation in my muscles that won't let me be still.

Too tired to sleep, too tired to stop. One step, another. I count them – one, two, three . . . fourteen, fifteen, sixteen . . . twenty-two, twenty-three, twenty-four, and turn.

One, two, three . . .

Light fractures, changes, the glass warps and curves around me.

Nine, ten . . .

My breathing changes. Slows and slows again, until it stops.

I'm swimming, trapped, circling back and forth and over again.

One eye open, one closed. Always searching, hunting, for the way out, even while I sleep. Even though I know there is none.

The glass walls have no end and they are strong, I know this. So I wait, I circle, I swim.

My patience isn't as infinite as the sea, but I know my time is coming.

Soon.

When?

Soon.

41

Bzzzzz.

What?

Bzzzzz. Bzzzzz.

I'm cold, stiff, and open my eyes, and it takes a moment to make sense of where I am. I'm stretched out on the floor, my back pressed against the cold glass wall.

Bzzzzz. Bzzzzz.

It won't stop – it's my phone alarm. It's five a.m. We're leaving for swimming training in half an hour.

Bzzzzz. Bzzzzz.

I get up, stagger to the dressing table and stab at 'Stop' on the screen. Sigh in relief when the noise it makes stops.

For a moment I'm tempted by bed: softness and warm blankets and sleep . . .

. . . which leads to dreams.

I shake myself and start getting ready to go.

I'm yawning and waiting by the front door when Ali comes down. He's dropping me on his way to London – an earlier start than usual for him also.

The unease I felt yesterday about going to this swim training has got worse. Is it the thought of being in a group with people I don't know? Is it the competing? Or maybe it's just the dreams and lack of restful sleep I had last night making me feel this way. I'm so tired, moving through air is like fighting my way in deep sand. How am I going to swim when I can barely walk? I don't even know what is bothering me the most, but my stomach is in knots.

'Good morning,' Ali says. 'Is this a bit early for you?'

'It's OK,' I lie. 'But I'm not sure about going to this training thing.'

'Simone says you're really into swimming, and from what I've seen, I agree. Isn't that right?'

'Yes. Being in the water is my most favourite thing: I love swimming.' It's an understatement and has always been true, but I've started becoming even more obsessed. With everything that has changed, the only place I still feel like *me* is in the water, and I think about it all the time when I'm not.

'You could excel at this, find a place for yourself there. Or maybe it won't go anywhere, but if it doesn't all you've done is spend some time doing something you enjoy with people who also enjoy it. So, what do you think? Do you want to give it a try, or go back to sleep?'

'Well, when you put it like that . . .'

He smiles. 'Come on.' We head out the door, walk to his car. Get in.

'This could be a good opportunity for you,' he says. 'I've looked into Wendy Wilson. She's the real deal. She has been behind some of the best swimmers to come out of the UK in the last decade. The swim school she told you and Simone about fast-tracks new talent to qualify for the British championships – and then, if they do well, on to the Olympics.'

The drive goes all too quickly and we're soon pulling up to the main doors of the swimming club.

'Here we are,' he says.

'Thank you,' I say. 'For looking into her and stuff. I'm always nervous about people I don't know.'

'That's all right. If you haven't worked it out yet, Simone and I will always be here for you, looking out for you. It's part of our job, and we haven't had the chance to do enough of it.'

I'm here, in this moment – more present than I have been with either of them for a while. I can feel in my gut how sincere he is. I've been holding it against both of them – particularly Ali – how they feel about Cate, but that's not really fair, is it?

I'm looking into his eyes, hesitating, then very quickly lean across and kiss his cheek.

'Have a good morning,' he says, smiling. I get out and he waves. I stand on the steps of the swimming club for a moment, watching his car go. Then head in through the front doors.

42

There's someone at reception, yawning. 'Good morning,' he says. 'Are you Holly?'

I nod, too tired to bother giving the spiel about using my middle name instead.

'Go on through. Most of the others are in the changing rooms. You meet at the pool at six – you've got less than five minutes.'

Once I'm out of his sight I slow, almost stop, hoping if it takes me a while to get to the changing rooms they'll be empty by the time I get there. I hesitate at the door, then push it open. There are some voices at the exit to the pool – that door shuts and then silence.

My suit is already on under my clothes. I take them off quickly and shove them in a locker. As I do so the door from the hall opens and a girl bolts through, cheeks flushed, like she's been running.

She nods. 'Hi, are you new? I'm Ariel.'

'Hi.'

She starts taking off her clothes and I turn to go to the door to the pool.

'Wait for me. Please! If I go in late on my own I'll catch it.' She grins and has the most infectious smile that I find myself smiling back, slowing my footsteps to the door.

She's pulling on her swimsuit while I wait, looking the other way.

'Ready. Let's go,' she says.

We step out through the door to the pool just as Wendy is counting down from ten.

'Just in time, Ariel,' she says, giving her a look.

'Sorry, Coach,' Ariel says.

'And everybody, this is Holly,' Wendy – *Coach?* – says. 'Say hello.'

Including Ariel and me there are eight of us – all girls – and a less than enthusiastic round of hellos. It's the moment when I should say, *Call me Tabby*, but I can't bring myself to say anything when they're all looking at me.

We start with gentle stretches and then slow lengths to warm up. No matter how tired I felt before, once I'm in the water my energy comes back; I can feel it flowing through my arms and legs, urging me on.

She has us doing different strokes – ten lengths each of front crawl, backstroke and breaststroke, and then stops us, giving individual tips to each of us on our technique. Then we do it all over again, at a gradually increasing pace. It's gruelling, and I love it.

I'm surprised the ninety minutes is up when she blows a whistle. We get out of the pool and do stretches. They're all chatting as we go into the changing rooms; Ariel starts telling me their names. I want to escape but there are only four showers and I have to wait.

When I finally finish, dress and come out, the receptionist says, 'Holly? Wendy has left your schedule here.' He holds out an envelope. 'Your mum is in the café.'

I open the envelope. Weights training? Really? Early-morning group swim sessions like today. One-to-one training sessions.

I put it back in the envelope and as I do, notice a scrawl on the back of it – a mobile number, followed by an A. Is that for Ariel?

In the café, Simone is reading, a coffee in front of her.

She looks up and smiles. 'Do you want anything?' she says.

'I want *everything*. I'm famished.'

43

Ali is late for dinner, Simone glancing at her watch. She's just signalling to have the first course brought in when he comes through the door, still in his suit.

'Sorry,' he says, and kisses Simone's cheek before he sits down, then loosens his tie.

'Was it the traffic?' she says.

'Sort of.'

'Sort of?'

'I left a bit late – there were last-minute security briefings. Then there were protestors on the way home – had to reroute.'

'Security briefings? Is something wrong?'

'Nothing to worry you.'

Simone's eyes narrow. 'Hmmm. I see. And the protestors – what was that about?'

He shrugs. 'Same old climate change refrain. And the latest proposed fracking sites.'

'I thought fracking was banned,' I say.

'It *was*. Overturned last week, thankfully,' he says.

'Thankfully?' Simone shakes her head.

Fracking: high-pressure liquids underground to force up oil or gas. Both the process and the product make climate change worse, not to mention what it does to the environment where it is done. And my dad does this? I've mostly managed to avoid

176

thinking about the fact that Ali works for Industria United, at first convinced he wasn't my dad so it didn't matter; then in too much shock that he was; then Cate's death. I flinch. Cate would have the words; I don't.

He laughs, looking between us. 'Like mother like daughter: the two of you have the same dismayed expression.'

'And so we should,' Simone says. 'Holly will have to live with the consequences of climate change after we're gone.'

'We're working on solutions, I promise you,' he says. 'Things will get better, and the protestors will have to find something else to object to.'

'Solutions? What kind of solutions?' Simone says, but he won't be drawn on it any further.

Later I'm in my room, at my desk, trying to read English lessons from the tutor. I open the laptop, dither for a while but can't concentrate.

The training plan that Coach left for me this morning is on the desk in its envelope. I turn it over and pick up my phone, then enter the numbers scrawled on the back.

Hello mystery A, I text.

Seconds later my screen lights up.

so v mysterious, aren't I! it's ariel. And u r? . . . just checking ;-)

Who am I, really? I don't even know. Perhaps I should just start over again as a new person, and use a new name – I seem to be stuck with it at swimming, anyhow. *Holly*, I reply, in the absence of a better answer.

so what did u think of training – coming back 4 more or is it 2 freaking early?

177

It IS early. But yes. I'll be there.

yay! c u in the morning byeeeeeeee

Using letters for words seems to be the thing to do, since both Jago and Ariel do it. I change what I'd started to text to *c u then*, and hit send.

I watch the phone for a while, but the screen doesn't light up again. It's late. Ariel is probably being sensible and going to sleep before *2 freaking early* comes tomorrow morning, just like I should be.

Jago: I could message Jago. I hold the phone in my hand again, read the ones he's sent me. It feels wrong to ignore him, but somehow I can't bring myself to reply.

I'm restless; my feet want to pace back and forth like I did last night, but I don't want to wake up on the floor again. I sigh, remembering. It was so weird: it felt like I fell asleep on my feet, my walking changed to a dream of swimming.

There wasn't enough time to write my dream down this morning, either.

I grab my notebook from the top of the shelf, make myself get into bed, then open it to the next blank page.

I stare at it, pen in hand, but I don't know what to write. When did I switch from being awake to being in a dream? It wasn't like there was a moment where before it, I was awake, and then after it, I was asleep. It's not like one blended gradually into the other, either. It felt more like I was awake and dreaming at the *same time*, and couldn't tell one from the other.

What would Dr Chang make of that? Maybe I should be telling her what is really happening. She might be able to help me make sense of it. But even though part of me thinks that would be the sensible thing to do, something else inside me screams *NO* – that I need to figure this out for myself.

Or maybe I'm just afraid of what she might say, or what might happen. Being different isn't how they want things in this world, just like Cate always said. Maybe they'd lock me up.

Thoughts of Cate sneak in, unexpectedly, like a kick to the guts – the pain an ambush that could knock me from my feet.

Cate, I wish you were here, I whisper. She'd know what to do, what all this means. Even if she didn't – even if she said it was for me to work out – just her being here would make me feel better.

They promised they'd let me know if they found out how she died, why; nothing has been said, and there's been nothing beyond speculation in the news, either. Maybe they'll never find the answer. Maybe I'll never know why she took me from my parents, either.

I keep coming back to that. Once I accepted she really had taken me away from my true family, despite the misgivings – and anger – I know Cate. I know what she did must have been because she felt it was right – I'm sure of it. All I can think of is that she must have thought she was protecting me from something. But I also know Simone and Ali love me and would never have harmed me, so why would she have taken me away from them?

Cate told me to think for myself, but I keep coming back to the same problem, the same question.

If I know two things and know both of them are true, but one contradicts the other, what does this mean?

Either they are both true, and I can't see the reason they can coexist.

Or I am wrong, and one of them is false.

More to distract myself than for any other reason, I try again to go back to last night, to remember my dream enough to write something down. But it's still too mixed up and weird; words won't come. Instead, I begin to draw, not thinking about what I'm doing, instead feeling, remembering – how walking became swimming, air became water. My room enclosed by glass: not just one wall, but all around.

My pen stills, my right eye gradually closes but the left sees nothing around me. Swimming, but not as I am now. *Power* runs through me and is around me at once. Both ancient and newly born: born for a freedom that has been denied.

The sea runs through me and I am the sea.

When my *2-freaking-early* alarm goes the next morning, the notebook is still next to me, the pen locked in stiff fingers so tight that I have to use my other hand to remove it.

I stretch, sit up, go to close the notebook. That's when I see it: the double-page spread covered with a schematic drawing of waves. It looks as if I've traced the same pattern endless times, but I have no memory of doing so.

Did I draw this while I slept?

Even assuming it is possible to draw in your sleep, could it be done so neatly? It looks like there is exact spacing between each line and the one next to it. I don't think I could be that precise if I tried when I was awake, so how could I do it in my sleep?

My hand is still stiff like it was holding the pen as tight as it could all night – I massage my fingers with the other hand, and that's when I realise.

The pen – I was holding it in my left hand. But I'm right-handed.

Unease walks up and down my spine, like an army of invisible spiders. But I shake my head, get up, push it away.

It's time to swim.

44

I get there first and dive off the side of the pool. Brief seconds of being airborne are followed by hands, arms then body slicing through salty cold. As soon as the shock of the water is all around me, I'm at ease, and I arc down deep, swim along the rocky bottom to the other end of the pool.

I do a kick turn then swim back until I'm nearly where I started. Aware now that the others are here, standing in the water, I surface and breathe in deeply.

'Glad you could join us, Holly,' Coach says from the side above us.

The faces of the other girls around me show varying degrees of surprise, even shock. Is that because I swam underwater without breathing for so long? 'Freak,' I hear one of them murmur, and a few sniggers follow. My eyes find Ariel; she nods, an appraising look in her eyes like she's trying to figure something out, and then she winks.

We begin swimming drills but I'm struggling to concentrate, wanting to lose myself in the depths of the pool and not swim along the surface. Wanting even more to leave the pool and swim out in the sea.

Someone taps my shoulder – it's Ariel. She points to the side where Coach is looking cross.

'Come here, Holly,' she says.

I swim to the side.

'I'd appreciate it if you could stay with the rest of us.'

'Sorry,' I say, and go back and follow along with the others.

I'd been so happy when I arrived to find out we were training in the outdoor saltwater pool today; relieved to be immersed in the water, to feel like me. I try harder after that and mostly manage to do what I'm supposed to be doing, but feel this sense of not being here, being someplace else, at the same time – like I'm dissociated from my body and surroundings.

The ninety minutes is soon gone. When it's time to get out, do stretches and head for the showers, I want to stay in the pool for ever.

45

'Lovely to see you, *Chérie*,' Elodie says. She's up out of her seat to kiss me and then Simone on both cheeks, then gestures at chairs next to hers. We're on a terrace; the table is set for lunch. Other tables are scattered between potted plants and sculptures but ours is almost secluded, with plants all around.

'Sorry we're late,' Simone says. 'Somebody didn't want to get out of the pool.'

'Sorry,' I say. Simone had told me to get out sharpish; when I was in the water I was too focused on being there to remember.

Elodie shrugs her shoulders. 'No matter. So. How are you both?'

'We're well,' Simone says.

'I can see that, but how are things, really? Now that some time has passed with the new living arrangements, are you getting along?'

'*Of course* we are,' Simone says. 'She's my daughter.'

'And I'm your mother, and we both know we get along better with different addresses.'

Simone stares at her a moment, then bursts into laughter. '*Touché*. But I really do think we're doing well, don't you, Holly?'

'Wait,' Elodie says. 'Aren't you called Tabby any more?'

'I remembered some stuff, about being Holly from years ago.'

'That doesn't change the question. Are you Holly or are you Tabby?'

'Both,' I say, feeling caught. 'I mean—'

'Who are you inside, when you think of yourself?'

I hesitate. 'Tabby,' I say, finally.

'I thought so.'

'It's all right, it's just a name—'

'Who you are inside is *everything*. But outside, too: you're dressed like a version of Simone.' I look at what we're both wearing and she's kind of right. I'd let Simone decide what I should wear to lunch today, not having confidence in what was right myself.

'Simone, she's your daughter, not a mini-me.' I glance at Simone, alarmed at how she might react, but she has a sort of long-suffering look on her face and says nothing.

'Haven't you been shopping on your own yet?' Elodie says to me.

'Uh, no. I don't really care what I wear.' Maybe I do a little, but there's been too much other stuff to think about.

'And we're related?'

She turns the focus to Simone now, demanding to know how things are with Ali, and why hasn't she gone back to work?

As I watch them spar with words – that is what it is – I wonder at how they get along behind it all. I like Elodie. I don't know what she's going to say until she says it, but she doesn't just talk without saying anything, or use words that have no meaning or hide a meaning you have to look for underneath.

'Now, Simone, isn't it about time you went to powder your nose?' Elodie says. 'It's a bit shiny.'

185

Simone rolls her eyes. 'Excuse me a moment,' she says, and gets up, walks out the way we came.

'At last we're alone. Tabby, I'm so sorry about Cate. That must have been a terrible shock.'

'I . . . ah . . .' There's a lump in my throat, and I swallow. 'Yes. It was.'

'There are some things even I won't say in front of my daughter or her husband. But I liked Cate. I never understood what she did – what her reasons were – but I'm sure she had one, even if it was misguided. And from everything I have seen, she has raised you well.'

'Thank you. I . . . I miss her.' I whisper that, as if it can't be said out loud.

'Of course you do. It's OK. If you ever want to say things you can't say anywhere else, try me. Trust me, there isn't anything that'll shock me. And despite impressions, I'm good at keeping secrets that need to be kept, I promise you.'

There are tears in my eyes now and hers are kind. She's holding my hand and gives it a squeeze.

Her eyes move over my shoulder; she nods and Simone is back.

46

'Hi, my name is Dina, and I'll be doing your massage today. Have you been with us before?'

I shake my head, standing in the doorway to a room with a kind of narrow bed in the middle of it, feeling very like walking in the other direction. But I know Elodie thought this was a special treat and I don't want to do anything that might upset her – not when she's been so lovely to me.

'You haven't had a massage before, have you.' She says it like a statement not a question.

'No.'

'You'll love it, I promise. Do you have any allergies?'

'Not that I know of.'

'Any health problems or regular medications?'

I shake my head. 'Just vitamins, and something to help me sleep at night from the doctor.'

Soon Dina has left the room so I can get ready. She said to take everything off except my pants and lie down on the table, face first. I'm feeling so uncomfortable being mostly undressed, only a towel over myself, with someone I don't know about to massage me, that I'm about to get up and get dressed again when the door opens – too late.

Music starts: no, it's not quite music, it's sounds – of nature? There are bird calls, water falling, the sea. And then there are hot stones, and oils that smell lovely. She starts on my back, gently and then more firmly, easing into my muscles and . . . it's *amazing*. It reminds me how it felt when Cate would sing to me when I was unwell.

And just like when Cate sang to me, I'm drifting, not quite here any more; sleepy, but not stressed like I have been lately when it's time to sleep. The sounds of the sea, the fragrances, the warm stones . . .

Gliding through warm water, a pure blue that is unreal — tropical? Languid. Drifting and dreaming.

Peace, shattered. Sounds of alarm through the sea and I wake fully. Fight or flight?

Flee.

Too late.

A net?

I'm thrashing for all I'm worth but can't get free

Tangled. Struggling for the surface to breathe. Panic —

I strike out, gasping, struggling to sit up but I'm tangled in towels. There are concerned faces. Dina? Simone is here too, and then the door opens and in bursts Elodie and two paramedics.

I'm still on the table. Nothing on but pants and a towel and I pull it up around me but I'm still half in my dream and I'm gathering myself to run, to get out of here and away from all of them . . .

Someone touches my arm and I pull away. 'Holly? Holly? Tabby!' It's Simone. I turn, try to focus on her. 'Are you all right?' she says, and with her voice, her words, I'm back to myself, and here and now.

My breathing slows gradually. 'Of course I am. I was asleep, that's all. What's going on?'

'We were called that you'd stopped breathing,' a paramedic says, looking at Dina with a sceptical look.

'She did, I swear it. I was doing back massage as usual – she'd fallen asleep and then I realised she wasn't breathing. I shook her, said her name and she didn't wake up. One of her eyes was wide open and staring at me!' Dina is scared, shaking. She's frightened – of me?

'I'm fine, really,' I say.

'We better check you out,' one of the paramedics says.

They check my blood pressure, oxygenation. Respiration. They say my blood pressure and breathing rates are unusually low, and ask if I'm an athlete.

'I'm a swimmer,' I say.

'She trains hours every day,' Simone adds.

'I'm sure I didn't get it wrong,' Dina says. 'She wasn't breathing. And the way she had one eye open like that, fixed and staring – it looked like she wasn't *there* any more.'

'We'll get our doctors to check her again,' Simone says. 'And she used to sleep with one eye open sometimes when she was a baby; perhaps she still does. I know it looks alarming if you're not used to it.'

They leave so I can get dressed.

Was Dina right – did I really stop breathing? I couldn't breathe in my dream – I was trapped and struggling underwater. Does that happen to me in reality when I'm dreaming?

What if they hadn't woken me up?

My dreams are scary enough without being worried that they might kill me.

47

'Hi, Tabby,' Dr Chang says. 'Take a seat. How are you feeling?'

'All right, I guess.'

'The report I've been given is that you've been checked over thoroughly just now and everything seems OK medically; in fact, they said everything is perfect. Now why don't you tell me what happened.'

I'm uneasy. 'I don't really know. I fell asleep during a massage, and when I woke up my mum and Dina – the massage person – were there, and then paramedics she'd called came in with my grandmother. Dina said I'd stopped breathing, but I got the feeling they thought she was mistaken.'

'OK. How do you feel about it?'

'She must have made a mistake,' I say. 'I'm fine.' *Am I really?*

'I hear that you've taken up quite intense swimming training?'

'Yeah, I have.'

'How's it going?'

'All right, I guess.'

She looks at me like she's wanting more, but I wait out the silence. She looks down at her notes.

'Have you been sleeping well lately?'

'Just fine,' I lie, and think how weird it is that I'm able to cope with the training with so little sleep. No matter how tired I feel, as soon as I get into the water, I'm fine. The only one who regularly beats me is Ariel.

Again, there is a pause.

'All right, then,' she says at last. 'Have you begun a dream diary like we've discussed?'

I shake my head, wondering at how good I've got at lying. As just Tabby, I was rubbish at it. No matter what name I get called now, since I've been playing at being someone else – Holly – I seem to have worked it out. I get the feeling that Dr Chang knows it, too. Why am I even bothering? Is there any reason not to tell her what she wants to know?

She sighs. 'You make it difficult to help you. Is there anything at all you'd like to talk about?'

'No. I'm good.'

'All right, then,' she says, and I've lost count of how many 'all rights' we've said between us. Two words that seem to cover just about anything, even when what they mean doesn't fit at all. 'We'll see you again in a few weeks.'

Simone is in the waiting room and seems surprised to see me so soon.

'Is everything OK?' she says.

'Yes. Can we go?' I'm impatient to get away and don't even know why. There's something about coming here. The more often I pass through the doors of the place, the more I want to get away from it.

'All right,' Simone says.

Another 'all right'.

I'm chasing food around on my plate at dinner, not hungry. Sitting outside with Simone on the veranda.

Ali comes out to join us, the cook behind him with things for an extra setting.

'I thought you were going to be working late?' Simone says.

'Wanted to come home and make sure you're both OK. What did the doctors have to say?'

'That nothing is wrong. She's fine.'

'Tabby, how are you feeling?'

'I'm good. Just a little tired.'

'Maybe this swimming training is too much too soon,' Ali says. 'Should you take a break?'

'No! Really, I'm OK. And—'

There's a noise, an odd mechanical sort of noise, and I stop mid-sentence. It sounds like it's coming from above us, but nothing is there.

Then something rises over the line of the roof behind Ali.

Ali turns.

'Everybody inside!' He grabs my hand and almost pulls me from my seat before I can react. We're up and running for the doors.

Whatever it is, it's closer now.

Simone is just behind us. She screams, and I turn.

She's covered in red; *red* that is splashed on my back, my arms.

Ali pushes me inside and goes to her and now I'm screaming too.

48

Ali is on the phone and he's furious. So furious he doesn't see me listening in at his open office door.

'It's paint. Red paint.'

'Yes, it's water soluble, but it could have been anything.'

'We're paying a fortune for security and I expect you to deliver. Keep my family safe.'

When Simone gets out of the bath she is angry also, but in a different way. With a different focus.

'What is going on, Alistair? Tell us.'

'It's just the usual—'

'No. It isn't, and it isn't just what happened here tonight, is it? There's something you've been hiding. Tell us.'

He's silent for a moment. Then turns to me. 'Tabby, can you give us a moment?'

'No. I want to know, too.'

He looks between us, then sighs. 'All right. There's been an increase in internet chatter that suggests something is going to happen – that the oil and gas industry in the west are being targeted. Also, there have been warnings sent – with increasingly stronger wording – threatening action if we don't do the impossible and stop all extraction immediately. We don't know how seriously to take it, but all levels of security in our sector are on alert.'

'Something is going to happen – like a drone with red paint?' Simone says.

'They're looking into it, but the warnings have been about action on a large scale. What happened tonight is unlikely to be related.'

'What if it was acid? Or a nerve agent?' And she's looking at me and the fear she has for me is all over her face.

'It wasn't, and it won't be. They're just trying to get a reaction.'

'You don't know that.'

'Think about it. Would an environmental group use chemicals? It'd be completely against what they're trying to achieve to use poison.'

'Maybe you're wrong. Maybe they're just desperate enough at all the inaction by governments on the whole climate change issue to take steps you wouldn't think they could take.'

He doesn't answer. He doesn't know, so how can he? Simone's eyes are locked on his, and he looks away first.

'For the time being, both of you stay inside and keep away from the beach,' he says. 'At least until they catch whoever controlled the drone.'

That night I can't sleep.

There was a banner dropped before the paint; they found it later, fluttering on the roof. It took a while to get it down.

Climate Change Kills, it said. Spelled out in more red paint: red for blood, for death.

When Simone screamed and was covered in it, I thought she'd been shot. Even when it splattered me, too, I didn't realise it wasn't blood.

I can't lose another mother. I can't.

49

The next morning I throw myself into training, giving it everything I've got and then finding some more. It's the only way I know to make the world go away.

We end with a race: eight lengths. When I touch the end of the pool I'm startled to see I got there first. I beat Ariel? She's in the lane next to me and when she gets there soon after, holds up her hand for a high five.

We get out as a group, do our stretches and turn for the changing room door.

'Holly?' Coach says. 'Wait a moment.' She pauses until the last of them have disappeared through the door. 'I've got some very good news for you. I'd like to invite you to our summer training programme. Get changed and we'll talk about it.'

I head for the changing rooms. Summer training? I remember she'd said something about it the first day she spoke to Simone and me, but she hasn't mentioned it since or said anything about what it involves.

I pause at the doors, take a deep breath as I go through. This is the part that I don't like: being in the changing rooms with seven other girls. They all chat and I don't know how to join in, or even if I want to. Sometimes one of them – usually Ariel – will direct a comment at me or ask me something. I think she's just trying to include me, but then they all look at me and I hate it.

But today is different. When the door opens it's like they were all waiting for me and crowd around.

'What did Coach want?' Ariel says. 'Did she ask you?'

'Ask me what?'

'About the SSS.' I must look puzzled; she rolls her eyes. 'Summer swim school.'

'Yeah.'

'Congratulations,' one of the other girls says. 'I'd kill to go.' She almost looks like she means it. But I'm getting pats on the back and one by one they move off, go to the showers, but Ariel stays.

'And? What did you say?'

'Nothing yet. She wants to talk to me when I come out. I don't know that much about it.'

'You'll love it. It's amazing, all cutting-edge training and breathing techniques – you'll be even faster by the end. And it's not just girls, either.' She winks.

'You've been before?'

'I went last year.'

'How many people go?'

'Last year there was about fifty, from all over the UK. At the end of it if we reach qualifying times we can compete at the British Championships. I just missed out last year; this year, I'm determined to make it.'

'Where is it, exactly?'

'On the coast, not far from Exmouth.'

I try to work out in my mind how long it will take to get there, but all I can get is that it is a long way. 'You must spend a load of time going back and forth?'

She shakes her head. 'It's residential. We're away for six weeks – most of the summer.'

I'm looking back at her, horrified. Simone is *never* going to let me out of her sight for that long. I wasn't sure she'd even let me come to training this morning, after what happened yesterday, let alone go away. Even if she would, do I want to do this? Go away to a new place with so many people I don't know?

'What's wrong?' Ariel says.

'I'm not sure I can go.'

'Got something better to do?'

'Well, no, not exactly. It's complicated.'

'Have you got secrets? Don't worry, I'll get them out of you eventually.' One of the girls comes out wrapped in a towel and Ariel goes to shower. I sit there, waiting for my turn.

Ariel's easy confidence with everyone and everything makes me more aware how awkward I am in comparison. School seems to have been dodged until the new school year, and I'm relieved. I'm not used to being around groups of people my age, or any age, for that matter. One at a time I can almost handle, but being away for six weeks with how many – fifty? How could you even work out who they all are?

But does it matter what I want or don't want to do? There's no point in even asking. I'll never be allowed to go.

I'm slow in the shower, not wanting to have to talk to anyone when I come out. The girls are all gone but Coach is still there waiting by reception when I come down the hall.

'Ah, there you are at last. I've got some information I can email you and your parents about the summer, and then—'

'Don't.' I shake my head. 'I can't go.'

Her eyes open wider – surprise? 'It's a tough six weeks, but I didn't have you pegged as a quitter, Holly.'

'I'm not! I . . . well . . . it's complicated. It's to do with my family. I need to be at home just now.'

Her head is tilted to one side; she looks at me so long that I squirm. 'All right, I hear you. But I'll keep the offer open for a few days; think about it some more.'

When I go up to meet Simone at the café, my feet are dragging. I'm trying to put the swim school out of my mind. She's happy, smiling, as I walk across and sit down.

'There you are. Ali just called with some good news.'

'What's that?'

'They caught them – the group with the drone. It's just a bunch of misguided teenagers by the sounds of things. Sorry if I freaked you out last night, talking about nerve agents and stuff. I guess Ali was right.'

She's trying to make me feel better but, behind it, I can tell she's still worried. And so am I.

I stare at the ceiling that night. OK, they found out who sent the drone, but is that the end of it? Ali said they were on alert, expecting something to happen. He made it sound like it would be something big.

He also said stopping all extraction was impossible. Why? Why can't everyone around the world get together and agree that it'd be a good idea to stop destroying the planet, and then do something about it?

Even with all of that to worry about, I can't stop my mind going back again and again to swim school.

Six weeks with nothing to do but swim.

Which would be worse: going, or not going? And I don't even have an answer.

Am I scared to go, is that it? I don't think so, not exactly; it's more a feeling inside me that says to be careful. I'm uneasy.

That's not the only thing I'm uneasy about, but I'm too tired to put up any resistance to sleep tonight.

Yet when I lie down, close my eyes, nothing happens. After a while I give up, get my laptop. The whole thing with the drone took it out of my mind yesterday, but did I really stop breathing when I fell asleep at the spa? Could it happen again?

Not if I stay awake.

I do a search: 'How long can you go without sleep?'

Someone lasted eleven days – that's some kind of record. Cognitive function is impaired by fatigue after forty-eight hours; no death has ever been recorded by lack of sleep.

That isn't the real question I want answered though, is it?

Another search: 'Can you stop breathing in your sleep?'

You can. It's called sleep apnoea. But the more I read on that, the less it seems to fit what happens to me. It's usually about the tissues in the throat collapsing and obstructing breathing, then being woken up by your brain to breathe properly; this leads to fatigue from frequently interrupted sleep. I don't have that.

Next search: 'Can a dream kill you?' I pause for a long time before I hit enter.

There's an uncomfortable lurch inside of me when I see that the answer is yes. But then when I start reading more, it seems it's from heart failure if you have a certain kind of heart problem; I've been checked over and they found nothing wrong.

Dr Chang might have been able to answer these questions; she might have been able to help. I just couldn't open up to her yesterday and don't even know why. That whole place makes me uneasy; it feels *wrong* just being there. Cate always said to trust those kinds of feelings.

When sleep finally comes, there are voices inside me arguing with each other, wanting me to choose a side. But how can I when I don't even know what they are arguing about?

50

'I understand you've been invited by Wendy to do this summer swim training,' Ali says.

When Simone called me on the intercom to come down for brunch, I got the feeling there was something they wanted to talk about. But I wasn't expecting *this*.

'She told you?'

'She also told me you said you couldn't go. I think we should talk about this. Why did you turn it down?'

'It's six weeks. I didn't think you'd want me away for that long.'

Simone reaches for my hand.

'Let me ask you a question, and answer it honestly,' Ali says. 'Don't think about what we want, all right? Is swimming your one thing? The thing that you want to do and succeed at more than anything?'

I'm looking back at him and I can feel Simone's worry and fear that I'll slip away from her, but I'm also thinking of how I feel when I swim.

'Swimming isn't just my one thing, it's the *only* thing. I love it.'

'I've spoken to both Sophie and Dr Chang at Penrose. We're all in agreement that this should be your decision. Security have checked the school and are happy with the arrangements for the safety of the students. Do you want to go?'

I swallow. Think. Trying not to feel Simone's panic or Ali's sense that there has to be something I excel at — I don't want to feel like that is what it is all about.

But right now, in this moment, away from what they want and hope for me: all I want is to swim as much as I can. Especially in the sea. I'd live in the water if I could.

'I want to go.'

51

The email pings into my inbox later that day; it's been copied to Simone and Ali.

Hi Holly,

We're so glad you've reconsidered and will be joining us for training this summer. All the information you need is in the following attachments. We'll see you there next weekend.

That soon?

There's an attachment called *What to Take.* I click on it; not very much. Gym stuff, trainers, casual stuff.

Another, *Directions*, shows how to get there, complete with a map: it's set in the grounds of an independent boys' school on the coast, not far from Exmouth. A third attachment, *Permissions*, says that if the participant is under eighteen, the following must be signed by their parents or guardians.

And the fourth is marked *Staying in Touch.*

I'm just starting to read it when Simone bursts through my bedroom door.

'Have you seen the email, the bit about staying in touch?' she says. 'I can't believe it.'

'I'm just about to look at it now. What's wrong?' She comes across the room, looks at the screen over my shoulder as I read:

To ensure total concentration and dedication to the training programme, personal phones and internet-enabled devices are banned and visitors are not allowed. Facility will be provided to allow one call home each weekend. There is a signal block at the school so no mobile signal is available.

'They *can't* be serious,' Simone says. 'No visitors for six whole weeks? And you can't even text or call when you want to – what if you need something?'

Even though I'm not used to phones and internet being everywhere, I'm surprised too. The world Simone lives in – and Ariel and Jago, too – seems to be all about being in constant contact with the people in their lives, even people they hardly know.

'I can't believe parents put up with this,' she says.

'I'm sorry, I didn't know.'

'We've just got you back, Holly. I thought we could text each other, talk whenever we wanted.'

'Maybe if we explain to them that you need to be in touch with me more often, they might make an exception?'

'We can't tell them why. Your identity has been protected. But I'll try.'

Later that day when I come down for dinner, I hear voices – raised voices – and pause outside the dining room.

'We've already said she can go,' Ali says. 'We can't stop her now. Think of Holly instead of yourself.'

'*How* can you say that?' Simone says. 'Holly is *all* I think about.'

'Maybe that's the problem.'

I clear my throat and they both turn, see me at the same moment.

'I'm sorry you heard that,' Ali says.

'Did you ask if they'd make an exception about the phone?' I say, and Simone nods. 'I guess it was a no, then. Look, I don't have to go.'

'Yes, you do,' Ali says.

Simone hesitates, then she nods, too.

Simone has a laptop out after dinner. She's on a map site and shows me the place I'll be staying from far above. Fences, green trees and fields, four blue-green pools. It's right on the coast.

'Will you be able to see me there? If I'm swimming, and look up and wave?'

'No, this is static – a satellite image from a point in time. I could do that if there was a webcam.'

'A webcam? What's that?'

'A camera that streams live images online. I doubt there'll be one there, though there might be one nearby. I'll check,' she says, and searches for cameras in the area.

'Look, Holly. There's this one on a beach a few miles away. There's a café there.' The webcam gives a view of the sea. Some benches. Someone walks across the camera.

'Wow. You mean anyone could go on this camera online and see whatever is happening there?'

'Exactly. It looks a nice place; let's stop for lunch on the way when we take you.'

'Are you sure you're OK with me going?'

'No. But I will be.'

That night I'm in bed, staring at the stars out of my window, when my phone beeps: a text?

It's Ariel. *so r u coming or what?*

coming. I think.

u think?

my mum isn't very happy about the only one call a week thing. I marvel as I look at two of the words I just texted: *my mum.* I've never referred to Simone like that before, not without thinking about it or feeling self-conscious.

She sends an unhappy face with eyes looking up. *MOTHERS. Don't get me started. u HAVE 2 come, it's such good fun getting away from home 4 the summer.*

Fun . . . thought was meant to be hard work training?

Bet u'll breeze through, like I do.

Not so sure.

u WILL!!!! And I told you boys go too, didn't I? Very fit – swimmer-fit – boys.

That isn't mentioned in any of the attachments. There's an uncomfortable feeling in my gut, half between excitement and dread. What do I know about boys, fit or otherwise? The only friend I've ever had who is a boy is Jago, assuming that he still is my friend when I haven't been answering his messages.

u'r coming, right? promise me u'll come, & I promise u'll have the best time, ever. I'll see to it.

uh . . .

PROMISE ME!

ok, I'll come!

good. text if u're weakening under parental pressure.

Sure.

Gnight.

I put the phone back on the bedside table. It's gone midnight, but I'm wide awake. These pills from the Penrose Clinic that are supposed to help me sleep don't seem to do anything, but I'm afraid to stop taking them in case it gets worse.

I wish I knew the right thing to do. More than anything I wish Cate were here to talk it over with, and there is this wave of pain that sweeps through me like it does every time I think of her. I wrap my arms around myself and struggle to stop the tears. It never hurts any less. The only thing that dulls it for a while is swimming, and even that is only when I get to the point when I'm almost exhausted but still pushing myself hard.

If Simone will miss me like I miss Cate, is it fair to do this to her?

It's not the same thing; Cate can never come back to me. I'm only going away for six weeks.

Anyhow, I know it isn't just Simone's feelings that are making me hesitate. Part of me is worse than reluctant, and I'm not even sure why. A new place, new people – fear of the unknown, not being sure I can cope with it – is that all there is to it? I don't know.

But if I'm not even sure I want to go, why make Simone so upset?

If I pull out now, Ali is sure to blame her. Ariel will send endless texts in capital letters if I even think of it. The thought makes me grin, lessens the ache inside me just a little.

Maybe what I really need is some friends.

I decide I will text Jago before I go. What happened to Cate isn't his fault. I know it isn't, that he did what he thought was right, that most people would agree it was right. It isn't fair or reasonable to refuse to answer his messages because of it.

I will text him, even if it is just to say goodbye.

I'm swimming, underwater.

Searching. What I want — need — I can't find. All I can do is swim.

I swim along the seabed, back to the surface to take a breath, down again to search some more. Over and over again I do this, but then the next time I swim up to the surface there is a cloud above me in the water, something blocking the sea from meeting the sky. I can't get through it to breathe. Panicked, I swim under it as far and as fast as I can, but it is still there.

52

The next few days go fast: packing, worrying, having bad dreams. At least I know that I've dreamt about not being able to breathe a few times and still woken up. Even though the dreams are hard to deal with, I'm less nervous about actually going to sleep.

There is just one last thing I need to do before I go.

I pick up my phone and click on Jago. How many texts has he sent? One a day or so since Cate died. All some variation of, *hi, hope u'r ok*. Guilt twists inside me as I read them. I want to answer him, but somehow I can't unless I say something that is hard to put into words.

Just do it already.

I reply: *hi Jago. Really sorry I haven't been in touch.*

He answers almost immediately. *r u all right?*

Am I all right? The honest answer is no, not when I'm walking around under the sun and sky on this earth without Cate. I sigh.

I'm getting there, I answer, though I'm not sure that I am. *But there's something I need to say.*

Go.

When you told the police I called you, it felt like a betrayal. And I know you did it because you were worried about me and thought I needed help. It wasn't your fault, but it led to the police finding us and Cate dying. And I loved her.

The tears are flowing now. *If we're going to stay friends, I had to tell you how I feel.*

I stare at the words, hit send. I'm starting to see why people like to text. It gives time to say what you want how you want.

But it's there for ever on the screen, too.

There's a long pause. Maybe he won't answer; maybe he thinks I'm crazy.

I'm so sorry, finally comes back. *I did it because you're my friend, and I care about you.*

He's my friend, and he cares about me – he said so, and it makes me feel warm inside. My first real friend, apart from Cate.

I know that. Thank you. Promise me something?

Anything.

That you'll never tell anyone anything about me again, no matter why you think you should.

There's another pause.

I promise. Of course, that means if I think u need rescuing, I'll have 2 come & do it myself.

I smile. *Fair enough. And now, I have some news. I'm going away for swimming training for the summer, and we aren't allowed phones. So you won't hear from me again for a while.*

Yegods. No phones?!? Isn't that teenager abuse? It can't be legal – it's a basic inalienable right to be able to text at all times of day and night.

We're expected to train and concentrate on swimming and stuff all the time. It's training to qualify for the British Championships.

Woah. Like, serious stuff? Maybe Olympics even?

Apparently so. Who knows where it might lead?

WOW *bowing to world class athlete*

211

Hardly, I say, but I'm secretly pleased. It feels different to be doing something that other people might think is impressive – not just other people, but Jago – even though I'm not sure I can do it.

Are you ok with being cut off like that without your phone?

I'm OK with it, not so sure about my mum. And I smile to see that I've called her that again, without thinking about it.

Mine would freak if one of my sisters went away for the summer. Me, on the other hand? She'd help me pack my bag and drive me to the station.

I smile. From other stuff he's told me about his family I know that isn't true.

I glance at the time. *Look, I've got to go. Phone will be off and out of action for six weeks now.*

All right. And again – I'm so sorry about Cate. Take care of yourself. Maybe when you're back, we could meet up? I could get my mum 2 drop me at a train station – she really totally loves doing that.

I smile again. *Yeah. I'd like that. Thank you.*

He texts back a happy face, and with that, I turn it off. I'm glad I did this. I wasn't sure I'd be able to separate Jago from what happened completely, but getting back in touch felt good.

I reach up into the wardrobe, take out my wave notebook from Cate. Last chance to decide to pack it?

I hesitate, then slip it back on the shelf with my phone. This summer is about swimming, and that's it. Weird-dream diary can wait.

My stuff is downstairs already and I get up, stand in the doorway to my room. I haven't been here very long, but it still

212

feels like I'm saying goodbye, like I've done so many times in my life.

But it's not the same thing at all. It'll be here when I get back, right?

As I head down the stairs I can't shake an uneasy feeling that I might be wrong.

53

'I've hidden a few surprises in your case,' Simone says.

'Thanks,' I say.

We're on a bench by a beach – me, Simone and Ali. It's the very one Simone showed me on the webcam a few nights ago. She had her phone out when we arrived to show me that we could see ourselves on it. It wasn't crystal clear, but you could tell it was us.

'We should go soon,' Ali says. 'I'll get the car.' I start to protest that we'll go with him, but he shakes his head, goes on his own.

Simone takes my hand. 'I can't believe we're about to say goodbye.'

'Only for the summer.'

'I know. But what if something happens?'

'Like what?'

'I don't know. It's just you've only been back with us for such a short time; I'm scared to lose you again.'

'That isn't going to happen. I promise.'

'What if you hate it there and want to come home and they won't let you call me?'

'If I wanted to leave, they couldn't do that, could they?' Cate's warnings echo inside of me: how the world is full of prisons and prisoners, that the bars are there even if they don't see them.

'I suppose not.'

'How about this. Cate and I did this sometimes: we'd have a place prearranged, and if anything went wrong, we'd meet there.'

'But how would I know if they won't let you make calls?'

'Well, I could leave and find a payphone.' She's not looking convinced. 'Or we could meet here, on this bench. If I hate it and want to come home and can't get in touch, I'll meet you here.'

She's smiling now to think of it.

'Whenever you're wondering how I am, look at the webcam; if I'm not on the bench you'll know I'm fine. If I'm on the bench come and get me. Right?'

'OK. I guess that'll do. But don't tell Ali, he'll think I'm completely bonkers.'

'It'll be our secret.'

I take off my bracelet. The only time I don't wear it is when I'm swimming, and that's mostly what I'm going to be doing.

'Can you keep this safe for me until I come home?'

'Of course.' She puts it on her own wrist, then her arms around me for a hug.

It's only a short drive and soon we reach the swim school gates. We go through, along the drive and park.

There are people milling around outside a building — teenagers, some adults that are probably parents — *so many* people. Panic starts to twist inside as we get out of our car, but then someone calls my name. I turn and there is Ariel, a wide grin on her face.

'You made it!' she says. 'I was starting to wonder; you were even later than me.'

Simone nudges me. 'Oh. Ariel, this is my mum and dad.'

'Hi,' she says.

'Are your parents here?' Simone says.

'My dad brought me, but he's gone now.'

Goodbyes are beginning to happen around us; parents getting into cars with a wave. Soon I'm hugging Simone and Ali – *Mum and Dad* – goodbye. If Simone is clinging a little too tight I don't notice, because so am I.

54

'Everyone, listen up,' a woman says. She waits for quiet, for all eyes to be focused on her, and smiles. 'Welcome. I am Christina Lang, director of the swim school. Before me I see the future stars of swimming in the UK: this can be *your* future, if you want it enough, and train hard enough. For now we'll give you your room assignments. Your personalised schedules are in your rooms.'

Then names are called, keys handed out, and all the while everyone is chatting as though they all know each other.

'Am I the only new one?' I say in a low aside to Ariel.

She shakes her head. 'It's about half and half.'

Instead of that making me feel better, I feel worse. I can't even tell by looking at them who is new and who isn't. I must stick out like a big awkward thumb.

My name is called; I get handed a key and pointed to the door that leads to the stairs: the card with the key says 'Level 3, Left Corridor, Room 4'.

I pull my case along on its wheels to the stairs, lift it in one hand and groan. It's way too heavy. We were told to only bring one bag so Simone found a big one, then kept insisting I might need tweezers, a hand mirror, or some other important thing I've never needed before.

'Do you need a hand?' a voice says, and I turn: it's a boy. Tall. Dark hair and even darker eyes.

'Thanks, I can manage.' I heave it up the steps, pause at the first landing to switch sides, then continue on more slowly to the second landing. This time I stop and put it down, roll my shoulders. He's following behind.

When he gets to the second landing, he puts his much more reasonably sized bag down. 'This is my floor. Are you sure I can't help? I can leave mine here.'

I shake my head, but he takes my bag and then pretends to stagger under the weight as he starts up the stairs. I walk along behind him.

'What on earth have you brought?' he says.

'I don't even know. My mum kind of took over packing.' We're soon at the top of the stairs. 'Thanks,' I say.

'I'm Denzi, by the way.'

'I'm Tabby. I mean, Holly. Sorry.' And now I'm flustered and don't know what to say; I can feel heat rising in my cheeks.

He smiles. 'Call yourself whatever you like.'

'Tabby is my middle name, but my parents call me Holly.'

Before he can say anything else, there's a commotion getting closer on the stairs – Ariel and two other girls laughing and dragging their stuff up to the same floor as me.

'Bye,' he says.

As he walks down the stairs past them, Ariel widens her eyes and winks at me.

We find our rooms – Ariel's is on the same corridor as mine, across and a few doors down. The rooms are rectangular, with a bed, a desk, a wardrobe. Shared bathrooms are down the hall, and there is a common room in the middle with sofas and kettles. Ariel says boys board here during term time.

It's OK and better than many places I've stayed, but have I got spoiled since I moved in with my parents? It seems cold and bare, and the sea view – if there is one – must be on Ariel's side of the hall. All I've got out of my window is the front lawn and driveway where we came in.

What now?

I lug my case to the bed, pull it up and unzip.

Inside is a card with my name. There is a sandy beach on the front and inside Simone says to have fun, Ali to work hard; they both say they'll miss me. And underneath it in the case is a giant slab of dark chocolate with a sticky note on it, that says, *I know you weren't supposed to bring food, but chocolate isn't food, is it?* Simone's handwriting.

I put the card on the desk and as I do, see a folder there – this must be my schedule.

I open it and see that it starts today – we've already done arrival and room assignments. Next up are a few appointments: first a health assessment, then a meeting with a sports psychologist. Dinner is after that.

The appointments are in a different building; there's a map showing how to get there.

And the first one is in ten minutes.

55

I bolt down the stairs, map in hand. Once out front, there is a path to follow between a few buildings. It leads to a gate set in hedges. Then there is a lane to cross, and there it is. The sign says it is the Centre for Sports Medicine and Excellence – it is marked as CSME on the map – but without the sign I wouldn't have known it was a medical kind of place. It's a rambling old building with ivy growing around it, grounds sloping down steeply behind. It looks more like someone's country house.

The door is blocked open to catch the breeze and one of the other swimmers is coming down the front steps.

She smiles. 'Yes, you're in the right place. It's down the hall and to the left.'

'Thanks.'

I go as she said and find a waiting room, with someone at the desk in a white coat. 'Your name please?' she says.

'I'm Holly Heath.'

'Come straight through.'

I follow her to a consulting room down the hall, am given a detailed health and lifestyle survey to fill in, and then blood is taken. I wonder if they'll notice it's weird? Then I'm weighed, my height measured. I'm assigned a fitness tracker that is fitted to my wrist and is to be worn all the time – it's waterproof, so even in the pool and shower – and I'm told they are the very latest and will monitor our activity levels, heart rates and a bunch of other stuff all the time, even while we sleep.

'Your individualised eating plan and supplements will be drawn up for you and begin tomorrow.'

'Eating plan? I think you were told that I'm vegan – is that going to be OK?'

'Absolutely. The kitchens here are completely vegan, so everyone will be on an optimised vegan diet. We encourage all swimmers to maintain this when they leave.'

'And what are the supplements?'

'Vitamins and nutritional supplements. They are tailored based on your blood test results to reach and maintain optimum health for fitness and your intense training programme. All vegan and natural also.'

'I've already got vitamins in the morning and another tablet at night from my doctors at home.'

'Yes, we have the details of those and will continue them, or not, based on our assessments. Any other questions?'

I shake my head, pleased that whatever it was the Penrose Clinic gave me will have another doctor's opinion. It has always felt weird taking stuff when I don't know what it is.

She shows me to another waiting area. 'Take a seat. The sports psychologist will be ready for you soon.'

'Thanks,' I say and sit down, not feeling keen to speak to any sort of psychologist, not if they are anything like Dr Rasheed or Dr Chang.

Another door opens; out steps Denzi. He sits down next to me, glances at my wrist. 'Is that the new fitness tracker? I get one next.'

'Yep.' I hold out my wrist in case he wants to look at it, but then the door he came out of opens again. A woman peers out. 'Holly?' I stand up. 'This way.'

We go in. She motions me to sit down.

'Hi, Holly. I'm Nadya. This is just a getting-to-know-you session, a check to see if you have any particular barriers to success that we need to think about addressing.' She asks me about how long I've been swimming, how I feel about it, that kind of stuff.

She doesn't seem to want to get in my head other than to see if there is anything that might hold me back in training or competition, but the ways I'm messed up all seem to help with that. And then she talks briefly about visualisation: imagining what I want to achieve in my mind as if it has already happened, and all the steps to get there, and how good it would feel to reach that goal.

Here it is all about performance, optimum health to make me a better swimmer. No one is asking what I'm thinking, how I'm feeling, or what I dream about.

I like it.

What comes next, not so much.

56

When I walk into the dining hall, most of the others are already there. Rectangular tables are spaced around the room and set for six or eight people, with separate tables for staff.

I'm scanning faces, looking for Ariel or Denzi – the only people I know so far. I spot Denzi on a table on his own across the room, nose in a book, and start a few hesitant steps towards him when Ariel comes in behind me.

'There you are!' she says, and links her arm in mine, drawing me towards a noisy table for eight in the middle.

Dinner is a buffet and we soon get up to fill our plates. Ariel tells me this is the best dinner of the summer – we can have what we like. Tomorrow it all gets rather more boring and healthy.

It's hard to eat with so many people around me. Every time I get some food into my mouth it's like someone says something to me and I'm trying to swallow without chewing enough. At one point this makes me cough and I reach for my glass of water, knocking my knife; it hits the floor with a clatter.

'Sorry,' I say, lean over to retrieve it and realise it has left a trail of mess on the bag of the girl next to me – I think Zara is her name. I grab my napkin and start to wipe it off just as she looks down and my head bumps into hers.

'Ouch,' she says, and then we are both rubbing our heads. My cheeks feel hot.

'Sorry,' I say again, and give her bag another wipe. 'I think it's OK now.'

'No drama,' she says, but there is annoyance in the set of her mouth, lips pushed together. Then she turns at an angle away from me to speak to the girl on her other side.

Later we go into another room across from the dining hall – the lounge, Ariel calls it – a big space with sofas and chairs, and double glass doors to the gardens at one end. There's herbal teas and water, and a few make a face, wanting caffeine, but are told that it is on the *not-allowed* list.

I wait until Ariel's attention is distracted, then step out of the doors into the gardens. I slip around the corner into the fading light, lean against the brick wall and breathe in, out, in, out.

When my eyes adjust, I see that I'm not alone. There's a still form lying stretched out, knees up, on a low bench. It's Denzi.

He swings his legs down and sits up.

'Sorry, I didn't realise anyone else was here,' I say.

'Just us three.'

'Three?'

He holds out his hand near the ground and a black cat rubs against it. Only his white socks and chin stand out in the dark.

'Usually he runs if anyone comes near; he must approve of you. This is Dickens.'

'Hello, Dickens. I'm Tabby.' I lean forward and hold out a hand and he leans just far enough to take a cautious sniff, then retreats under the bench. 'Whose cat is he?'

'He belongs to the school, or the school belongs to him. He comes and goes as he pleases and takes care of mice and other pests. I take it that you've decided your name is Tabby, then?'

I tilt my head to one side. 'I prefer it.'

'So, Tabby, why are you out here with a loner and a cat instead of inside with everyone? Have you run away from them, too?' he says.

'I guess so.'

'So much fake friendship makes my skin crawl.'

'Fake? What do you mean?'

'Well, that's not true of absolutely everyone here. But most of them just try to get into your head to undermine you. Qualifying for the British Championships – winning at any cost – is what it's all about.'

There are footsteps, voices; they're getting closer.

'There you are, Holly.' It's Ariel.

'Do you know—' I start to say, turning back to the bench where Denzi was. But he's gone.

It's lights out at ten. I'm relieved to be alone in my room, lying in the dark. There are murmuring voices through the walls from another room – some of them are breaking the rules already.

There's no phone, no laptop to keep myself awake with or to fill the time if I can't sleep. I smile at myself and shake my head, amused at how soon I got used to having those things. Cate and I never needed phones and laptops, did we? We read books, we talked. I wrap my arms around myself, trying to hold the sadness inside. Will it always hurt this much to think of her?

I feel so out of place. I don't know how to talk to people; I don't know how to fit in. What made me think I could come here and be like everybody else? I'm not. I don't even know who I am any more. I'm not like Ariel, but I'm not like I used to be, either. I don't fit in *anywhere*. The only person I felt I was being myself with was Denzi, and from what he said, he's a loner, too.

Cate would say, stop feeling sorry for yourself. She'd say, the only person you can be is who you are.

She also said to never let anyone know your name or anything about us, to keep away from people like Sophie, hospitals, the police. I sigh, imagining how horrified she'd be at all these different medical places having my blood and details.

I feel lost, adrift. Being in my parent's house – their home, and OK, I guess it is my home now, too – has been a bit like being in seclusion. Hiding away from the world, from working things out.

I miss being there; I miss my room. Is that what it feels like – to have a home, one you can go back to? Am I . . . homesick?

Somehow thinking that – being able to put a label on these feelings – makes me feel better. Even though it is new for me, being homesick is a normal kind of thing.

The only other time I've felt anything like this is when we moved away from the sea.

I swim along the glass in endless circles, looking for weakness, but nothing ever changes.

I sleep. Half of me is here, watching and waiting, and half in another place, another time. With the kin. The contrast between the two just twists the blade harder, but I can't stop the memories.

Do they remember me still? Do they watch and wait for my return?

Hope is alien to where I am, but somehow, I still have it.

Watch.

Wait.

Swim.

57

'Good morning, swimmers! I'm Becker, your trainer for all things on dry land. Not so dry today.' He grins like that was the best joke ever, as we shiver in the rain, huddled in a barely awake group in front of him. It's all of us – fifty or so. Going by the schedule, this and meals are about the only things we do all together.

'This morning – every morning but Sundays! – we start with a six a.m. run around the perimeter of the grounds. Try to keep up with me. Anyone who beats me gets a lie-in tomorrow.'

'Why do we have to run? Why can't we just train in the pools?' Zara says, and groans. 'I *hate* running.' Exactly what I was thinking.

'It improves the action of your heart – making it work against gravity when you are upright instead of prone and supported in the water,' Becker says.

I guess that kind of makes sense, but I can't say I still wouldn't rather be somewhere else. If you're swimming outside, rain doesn't matter; somehow, when you're running, it does.

Becker takes us through some dynamic stretches and then a slow jog to warm up, and then away he goes with the rest of us following behind.

It soon becomes a race, one I stay out of. Denzi is up ahead; so is Ariel, and others whose names I've forgotten.

Last night, Denzi said everyone here was all about winning. Am I competitive like that? I don't think so; at least, not in that must-win-at-everything kind of way. I don't care at all if I win at running even with a lie-in at stake.

Swimming is different. It isn't about winning there, either; it's about going faster and faster still, pushing beyond anything reasonable to leave myself behind, to become something *else*.

But I'm with Zara on the running. Somehow, I'm not made for it, and it's nothing to do with fitness; I feel clumsy on dry land. Even not so dry land, in the rain and mud like today.

Denzi, on the other hand, runs with a kind of grace – long arms and legs in harmony. He's ahead of the pack now; only Becker is in front of him.

Most of them disappear around a bend. There is a familiar pull inside me and I run faster, go around and down to the left, and then there it is: laid out as far as forever. The sea.

Is there a way down? I slow, and the last few behind me go past. There's a fence below and what looks like a gate, but when I go to it there is a sign – *Keep Out. Dangerous cliffs. Risk of rock falls.* I stand there and trace the way I could go down with my eyes, hungry for the scratch of sand and salt.

The rain pounds down harder, reminding me where I am and what I'm supposed to be doing. I run back up to the path we were following and around the next bend – no one is in sight. When I finally catch sight of the group they're back where we started, doing stretches.

Becker sees me and starts doing a slow clap of his hands – everyone turns to look. I stop paying attention to where I'm going and my foot catches on something – a rock? I fly through the air and land on my hands and knees with a thud.

Denzi sprints over. 'Are you all right?'

'I think so.'

He holds out a hand but mine are filthy – I've landed in mud. I shake my head and get myself up.

'You've got a cut,' Denzi says. There's blood trickling down from my knee.

'Did you enjoy your trip?' Becker says, and there is laughter from some of the group behind him. 'What took you so long?'

'I, ah, was looking at the sea.'

'You're not here to admire the view! And I forgot to mention at the start,' he says, and grins. 'Whoever is last has to run the perimeter again while the rest of us shower and have breakfast.' And now there is more laughter.

Denzi scowls. 'She needs medical attention, not another run in the rain.'

I shake my head. 'I'm fine.'

'Denzi, how noble! You can go with her to make sure she's all right. Don't just stand there you two, get going! If you're fast there might be some breakfast left when you're done. The rest of you, head for the showers.'

I start to run the way we started, my leg smarting when it jars down on the path. I'm a mess, and not just from the mud. It was Becker, what he said, and everyone staring and *laughing*. And then there was Denzi; talking back like he did on my behalf just made me feel worse, as if I can't look after myself.

I hear Denzi's even long steps thudding behind me now, and then he catches up, and starts to run alongside me.

229

'What a twanker,' he says. 'Are you sure you're all right?'

'I'm *fine*. And I'm sorry you got sucked into this, but I don't need someone making sure I'm all right. Go on, you know you can run faster than I can. Go!'

He looks startled, but then speeds up, pulls away from me easily enough.

Guilt stirs inside me as he disappears from view. He was just trying to help; I shouldn't have snapped at him like that.

After a while the rain slows to a drizzle. When I reach the bend with the sea beyond, I can't resist going down for another look. The gate is locked but the fence would be easy enough to climb. I'm studying the way down again when I hear running footsteps approaching; it's Denzi.

He comes to the gate. 'Don't tell me you've lapped me,' I say.

'No! I diverted.' He holds up a small bag. 'Sit on the fence and let me look at your knee.'

I sit, but mostly because I'm tired.

He produces a bottle of water and uses it to wash the mud off my knee. Next? Disinfectant spray. Then a square bandage.

'Good as new,' he says.

'Thank you. I'm sorry if I sounded . . .' I shrug.

'Bitchy? Ungrateful?' He grins. 'Should I keep going?'

'No, that'll do.'

'Don't mention it. You looked like you were working out the way down?'

'I was thinking about it. You interested?'

'I haven't got a death wish. Seriously, there've been many rock falls here — the coast is eroding. A few years ago the path was open, but the whole coastline has changed since then. There

230

used to be a stretch of beach below the rocks; it's underwater even at low tide now.'

'A few years ago – do you live near here?'

He shakes his head. 'No, but I go to school here, and have done for years.'

I look down again. 'It's so close but we can't get to it.'

'Well, there is meant to be another way.'

'How?'

'The CSME – the Centre for Sports Medicine and Excellence – is one of the oldest buildings in the school grounds. There are meant to be cellars, and stairs that lead from there down to caves and then to the beach at low tide – or at least they did when the water line was lower. Legend has it that smugglers used the caves and cellars.'

The drizzle has stopped now, the sun is peeking out. 'I guess we'd better get going if we want to eat anything,' I say.

When I get to the dining hall, after the fastest shower in history, everyone is still there. Almost all look up from their breakfasts. There is scattered applause, even a few whistles, and I stop short – wishing I was invisible.

Then Ariel waves from the same table as last night, and I go over to her. 'I got your breakfast in case you didn't make it in time, but they wouldn't give me your supplements – they're over there.' She points to a table with a woman waiting.

As I walk across, Denzi comes through the doors, and I beckon him across. She checks our names, gets us to put our initials on a form and then gives each of us a small cup of pills and a glass of water.

'What is it?' Denzi asks her.

'Vitamins and minerals, tailored for your specific needs.'

We shrug. Denzi clicks his paper cup against mine. 'Bottoms up,' he says. And the pills slither down my throat with the water.

58

We are to meet by the outdoor pools an hour after a breakfast I ate so fast that it's sitting in a lump in my stomach. Or maybe being around so many people is mucking with my digestion.

I take my time getting changed, thinking I'll go at the last moment to avoid hanging around with everyone beforehand. I'm counting down the last five minutes when there's a knock on my door.

It's Ariel. 'Hi! Ready to go?'

Not having any reasonable reason to say no, I nod, and we start down the hall together.

'I'm sorry I didn't tell you what happens if you come in last running,' Ariel says. 'You're so fast in the pool I figured you'd be the same with that.'

'It's OK. Knowing wouldn't have made any difference.'

Outside, the heat of the day settles around us in a warm, muggy embrace; it will be a relief to get in the water.

'It's freaking hot,' Ariel says. 'Can't check the weather forecast without my phone.'

'Look up and around: hot and sunny?'

'I like to know the temperature to know how hot I actually am.'

'Do you miss having your phone?'

'I did last year, especially at first. I kept thinking things like,

I need to post a photo of this, or tell a friend about that. Or look things up – like the weather. But after a while I got used to it. And it is kind of a break from all of that, you know? I feel more chilled without it.'

When we get to the pool area it's just like I remember from the webcam Simone found: four full-sized pools, fields on one end and trees and benches on the other. In the shade of the trees are four coaches with clipboards, and one of them is our coach from home: Wendy.

They take it in turns to call out names to put us into four groups, one coach and group for each pool. Wendy calls out Ariel's name and I'm hoping to be in the same group – after the way Becker was this morning, better someone I know. She's near the end of her list when she finally says, 'Holly Heath'. I breathe a sigh of relief and step forwards.

When they're all done there are two groups of girls, two of boys. Each group has about a dozen.

Wendy gathers us to one side, gets us to introduce ourselves to each other and say where we're from. My name is a point of confusion, and where am I from, really?

Almost all of them add other details about themselves – the school they go to, stuff they like to do. I manage to say, 'Holly, Dorset,' but neither really feels true.

We dive into our pool. As the cool water closes around my body the doubt is gone. I *feel* who I am, and what I should have said: that my name is Tabby, I love to swim, and I'm from the sea – the only constant in my life. But imagine what they'd make of that?

Training goes beyond what we did at our swimming club: three hours of pushing as far and as fast as we can.

When we think we are done we are told that there will be races. Teams are sorted by the coaches – two girls and two boys on each team, each from a different group. Today we're doing relays; everyone is to do two lengths in their preferred stroke, and it is up to us to agree the order.

Zara sighs when she sees I'm on her team. She decides she is organising us and tells me I'll swim fourth. Probably so if we lose it'll be me coming in last again.

Denzi's team is in a lane next to us. He's going fourth also, but probably not for the same reason.

The whistle goes and the first swimmers dive in, swim to the end and back. It's Zara who is first for our group, and she's ahead of the others when the second swimmer dives in. He's a little slower and we're maybe a fraction behind Denzi's team but still running second when the third swimmers dive in. Everyone is shouting for their swimmers to go faster.

We're almost exactly even with Denzi's team when I dive into the water. When we get to the end of the pool and do kick turns is Denzi just slightly ahead?

I push myself further, going deep inside – to the place I always search for but can't quite reach. When I touch the end of the pool . . . I'm first? My team is jumping up and down; one of the boys gives me a hand out of the pool. Denzi is up now too. Even Zara looks happy with me.

Denzi's eyes – are they full of surprise? 'Congratulations, Tabby,' he says.

Coach is here now also and hears what he said. 'Tabby?' she says.

'Mostly I go by Tabby – I prefer it. It's my middle name,' I say, buoyed up by our win and my part in it enough to say this out loud.

'Want us to change your records?'

I smile. 'Yes, please! Thank you.'

'Everyone, listen up,' Coach says. 'Holly is now Tabby.' And everyone is looking at me again, but it doesn't bother me as much as it did before.

Ariel tilts her head as if thinking, then nods approvingly. 'You somehow *look* more like a Tabby.'

59

'Good afternoon, swimmers. I'm Malina, and I'll be your apnoea coach. Does anyone know what apnoea means?'

Ariel waves a hand. 'Apnoea means to stop breathing.'

'Yes, that's more or less correct. It's a temporary cessation of breathing; we're going to challenge you to see how long you can go.'

'Please lie down on one of the mats. Most find it is more comfortable to lie on your back, with or without your knees up. Now, close your eyes.

'Imagine yourself in your happy place.'

Somebody whistles.

'Not *that* kind of happy. Choose a place that makes you feel both happy and relaxed. A place from your childhood or a summer holiday, maybe, or an imagined place from your dreams. Let your breathing slow naturally while you listen to my voice.'

Malina's voice is rhythmic, calm, and I'm focusing on the sound of it as much as the words.

'Remember every detail of your surroundings and fill them in in your mind.'

My happy place – of course – is a beach.

'Feel it – touch it, yes – but also how it makes you feel inside.'

Not just any beach, I decide; the one where I met Jago. Lying on the sand with my eyes closed, listening to the music of the waves.

The gym mat I'm lying on is gone, replaced by the scratch of sand. There is salt on my lips. I'm losing touch with where I am, breathing in time with remembered waves.

'Now. Breathe in a little deeper, and when you breathe out, empty your lungs completely.'

A wave higher than any before, breathe in deeper; then the sea falls back, back, back until I have no breath left inside me.

'Then breathe in, fill your lungs all the way, and hold – hold the air inside. Stay in your happy place as long as you can.'

The next wave rushes up the beach, higher and higher; it'll sweep me away – and then, it holds. The sea surrounds me, it has stilled, my breath stays inside me . . .

The sea runs through me and I am the sea.

I'm on the floor of the ocean now, cradled, still . . .

The water, so pure and deep – there is barely a glimmer of sun in sky far above.

I want to stay here for ever. But something is pulling me away?

Cate is whispering in my ear. 'Let the sea fall back where it belongs.'

'It belongs with me.'

'Don't honour it above the other points of our compass. Let it fall.'

I sigh, breathing out slowly. Gradually the water falls back until it is gone.

I breathe in.

'Tabby?'

I open my eyes. Everyone else is sitting up on their mats, looking at me, and Malina is on her knees next to mine.

I sit up, my head spins a little.

'How are you feeling?' she says.

'Fine. Better than fine – amazing,' I say, and it's true. It's as if so much energy is flowing through me that I'm tingling. At the same time, I'm completely relaxed.

She gets up. 'Let's call it a day. But stay a moment, Tabby.'

The others in my group are getting up; no one is saying anything and, after being the centre of their eyes, now no one is quite looking at me either.

'What's wrong?'

'What do you think it is?'

'I don't know.'

'In that directed breathing exercise, you lost consciousness – but still held your breath – for far longer than you could have if you were conscious.'

'I don't understand.'

'I'll show you. Do as you did before: breathe in fully, then out fully, then in. Hold your breath, and I'll time you again. OK? But this time keep your eyes open and on mine.'

I nod and do as she says, holding my breath as long as I can. I know I can do this longer than most people, but after a while it gets harder and harder, and finally I let go.

'Impressive.' She shows me her stopwatch: four minutes, ten seconds. 'That is more than almost everyone else in the room this afternoon, and amazing for someone who has never done apnoea training before. But earlier? See this back button on this digital stopwatch – if I press it, it shows the previous time, which is yours.'

She presses the button and shows me the screen:

Nineteen minutes, fifty-two seconds.

'There must be a mistake.'

She shakes her head. 'No mistake. Take care, Tabby; don't try this when you're alone. If you don't wake up in time . . . well. I was monitoring you and your heart rate through your tracker. If it had faltered, I was here and could have done what was necessary to make you breathe.'

I head back to my room. There was that time at the spa when I was having a massage and the masseuse freaked, said I wasn't breathing. Was I doing the same thing then?

Malina said not to try this when I'm alone. But that time – and other occasions, when I woke from a dream – I didn't *decide* to hold my breath, I just did it.

Almost twenty minutes? Seriously? I'm missing my laptop – I want to search how long breath can be held. That seems insanely long.

Back in my room to shower and change, I find a card that has been pushed under the door: I've got a sports psychologist appointment with Nadya before dinner.

60

I open the gate and cross to the CSME, remembering now what Denzi said about there being cellars with stairs that lead through the cliffs to caves. Could that be true, or is it just a tale passed around by bored kids at school?

Inside at the desk when the receptionist asks my name, I say Tabby Heath, and she enters that I'm here on the screen without comment. Have my records been changed already? That was fast.

A moment later, Nadya calls my name and I go in.

'How're you finding the place?'

'OK. Good mostly.'

'Hmmm. I heard you got Becker annoyed. He thinks you weren't trying at running this morning. But I checked with both your swim coach and your apnoea coach, and they say you're doing very well: exceptionally well, in fact. So was Becker right?'

'That's not really true; I did try. I'm honestly not very good at running. I seem unco-ordinated when I'm upright, like my legs get tangled up or something. It's hard to explain.'

'What did you mean when you said, *not really true?*'

'Well, I did stop to look at the sea when we got around that side.'

'It's a gorgeous view there, isn't it? But maybe save that for your downtime. I'm not sure Becker appreciates the beauty of nature.' Judging by the look on her face, I wonder if she thinks he's a twanker, too, like Denzi said.

'As far as your running goes, do you remember when we talked about visualisation?'

I nod.

'Try applying that to your running like this. Close your eyes. Now picture yourself tomorrow morning.'

'Without rain?'

'Sure. This is your mind, make it how you like. You love running! Picture yourself getting ready, then stride out with confidence, enjoy the feeling of power in your legs. Now see yourself going faster, overtaking – who would you like to overtake first? Someone who was towards the back this morning?'

'Zara.'

'She sees you coming and pushes herself, but no, you're stronger, faster. You go past her. And every day visualise this – passing other runners – until you're at the front of the pack.'

I open my eyes now. 'Not sure that'll happen.'

'The only way to find out is to try. Will you?'

'Yes.'

'Excellent. While you're here, let's see what your tracker has to tell us.'

I go to take it off but she shakes her head. 'Leave it on; it downloads data remotely. I'll show you.' She taps at a tablet, selects my name from a list. 'OK. So we can see graphs of your heart rate against activity levels, things like distance travelled and speed. And I can see when you were running and then stopped for the view here, see? And I can also see that you were working very hard when you were running. Later in the day, when you were swimming, your pulse rate didn't go up as much.'

'Does that mean I should be working harder when I'm swimming?'

'Not necessarily. Swimming and running are very different activities, of course, and your body is used to swimming and not running, so it makes sense. A high level of effort that doesn't appreciably raise your heart rate is ideal for training. It shows your heart is healthy.'

There's loads of other numbers on the screen, and I'm curious. 'What is all the rest of this?'

'We can also see how long and how deeply you've slept.' She clicks on another indicator and another graph appears on the screen, with different phases of sleep marked. Before I can ask her any more questions, she closes the screen.

'Now, one last thing,' she says. 'How is your knee?'

'My knee? It's fine,' I say, surprised. 'Just skinned a little.'

'I was told that one of the boys – Denzi – came by to get a dressing for it this morning. If anything like that happens again, we like to check even minor injuries. And you should have been sent straight here after you fell. Becker has been updated on this aspect of our duty of care.'

Uh-oh. Does that mean he's going to be annoyed at me?

'We'll get a nurse to check your knee now,' she says.

She shows me to a waiting area down another hall. After a short wait a nurse gets me to sit on an examination table while she takes the dressing off my knee. There's some blood inside the dressing, but my knee? Barely a shadow of a mark on it. That's weird; it bled enough for there to be more to see than that.

She raises an eyebrow and puts a normal-sized plaster back on it.

61

I wait outside the dining hall, not hiding, exactly, but off the path, in the trees. The others are trickling in for dinner, most in twos and threes.

I can't decide if it would be better to go in now, before they all get there, or to wait until the last minute.

Something touches my leg and I jump, almost cry out.

It's Dickens.

He makes a grumbly sort of noise in his throat, and I step out from behind my tree, bend down, scratch behind his ears.

'Tabby? What are you doing?' It's Ariel.

'Making friends with a cat,' I say. Dickens runs off as she approaches, and I stand up.

'Ah, strangely I thought you were hiding in the trees.'

'Now why would I do that?'

She raises an eyebrow.

'Well, OK. After that breathing thing, I'm not sure how everyone is going to be.'

'Jealous, if anything; you aced it. Come on, we can walk in together.' She links her arm in mine.

We walk up the path and go through the doors. People are milling about, chatting, starting to sit where they usually sit. When we come in, heads turn to see who is there, then back to who they are talking to and it seems like the volume goes down a little, as if they are saying things they don't want to be heard. My stomach twists in a knot.

The others at our table are all there already when we sit down, and all eyes are on me.

'Wow. Like major wow. Is it true?' Zara says.

'Is what true?'

'That you held your breath for a really long time, way longer than everybody else?' she says. Zara isn't in our group, so if she knows, everyone must.

'Almost twenty minutes,' Ariel says.

'That's . . . I don't even know what to say. It's beyond . . .' Zara says, and I squirm under their eyes.

'Have you had apnoea training before?' another girl asks. She is in our group so was there: Isha is her name.

'Not like that.'

'So you *have* trained,' Zara says.

'Not exactly – I mean, not formally. It's just something I can do.'

'Like swimming,' Ariel says. 'Tabby had only been at swimming training for a week before she got invited to—'

A bell rings, interrupts her. Dinner is ready and we go across to the serving hatch.

When we are all getting back with our personally labelled plates, I'm nervous that the interrupted conversation will continue. Cate always said that if people are curious and want to ask you questions, the best way to distract them is by asking *them* questions. If you are evasive, they just get more curious. I'm searching my mind for something, anything, to ask, and delaying by looking at my dinner.

'What actually is this?' I say, and stab a slab of *something* over veg and rice and hold it up on my fork.

'I don't know, but it looks gross,' Zara says.

'It's a vegan protein substitute grown in a lab,' Ariel says.

'Seriously?' I say.

'I refused to eat it last year until they said what it was. It's not so bad if you cut it up and mix it in with the rest.'

Isha has a small piece on her fork and tries it. 'It's OK – tastes a bit coconutty?'

I cut off a slice to try. 'Mine's nothing like coconut – more like seaweed. Actually, it's a different shade of *bleugh* to yours.'

'You know what I could really go for right now?' Zara says. 'Pizza. Italian pizza! Thin, crispy, with just basil, tomatoes and scattered mozzarella. Hmmm.'

'No, skip the main course,' Ariel says. 'I'd kill for a chocolate buffet.' She starts describing every possible use for chocolate.

By the time everyone has gone through their fantasy food, dinner is over.

I fake a yawn to escape. 'I'm beat. I'm heading back now.'

'Are you all right?' Ariel says.

I nod and look around us to make sure no one is close enough to hear if I lower my voice. 'It's probably against the rules, but I've got chocolate in my room if you want some.'

Her eyes widen. 'No way! I'll come by after lights out. Or will you be asleep?'

'That'll be fine.'

I head out and down the path towards the hall of residence. There are footsteps following behind me, hurrying and then closer.

246

'Tabby?' It's Isha. 'I'm heading back also. It's been a long day.'

'Yeah.' And it really has. So much has been crammed into it since this morning that it's hard to believe it is the same day. But I'm not the sort of tired that needs sleep; I just want to be alone.

We walk up the path, inside and up the stairs to the third floor.

'Can I ask you something?' she says. 'Ariel said you'd only been to swimming training a week before being invited to come here. Is that true?'

'Um, yes. Though I was always into swimming.'

'Me, too. But then how did you end up here?'

'It was one of the coaches – Wendy. She spotted me, invited me to training—'

'And then said, you're a natural; come to summer swim school and you could be in the Olympics. And here you are.'

'How did you know?'

'It was just the same for me.' She hesitates. 'I've always felt like a freak. And I could tell at dinner when we were asking you about holding your breath for so long that you felt the same. I just wanted to tell you that you're not alone.' Her eyes on mine are warm and genuine.

Goosebumps run up my spine.

That's exactly what Cate used to say to me: the same words, the same look in her eyes when she said them.

And I can't say *anything*. I give her a quick hug, then run to my room and shut the door.

62

After lights out there's a tap on the door.

Ariel comes in and shuts it behind her. 'I'm actually drooling,' she says. 'Are you sure you want to share?'

'It's huge; I can spare some. Haven't touched it yet. Ta-da!' I say, and produce the huge bar of vegan organic dark chocolate from a desk drawer.

Her eyes open wide. 'Oh *yum*, I love this kind.'

'I haven't tried it before. It was a surprise: my mum hid it in my case.'

We sit next to each other on the bed. I rip the wrapper, break off a square, hand the bar to her and she does the same.

She holds hers up against mine. 'Cheers. Now, just one square at a time, and you have to let it melt on your tongue.'

I put it in my mouth. It's lush, creamy, just sweet enough and completely delicious. It's hard not to chew it all at once but this way draws it out.

'Wow,' I say when it's gone. 'That is *so* good. Here, have some more.'

'Are you sure?'

'Yes. Actually, I wanted to say thank you.'

'What for?'

'I'm not very good at getting on with people like you are. You've gone out of your way to include me in stuff.' Even if I haven't always liked it, I appreciate it anyhow.

'Good at people? *Me?* Nah. I'm just good at faking it. I've always been the odd one out.'

No way. Ariel? The odd one out? 'That doesn't sound like you.'

'People aren't always how they seem on the outside, you know. Like you've got this lovely set of parents,' she says, 'leaving surprises of chocolate in your case. And the way they didn't want to leave you – your mum, especially – was so clear. I've never had that. I live with my dad – hardly see him, though. I barely know my mum. I get shuffled off to boarding school and then here for the last few summers – which beats being on my own at home by miles, anyhow.' She shakes her head. 'I don't know why I'm telling you this.'

'I won't tell anyone.'

'I know, and that's probably why I am. But I've always felt like I'm different to everyone else. I feel more like I fit in here than I ever do at school though, and do you know why?'

I shake my head.

'Here is this big bunch of people with the same swimming obsession that I have; away from here, we're different to the world around us. So we've all got that in common straight away.'

I think about what she said, then nod. 'You're right, I get that. But not so much the other stuff you said. You always seem so confident.'

'You don't. Learn how to fake it, it makes life easier. Especially at school.'

I hesitate, then confess. 'I've never been to school before, but I have to start in September. I was home schooled.'

'Really? Wow.'

'I was meant to spend the summer studying, which is why I wasn't sure I could come here.'

'I told you I'd get your secrets out of you!'

There are so many more she doesn't know, that I'm not supposed to say, but something about being here, after hours and sharing secrets and chocolate makes me want to tell her more. I'm thinking about if I should, or what to say, when she breaks the silence.

'Look, as far as school goes – everywhere, really – it's about how you present more than how you are. Here's an example. When you came to breakfast late this morning and some people applauded, how did you feel?'

'Like I wanted a cloak of invisibility.'

'That's OK, but that was how you looked, too. That's not OK. If you'd smiled, waved and taken a bow, everybody would have laughed, and it'd have been fine.'

Later I'm thinking about what Ariel said. It's hot tonight and the window and curtains are open – the sky is dark apart from stars – but I'm wide awake. Ariel seems so poised all the time, but she says she fakes it?

From what Ariel said, if I'd reacted differently at breakfast it would have been better. Do I have it in me to be different? I don't know. I'm not even sure I want to fake it; the only person I know how to be is me. But if whoever I am could be more like everybody else it would make things easier.

Isha said she feels like a freak, too. Her story about how she got here was so like mine that it's weird. When she said *you're not alone* there was a knot in my throat and I didn't know what to say, or how to say it.

Swimming is easy; people are hard.

I miss Cate so much, in so many ways. Most of all I miss having someone I can say anything to, without worrying what I should or shouldn't say.

Movement at my window catches my eye. I sit up, heart beating faster. Something moves again and I make out the dark shape of a cat against the stars, peering in from my window ledge: Dickens.

I get up, taking care to move slowly; I hold out a hand and he sniffs it cautiously. I lightly stroke his head, along his ears, and he leans into my hand a moment. He turns fast as if he hears something and then he's gone, running along the gutter and out of sight.

You are not alone.

Wherever you are, you have the sun in the sky above you, the earth under your feet, the sea that calls you. The voices that say these words then, now and always:

Sun, sea, earth, sky.

You are not alone.

63

'Wake up!' Loud words are barked in my ear and I jump, open my eyes. It's Becker.

'I wasn't asleep,' I protest. I'd been doing what Nadya said to do while we were stretching: visualising running, doing it well, not being last.

Some of the others are laughing and I try to do what Ariel said to do, smile and take a bow, and I'm wondering if that was right when they just laugh even more.

Now Becker is furious. 'Thanks to sleeping beauty here, there will be a special treat today: whoever comes last gets *two* extra laps around the P.'

He thinks it will be me, but I'm determined: it won't be.

I start well.

Not only am I ahead of Zara, I'm somewhere in the middle of us all. I'm moving easier, faster. The hardest part is going past the sea without stopping to drink in the view, but I manage it by promising myself that I'll walk back later.

It feels good. Especially when I see the stunned look on Becker's face when he sees me at the finish.

We wait as the rest of us come in: who'll be last today?

It's Zara. Her face is red, she's breathing hard when she reaches us. Becker is about to congratulate her when someone else comes around the bend.

No way. It's *Denzi*? He must have hung back on purpose.

He waves as he heads off for the extra laps, putting on so much speed now that he's soon out of sight.

I'm watching for Denzi, to see if he makes it in time for breakfast – he does, by about five minutes. Zara must have been watching for him too – she gets up and goes to thank him – and he shrugs it off like it was nothing, says he needed the extra laps.

Denzi told me he was a loner that first night in the garden, yet he does things for people, like Zara today and me yesterday morning, and helping with my case.

He is also the one who said fake friendship makes his skin crawl.

And Ariel said she fakes it all the time to fit in. How many others do? Maybe, he's got it right. Maybe you can only judge people by what they do and not by what they say.

Someone is standing and waving for attention at the staff table. It's our coach, Wendy.

'Good morning! Would my group please meet for our free swim by the front entrance in forty-five minutes. Thanks.'

'What does free swim mean?' I say, hoping but wanting to be sure.

'It means a field trip!' Ariel says. 'To swim in the sea.'

My stomach does little flips – butterflies – of happiness, and I can feel the grin taking over my face.

Isha and Ariel's faces are the same as mine; those in other groups, like Zara, have stark envy on their faces.

I am not alone.

64

We're all early, excited to be going. It's been torture having the sea so close but out of reach.

A small bus pulls in, a boat on a trailer hooked behind it. We get on in a hurry and head down the lane to the gates.

I glance back as they close behind us. The fences and gates are too high to climb; there is even twisted wire at the top. No one gets in or out of this place easily unless they are meant to. Being shut in like this makes me uneasy, but I'm too happy about where we're going now to dwell on it for long.

It's quiet on the bus; everyone seems as intent on where we are going as I do. It's not a long drive but it feels like it is. When we finally turn down towards the sea and pull in along a beach, I see that it's *the* beach – the one where I stopped with Simone and Ali, with the webcam and bench.

Suits on underneath already, we shuck off our clothes. The surf is thundering through my blood. The salt is on my lips. The need to be in the water is so strong that it's hard to hear anything but the breaking waves on the sand. Vaguely I'm aware that Coach is pointing out buoys in the water that she wants us to swim between. That she and an assistant coach who came with us will be on the boat keeping an eye on us all.

When at last we're told we can go, I walk fast, almost running into the surf. Without thinking about it I exhale completely, breathe in to capacity and dive under the first big wave.

I head out – *further faster longer* – skimming the ocean floor, savouring touch, feel and taste. The sun and waves above become less real, more remote.

That's when they come. A beautiful silver sheen in the water, eyes that are intelligent, curious. A half-dozen young dolphins.

They circle at a distance at first. One holds my eyes and something twists inside me – both joy and pain – when she comes close enough to touch.

They are playing a game: tag and chase. I try to join in but they're faster and circle around to urge me on. And I'm laughing as we tumble through the water, feeling *alive*. *All* of me, in a way I never have before. Nothing away from the sea can ever compare to this feeling.

At the same time something is niggling away at me inside; there is something I need to do. Reluctantly I kick up slowly, bit by bit, exhaling a steady stream of bubbles as I go until my lungs are empty, my head is light. I break through the interface between here and there, and breathe in deeply. My new friends swim away, jump out of the water in beautiful arcs and I want to follow.

But nearby a motorboat is bobbing on the waves.

It's Coach. She waves. 'Not so far out please, Tabby,' she says, and when I look the other way to the beach I can't believe how far away it is. I came all this way, against the tide, on one breath?

I swim more slowly and stay on the surface now, heading towards the buoys near the shore.

What was I thinking – swimming straight out to sea like that?

I wasn't thinking; I was *feeling*. It was almost like one of my weird dreams, the ones when I'm swimming and everything inside me is pulling me out, out, to deeper water. The joy I felt swimming so far under the surface is still running through me. I feel giddy, energised, almost as if not having enough oxygen has the opposite effect from what it should.

I reach the buoys and begin swimming back and forth around them with the others. Coach's motorboat stays beyond where we swim; it reminds me who I am and what I'm doing, even as something wild inside me rails against the constraint.

65

That afternoon we're told to meet Malina at the pools for more apnoea training: this time, in the water.

We're to work in pairs, taking turns; I'm with Isha.

'It's easier to hold your breath longer when you're underwater,' Malina says. 'It subdues your breathing reflex.

'First float on your back, relax completely. Then, when you're ready, breathe in almost fully, breathe out fully, then in fully. Then your partner pushes down gently on your shoulders until your face is underwater. Raise a hand when you've had enough and your partner will release you.'

I tell myself: I'm *not* zoning out this time. I'll stay awake, focused on what I'm doing.

But floating limp and relaxed in the water like this, it's a struggle to stay conscious. Almost like I'm doing that thing when you're falling asleep sitting up no matter how hard you try not to. Eyelids drooping – or is it more that eyes roll back? – head drops, the movement makes you jerk and wake again. Like that. But now it is more my consciousness slipping back and forth, making my thoughts jump from one thing to another that wakes me each time. And it is also the thing that says, *enough* – and makes me raise a hand, let my head rise from the water as I breathe out, then breathe in. Stand up in the pool.

When I do so, I look around, everyone else is standing, waiting. I look to Malina.

'Five minutes twenty seconds. Very good, but why so much longer the other day?'

'This time I stayed awake.'

Isha frowns. 'But how can you hold your breath any other way? Surely if you're asleep, you'll automatically breathe?'

'Not necessarily, but it is a difficult skill to learn,' Malina says. 'One that Tabby seems to have quite naturally. Now, switch places with your partner.'

Isha floats on her back in the water, open eyes looking up at mine. She doesn't look very relaxed when it is time, but she breathes in, out all the way, in all the way, and I hold her under the water. It is less than two minutes before she raises her hand and I release her. She gasps and coughs when she breathes in, as if she'd started before her head was above the water.

We start doing what Malina calls tables after that. Hold breath a minute, one breath in and out, hold breath another minute, repeat. Getting used to lack of oxygen. Next time we'll do active tables to get used to a build-up of carbon dioxide.

'I don't get *why* we're doing this,' Isha says to Malina.

'The more you can swim without oxygen, the more you're getting used to both low oxygen and increased carbon dioxide.'

'But this isn't swimming.'

'No. It's a skill you use in swimming, though, even if you're not aware of it.'

That night I can't sleep. I'm lying in bed, staring at the ceiling, wishing Dickens would appear at my window again so I won't be alone with my thoughts.

When I'm not thinking – when I'm *feeling*, instead, like today in the sea – I can hold my breath for ages. Was I asleep? Well, not unless I can swim in my sleep. I was aware – *hyperaware* – of where I was and everything around me, but it's also kind of like being away from myself, almost like my body has taken over from my brain, or I'm dreaming but aware of it at the same time. But then today in the pool when I stayed focused on who I am and what I was doing, I couldn't hold my breath for anywhere near as long. It was still pretty good at over five minutes, but much less than before.

Malina said this was a skill that can be learned – holding your breath when asleep. But I'm not sure I understand how that can be possible. Surely some part of me must still be conscious and aware enough to stop me from breathing? Maybe *asleep* isn't the right word for what I've been doing.

Then I'm remembering how it felt to go to the sea today, to dive underneath the waves. It was so *unbelievable* that there aren't any words big enough to hold how it felt inside of them.

I asked Coach on the bus back when we'd next swim in the sea: she said in seven days. We go once a week all summer.

How will I wait that long?

I haven't been this bad before. This longing for the sea is always with me but before it wasn't controlling my thoughts and feelings the way it is now.

Is this obsession with the sea healthy? Is it normal?

If *normal* means being like everybody else, then no – but I don't care about that. Even though not fitting in can be difficult sometimes, I've never been like everybody else, so why start now?

Is it healthy? It is, if I'm near the sea. If I'm not . . . I pine. I imagine it's how Juliet felt when Romeo wasn't there. If I were locked away and couldn't go to the sea, I'd die. And it sounds crazy to even think that, but I know in my gut that it's true. It's not that I'd kill myself like Romeo and Juliet did — at least, I don't think I could ever take that step — but this need inside me keeps growing stronger. Being kept away from the sea is like having no oxygen.

Even I can only hold my breath for so long.

66

It's days later when it happens again.

I'm floating on my back in the pool, relaxing every part of me, breathing out all the way, in all the way. I turn over so my face is in the water, and *hold*.

Now that we're doing our apnoea training this way, no hands are needed to hold us under. But we are still in pairs so I know Isha is watching over me.

I've been trying different ways of keeping my mind busy but quiet, like making mental lists, counting backwards – things that don't require much thought but keep me conscious. So far it has only worked to a point. My breath holding goes up a little at a time – seconds, tens of seconds, longer – but nothing like I've done when I disconnect. But I'm sure there is a way to do what I'm trying to do without going to sleep, or whatever it is that I do, when I can hold it far longer.

Even though I don't fully understand why we're doing this, it's a puzzle, a challenge, one I want to solve. How long we can all hold our breath has become another competition to a group of people who are ultra-competitive by nature. It's almost like that aspect stops them from asking questions about why we're doing it at all.

No counting this time. Instead, I see me, as I am – visualising my body floating in the water with Isha standing close by and the others all around us. I pull away further, rise ever higher in the sky, until all the schoolgrounds are spread out below. Now I can see the sea, and my thoughts are drifting . . . separating . . .

I plunge down to its depths.

At last I'm back in control. She resisted me for so long.

I'm amazed that she doesn't understand the most basic things that even a newly born calf grasps instantly.

With knowledge comes strength: so long as she doesn't know what she does, I will always win.

The craving to breathe is strong, getting stronger. The temptation is there to refuse, to make everything stop.

But this time, I let her win.

I turn in the water and throw my head back, to breathe in deeply again and again, still floating in the water. It happened again: I was unconscious or disconnected or *something*.

It was almost like I was dreaming, and I was someone or something else, and they were in charge. Even to the point that whether I breathed or not – lived or died – wasn't under my own control.

'Tabby? Are you all right?' It's Isha.

I drop my feet down and stand up in the pool, though it feels unnatural to do so and my head spins. 'I think so,' I say.

Around us, everyone isn't looking at me this time; instead, they're focused on Ariel. She's still face down in the water.

Malina is in the pool next to her, concern on her face but then Ariel moves, turns, breathes in again and again like I did.

Malina has still got her stopwatch in her hand. She grins.

'Ariel: twenty-six minutes twelve seconds. Tabby: twenty-four minutes forty-six seconds.'

Later everyone crowds around Ariel, asking how she did it, and I'm relieved to be forgotten.

Ariel's eyes find mine over the others. Does she understand what happened any better than I do? But there's only a confused question in her eyes for me, one I can't answer.

At dinner we find out we're not the only ones. In other groups today there are three more that cracked twenty minutes.

There is a strange feeling around the staff table, an air of excitement – almost an *electricity* – as if some waited-and-longed-for thing is happening.

Ariel checks around with everyone and comes back, a smile of triumph taking over her face. 'I was the longest. Tabby was second.'

She's really pleased, but all I can think is that she was the closest to dying.

67

The next morning I'm yawning, out front as always for our early-morning run . . . but Becker isn't here. Nobody is, and I'm wondering if I'm late and they've gone without me. I check my tracker; I'm a minute early.

'Hi,' a voice says, and I turn to see Denzi, walking towards me. 'I didn't think you'd come today,' he says, and I must look at him blankly. He laughs. 'It's *Sunday*. Running is optional.'

'Damn.'

'But you're here now?' There is a glint of challenge in his eyes and an answer in mine. We set out at a fast pace that I'm not sure I'll be able to maintain but I'm determined.

So if today is Sunday . . . we've been here an entire week? And it is today that we can call home. I'm surprised – I've been so focused on each day, as it happens, that I hadn't been thinking about it.

When we clear the corner that leads to the view of the sea, I'm close to having to admit I can't keep this pace up any longer. Then Denzi gestures at the gate. 'Take a break?' he says.

'Well, if you need to,' I manage to gasp out, and he laughs. We slow, go down the path to the gate, stand there next to each other and gaze at the sea as far as forever. Something constricts inside. The only way I've been able to go past this every morning is by keeping my eyes straight ahead, not straying from following whoever is in front of me at the time.

When I glance up at Denzi he is staring at the sea with a rapt expression of longing that is both naked and real – and so much like the way I feel that I wonder that anyone else could be the same as me. And just as I'm thinking this, he turns and his eyes look into mine.

'It's torture,' he says. 'It's so close and we can't taste it, touch it.'

In this moment, I feel understood. Like Denzi gets me and I get him. He moves a little closer and he's looking at me a different way, like he feels that also. My eyes are still meeting his and he's smiling, and it's like the world is falling away and there is only Denzi, me, this moment.

A sound intrudes – footsteps above? – and I'm startled. We both turn to look up. It's Nadya, the sports psychologist. Out for an early Sunday run, too?

She sees us and waves.

'Guess we better go,' Denzi says, and there is something about the way he says it – a mixture of annoyance, regret. Feelings that I share. What would have happened if she hadn't interrupted? I don't know, but I want to.

We run up the path to join her.

After showering and heading to the hall I'm thinking maybe today I'll sit with Denzi for breakfast. He always sits quietly on his own, much like I do but I'm within a noisy group, and just now some peace – a space that doesn't always have to be filled with words – is what I want. But when I get there, Ariel is standing, talking with a few others near the door; she links her arm in mine.

Once our supplements are taken and we've collected our breakfasts, I'm swept up with them to my usual place. As I sit down I glance back to Denzi; he's watching me. He smiles and shakes his head in a what-are-you-like kind of way, as if he knows what I am thinking, and I smile back.

'What?' Ariel says, and follows my eyes. 'Is there something going on between you and Mr Antisocial?'

'What? No. We're friends, that's all.' But as I say it, I wonder: is there something between us?

'First time for everything for him, I suppose.' The way she speaks of him is dismissive and I want to argue, tell her she's got him wrong, but while I'm thinking what to say, Malina stands up at the staff table, waving a hand for attention and quiet.

'Good morning! For those of you who haven't met me, I'm Malina, from the CSME. After breakfast and your calls home, it is a free morning. For the next stage in apnoea training, if this is your first summer with us, we want to see you individually to assess where you are and if you are ready to proceed. Appointments have been scheduled starting this afternoon, so check the list before you go. If you're not on the list first up, go to the pools at the usual time after lunch.' She pins the list up on a noticeboard by the doors.

When it's time to go, we stop to check it. There are six names on it for today, and there I am: Tabby Heath, lucky last. Just before dinner.

But before I can wonder what it is about, first I need to make a call.

68

The phone rings. Once, twice – but it cuts off mid ring.

'Hello?' Simone's eager voice.

'Hi.'

'How are you? Do you like it there? Are you making friends?'

The questions follow thick and fast and I do my best to reassure her that everything is good, but both where she is and who she is feels remote. I guess I haven't known her for long this time around, have I? A week apart and it's almost like I was never there at all; a week that has been so *intense* that it feels both longer and more significant. It's driven thoughts of anything outside this place from my mind.

I manage to get in a few questions of my own: have there been any more drones, or anything else? Anything more about what Ali said about warning letters and being on alert? The answer to both is no, though the way she hesitates on the second question I'm not sure that she's said everything there is to say. Then Ali comes on the line and it's even more awkward.

Finally our time is up. Simone's final words, 'I love you, Holly,' are followed by a pause, and I know I should say it, too, but somehow the words won't come.

Pain twists deep inside: it isn't just my parents I've been forgetting; I haven't thought about Cate in days, either. There was no knowing that Cate was going to be taken away from me, that after that she would soon die. There were so many things I would have said that last night if I had known, but there was no second chance.

I wish I could have given more to Simone just now. More of myself. But I can't speak to her again for a week.

I'm not sure what to do with my free morning. I want to go back around the grounds to see the sea again, but what Denzi said is right: it's torture, being able to see but not reach it. It's a different kind of homesickness.

Instead I wander around the quiet places of the school grounds, behind buildings, through gardens – looking for a corner to be on my own.

Movement in long grass draws my eye – it ruffles like something moves inside, out of sight. Is it Dickens?

I make soft noises, say his name and a tail tip appears over the top of the grass and he pokes his nose out, comes to me. He lets me stroke him but his nose is sniffing the air and he turns away, bounds behind a few trees.

I follow and behind them is Zara. She's on a bench and Dickens is next to her now, rubbing his head against her hands. I hesitate, about to turn back but Zara looks up and sees me.

'Ssssh, don't scare him away,' she says. 'Puss, want a treat?' I come closer – he's purring loudly. She opens her hand and holds out a small piece of something on her palm. That's when I notice something I haven't before: her hand. A few of her fingers are joined together, like my toes. Am I staring like people do at my feet? I blink and look away but she doesn't seem to notice.

Dickens half climbs into her lap to get to the treat.

268

'What is it?'

'Cheese. He loves it.' She strokes him and I make a mental note to keep back some cheese at lunchtime in case he comes to my room at night again.

'He's called Dickens,' I say and he turns at his name. I sit down with Dickens between us, and scratch behind his ears.

'Suits him,' Zara says, still looking at the cat and not up, but now I'm there next to her I can see her eyes are red. Has she been crying?

Should I pretend not to notice and leave her alone? I hesitate. 'Are you all right?' I finally say.

She shrugs. Drops her eyes to Dickens again. 'I'm fine,' she says but the way she says it, she so obviously isn't. I leave the silence for her to decide to talk or not.

She sighs. 'It's just . . . well, I guess I'm homesick, though I don't know why. And the call home today; it rang out. No answer. I mean, it's not unusual, but somehow I thought with me being away . . . Well, never mind.'

'Oh. Sorry.'

'Not your fault. My mum is really into her work. She's probably away somewhere and forgot to take her phone.'

'What does she do?'

'Geologist.' She looks at me sideways, shrugs. 'Oil and gas exploration,' she adds, like it's a shameful secret – and it kind of is. Finding new deposits to exploit will only poison the planet more than it is already. But I have one of my own.

'My dad works for an oil and gas company,' I say. 'He kind of runs it.'

She's surprised. 'What are the chances? I mean, there's Isha.

269

Her mum is also a geologist. And Ariel's dad works for an energy company, too.' I'm surprised; for all the time we've talked it's odd that Ariel and me have never said this to each other. She talks a lot without saying anything most of the time, though.

'I wasn't sure about coming away for the summer,' Zara says, 'but I like being here. Focusing so completely on what we're doing.'

'It makes the world go away.'

'Yeah. But I had to decide whether to come or not so fast I didn't have time to really think about it. I only got invited a week before I came.'

'Really?' I'm remembering what Isha told me, her story so like mine. Is Zara's, too?

'Did you train for swimming before you came?'

She shakes her head. 'Not really. I mean, we have a pool at home, and I've always spent more time in it than out. Though I like swimming in the sea the most.'

There's something weird about all the things some of us have in common. It makes me uneasy without knowing why.

69

I cross the lane to the CSME. It's even hotter today and even though I've just showered, sweat is already trickling down my back. The front door is propped open; all the windows are open, too.

My name is taken at the waiting area, but Malina comes in before I can sit down.

'Hi, Tabby, follow me.'

We go along the hall and then down a flight of stairs. There are more stairs down but we stay at this level, and go into a small room with no windows; it's stifling. There are gym mats on the floor but apart from that the room is empty and the lights are dim.

'Are you feeling the heat?' Malina says.

'Aren't you?'

She shakes her head, and no matter how unbelievable that may be she does look calm and cool.

'It's all a state of mind,' she says. 'That is exactly what we are examining today. I will show you.'

She sits cross-legged on the floor and gets me to do so also, facing her.

'First, we visualise. Close your eyes, relax your body. Starting with your fingers, toes, relax each muscle . . . Then continue up your arms, legs . . . Shoulders, hips . . .' Her voice is soft, she speaks slowly and I'm doing as she says, imagining every muscle relaxed. 'Now your core . . . Neck . . . Your face and scalp, too . . .

'Now I guide your breathing. When I say in, breathe in; out, breathe out.

'In . . .

'Out . . .

'In . . .

'Out.' Her soft voice gradually becomes quieter so I have to focus on it to hear her at all.

I breathe slower and slower, following her words.

'Now breathe in all the way and hold the air in your lungs . . .

'Quieten your thoughts. Listen only to my voice; there is nothing else. You are not your body. Your mind can be where you want it to be. Floating, relaxed, in the cool sea. Suspended in the water, your breathing is suspended, too. You rest completely, but you are still *you* inside. When you are ready, you may decide to breathe again.'

There is peace inside me, a feeling of complete wellness and of being somewhere else. Floating in the water. Suspended, arms, legs splayed.

But then I'm not me, I'm drifting away from myself . . .

There is a sharp sound, and I open my eyes. Malina's hands are held up – did she clap to startle me?

'It's time to breathe, Tabby,' she says, and as she says the words I exhale the air locked inside of me, gasp air in, and cough, and breathe in again.

'You went too far, Tabby. What happened?'

'I don't know. I was concentrating on your voice, like you said. It felt sort of like I disconnected.'

'From yourself?'

I nod, freaked out. There are goosebumps on my arms, my legs, and I realise I'm not hot any more. If I'd been alone could I have held my breath until I died? It just doesn't make *sense*. Surely if I'm unconscious, my body is free of my mind controlling it and it's going to breathe because it needs to?

'Don't be nervous or uncertain,' Malina says. 'I'm here – you are safe.'

There is something about her, and her voice – I trust her, and I nod. My heart rate slows and she smiles.

'We will do this again, but this time, Tabby, I want you to visualise something else. A chain that you hold in one of your hands that you can never let go. It reaches between the halves of yourself. If you start to disconnect, you pull on the chain to bring yourself back together. Do you understand?'

'I think so.'

'All right. We begin.'

We start as before; I breathe in and out, slower and slower, on her words, then finally breathe in and hold. But when it gets to focusing on her voice and completely relaxing, I'm resisting, wanting to stay in control . . .

I'm trying to both relax and float and be present at the same time, but the two requirements fight each other. The desire to stop doing this at all, to breathe, is getting stronger, but then . . . it is like there is a fracture, a split. A moment when I can decide to drift or stay in the now – but I can't hold my breath if I stay in the now.

The chain. It's silver-grey and thick – warm in my hand. I drift in the sea and hold on to it tight at the same time.

It's so beautiful here in the water, in the flickering half-light.

Tabby, can you hear me? a voice says.

I frown and want to push it away. It says more things but I stuff my hands in my ears so I can't hear and, as I do, something I was holding falls away. A chain? It's pretty, a shiny, slender snake; dancing and drifting in the current.

I reach out for it, but it's too far away. Then the water surges around me, I'm caught in a whirlpool; my whole body is shaking but it's wrong, it's not who I am. The chain is caught in it, too; it's alive and wrapping itself around my neck and I'm clawing at it to breathe.

I sit up, gasping again and again, taking air into my lungs in big greedy gulps.

'Very well done, Tabby,' Malina says. 'I think that's enough for today.'

I nod, shaken. She helps me stand. 'And did you notice something else?'

'What?'

'You're not too hot any more.'

She's right.

In the bathroom upstairs, I splash water on my face and look in the mirror.

My face stares back, but it feels alien somehow – as if it isn't who I really am. No, that's not quite right: it isn't *all* of who I am. Goosebumps rise on my arms, my neck.

Scratch marks are livid and red on my neck. I didn't just imagine I was clawing at my throat, did I?

Well done, she'd said. For almost suffocating and then clawing at myself?

As I head for the exit, I go past the stairs that lead to Malina's room. There were more stairs going down past the first landing.

Maybe – if it actually exists, that is – I can find the way down to the sea that Denzi mentioned.

Before I have time to think about it, I open the door and go down, taking care to step quietly.

I go past the first landing, down another flight of stairs. At the bottom of the stairs is a hall with a few doors. I listen carefully at the first door; it's quiet. I open it. Inside is a locker room, with white coats hanging on hooks.

I close it and go to the next door. I try to turn the handle but it doesn't budge; it's locked.

Before I have a chance to walk away and look for another way, the locked door opens. A woman in a white coat stands there; her eyes widen when she sees me and she steps back.

'Can I help you?' she says.

'I think I'm lost. I just had an appointment and thought I knew the way out, but I was wrong.' Will she buy that? Even the most clueless sense of direction would know going down more stairs couldn't be right.

But she doesn't seem bothered. 'Ah, I see. I'll show you. It's quicker this way.' She turns back to the door that has shut behind her; there's a pass clipped to her white coat that she swipes against a plate on the door and it clicks open. She has me follow her through the door, across a room to an external door.

'This leads to the back gardens,' she says. 'Just follow the

275

path around to the right and go up the hill, and you'll get back to the front of the building.' She opens the door.

'OK, thanks,' I say. As I do I glance back towards her, and that's when I see it over her shoulder – across the room, on another door. The four-leaf clover symbol of the Penrose Clinic.

70

I cut across the grounds to the back of the dining hall. There is a bench in a shady corner and I sit down, wrapping my arms around myself.

Could I be mistaken? I only had a quick glimpse of the door. Yet I know what I saw – it *was* the Penrose Clinic symbol.

I thought I had got away from them, and yet here they are.

But *why* would they be here? And why would they be hidden away behind a locked door?

And what about that session with Malina this afternoon? It all seemed perfectly reasonable when I was with her, but not once I left. And it is like the alarm at the Penrose symbol and what happened with her are magnifying each other and everything else, including all these strange parallels between what some of our parents do, and how Zara, Isha and I were all spotted and brought along without having trained before. Do these things somehow fit together? *How?*

Whatever we were doing when I was with Malina wasn't just visualisation. It was like she took me someplace else – as if I was dreaming and awake at the same time. Was I hypnotised and imagined it all?

Somehow I know it isn't that simple. It is too like what happened in the pool yesterday.

There is something different inside me. It's always been there, but I've never fought against it like this. This afternoon I felt like I almost knew what it was; that if I'd been able to hold my breath a little longer, maybe I would have done.

But would I survive?

There are footsteps, getting closer, and I don't want to have to try to talk normally to anyone right now. But then Denzi comes around the corner. Maybe talking to someone is what I need – if the someone is Denzi.

'I saw you dive back here. What's wrong?' he says, and sits next to me on the bench.

'I don't know if anything *is* wrong. I saw something that surprised me, that's all.'

'And it worried you? What was it?'

I hesitate, but maybe, if I say it out loud, it'll seem less weird.

'There's this medical clinic near where I live that is doing some sort of longitudinal study that I'm in. I just saw their symbol on a door downstairs in the CSME. It was behind a locked door, like it was hidden away. I didn't know they were here.'

'Why were you downstairs and how'd you get through a locked door?'

'I was looking for the way into the cellars you mentioned, to see if there was a way down to the sea,' I say, a little embarrassed to admit it. 'Someone came through the locked door; I told them I was lost, and they took me across that way to an outside door.'

'What clinic and what is the study?'

'I'd rather you didn't mention this to anyone else. It's the Penrose Clinic. Have you heard of it?' He shakes his head, no. 'They help people who can't have children, like my parents.

They've been doing this study, tracking the babies born from IVF over time.'

'So what are they doing hiding in a sports-medicine centre at a boy's school?'

I shrug. 'I have no idea. It seems kind of weird, though.' I hesitate again, but now that I've started, I want to know what he'll make of the rest of it. 'And that's not all. There's some strange coincidences with some of us.'

'Like what?'

'Like Zara's mum and Isha's dad are both geologists. And Ariel's dad and mine both work for oil and gas companies.'

'That is a bit odd. Though my dad is a politician, which is even more embarrassing.'

'That's not all. Isha, Zara and me were all spotted by a swimming coach and invited here a week or so before the summer school started. We were all into swimming, but none of us had trained before we were spotted.'

'Really? If this is meant to be an elite performance boot camp for future stars of the sport, why would they invite swimmers who have barely done any training before they got here?'

I tilt my head, thinking. 'I can see why you say that; I was thinking the same thing. But I've always had this connection to water and swimming. What happened with me seemed natural as it happened. It's hearing similar stories from others that has made me question it.'

'I'm not saying you're not talented, that you don't have amazing potential – you clearly do. But I don't buy that kind of thing happens randomly on this kind of scale. I trained for years before I got here.'

'I think Ariel has too – at least she was here last summer.'

'Maybe it's a diversity thing. Trying to get people involved in sport who wouldn't otherwise get the chance. I mean, if you look around at who is here this summer, it's a pretty even mix of all races. So maybe they've gone looking for talent in different places, which is cool.'

I think about what he said, then nod. 'You're right. But that doesn't explain why so many of our parents seem to be in oil and gas . . . and politics.'

'Yep. Diverse, but not a disadvantaged group as far as money goes.'

'Maybe what some of our parents do – and that some of us are so new to swimming – are just weird coincidences. But I wonder what we'd find out if we talk to some of the others, see what their stories are?' I say. 'Though what it means if there are more of us with similar backgrounds, I have no idea.'

'Me either,' he says. 'But going back, what is it about this Penrose Clinic being here that worries you?'

It's a warm evening – hot, really – but the prickles running up my spine again now make me shiver.

'It's hard to explain.' I sigh. 'Having to go there always gave me the creeps. I thought I had got away from them for the summer, yet here they are.'

'If you don't like going there, then why do it?'

'My mum said they agreed to it before I was born.'

'But *you* didn't agree to it, did you?'

'No, but—'

'You're old enough to decide what doctor you do or don't go to.'

I think about it. Could it really be that easy? I smile at Denzi. 'You're right. Thanks.' And it feels so good to talk to Denzi like this, being honest about what I think. It feels so good to have a friend. And I'm looking into his eyes and there is something there, the same warm feeling I had when we were by the sea. A belonging – a connection? I don't know quite what it is, but I like it.

'Someone's coming,' Denzi says, and then I hear it also – footsteps on the path near us.

Then Nadya walks around the bushes to our bench. Interrupting us, *again*? Unbelievable.

'Hello, you two. Isn't it time to go for dinner?'

'Aye, aye,' Denzi says and gives a salute, his annoyance clear. As we get up I glance at the time on my tracker. We've got another few minutes still, really, but we follow Nadya to the dining hall.

That was odd. It felt like somehow, somebody knew where we were and what we were talking about – and sent Nadya to break it up. The same way she appeared when we were running and stopped by the sea.

I shake my head. Now I'm definitely being paranoid. I can't think anything we do or say is of much interest to Nadya unless it interferes with our performance.

71

That night I can't sleep. The sea is calling me and after a while I give up, get dressed quickly and slip out the door, down the hall and stairs and then outside.

I avoid the motion lights in the garden and go the long way around the perimeter fence of the school grounds, the way Becker has us run. The skies are clear, a half moon and the stars giving enough light to see my way.

I feel the sea getting closer and when I round the bend where I'd normally see it stretching out, far below, there is a wide-open expanse of darkness.

I go to the gate, sit on it. It's a still night, almost unnaturally so. Now I'm closer, I can see the moon and stars reflect in the water below with waves that barely ripple the surface. I can smell the sea; I can see it. I want to touch it, taste it, feel it on every inch of my skin.

Despite what Denzi said about rock falls, the climb down looked almost possible in daylight; at night it would be suicidal. I'm holding the gate tight as if by doing so I can stop myself from taking steps I know I shouldn't take.

How long I sit there, staring at the dark water below, I don't know. But then there is something – a slight noise – behind me? Then another.

I twist round on the gate, heart pounding and adrenalin

racing, and peer into the darkness. Someone is there, walking towards me from the path above. As they get closer I can see who it is: Malina.

What on earth is she doing here?

'Sorry, did I startle you?' Malina says.

'A bit,' I say and try to compose myself, to keep my thoughts from my face. There's no way her finding me here is random – it can't be.

She walks closer. 'What are you doing out here so late?'

'I couldn't sleep, so I came for a walk.'

'Me, too. It's so still tonight, isn't it?'

'Almost like the world is holding its breath, waiting for something.'

'Maybe it is. But in the meantime, morning will come soon enough – we should both be asleep. Come on, I'll walk you back.'

'All right.' I hop down off the gate and we start the walk back.

'You shouldn't wander out at night on your own. What if you'd fallen and hurt yourself? I won't tell anyone you've been out after lights out this time, but don't do it again.'

'Sure, I understand.'

She walks all the way back with me, up the stairs to my floor. She even waits while I walk to my door and open it. 'Goodnight,' she says softly as I go in my room.

I shut the door and lean against it, standing there in the dark.

Whenever I've been not quite where they might expect, someone from the staff has come to check on me. First it was

Nadya when Denzi and me were out early for an optional run; Nadya, again, when we were speaking in a tucked away corner of the gardens; tonight it was Malina.

It can't be coincidence. Somehow, they always know where I am.

I feel uneasy, like there might be a camera in my room. I switch the lights on and search but find nothing.

Feeling foolish I quickly change into PJs, turn off the light and get into bed.

I glance at the time on my fitness tracker: it's two a.m. Only four hours to go until our morning run. I wonder if I'll manage to—

Wait a minute. Could it be this – my tracker? I know it monitors my heart rate, the activity that I do – running, swimming – how far I go and all that, but how does it do that unless it knows where I am?

Do they always know where we are, what we are doing – maybe even what we are *saying* – because of these?

Maybe they can even tell what I'm dreaming about by my heart rate. What I'm thinking.

I reach to undo the strap – but no. If I take it off, they'll know, won't they? The heart rate data will stop. Would someone come running again – to my room – in the middle of the night? I'm afraid to find out.

Maybe I'm just being paranoid. Growing up with Cate made me distrust authority keeping track of me in any way. Maybe this is normal to everyone else.

I need to talk to somebody who understands how things are, who can either explain it away and put my mind at rest, or be as horrified as I am at the thought of our locations being tracked along with our fitness.

Tomorrow I'll talk to Denzi, see what he thinks. Though we'd better make it fast before someone comes along to stop us.

In the meantime, I count down the minutes, then hours, as the night goes slowly by.

72

The next morning I'm yawning more than usual when I get out front for our six a.m. run. It's hot already; there's no breeze at all. Most of us are here, others trickle down in ones and twos, but there's no sign of Denzi. Becker isn't here, either.

It's a few minutes past six when Nadya appears.

'Hi, everyone,' she says. 'Becker couldn't make it this morning, so you've got me instead.'

We set out. Where is Denzi? Has he overslept?

We run and I'm half expecting him to come up behind us, wave as he speeds past. He doesn't.

He's not at breakfast, either.

When I go to get my supplements, I ask the woman who hands them out if she knows where he is. She doesn't, but says he mustn't have been expected for breakfast. His tablets weren't sent down.

I'm distracted during swimming training that morning, worried about Denzi. I keep trying to look across at the pool his group uses to see if he turns up late.

He doesn't, and he doesn't come to lunch, either.

Where has he gone?

By lunch I've lost my appetite, and push food around my plate. Soon everyone is getting up and leaving now. Someone says my name and I turn; it's Nadya. She's still at the staff table; all the other staff have gone. I walk over to her.

She pulls out a chair. 'Let's have a quick chat. Is everything all right?'

'I don't know. Where is Denzi?'

'Ah, I see. Were you friends?'

I nod and wonder at the question since she's come by twice when we've been talking.

'I'm afraid I can't discuss other patients with you. But I can say this. Occasionally a swimmer decides the approach of the training programme here isn't for them and chooses to go home. Is there anything else that is concerning you?'

Yes. But maybe you're part of it, so I can't say anything. Instead I just shake my head.

'I'm here if you ever need to talk. Just ask at the CSME reception and if I'm not free they'll arrange an appointment.'

'OK. Thanks,' I say and get up, head outside for a walk before afternoon training.

She didn't say what happened with Denzi; she implied he decided to leave. Without saying goodbye? I can't believe he would do that. And why would he leave? He was doing well here, seemed to enjoy all the training side of things.

It just doesn't *feel* right.

Cate always said to listen to your gut: if something feels wrong, it usually is.

There is an hour to kill before meeting at the pools for apnoea training and I wander around the grounds. My feet take me towards the lane we cross to go to CSME. Was that *really* the Penrose Clinic symbol that I saw?

If it was, I don't want them to know I'm on to them. I walk on, following a path along the hedge next to the lane. I still

287

can't shake the feeling that I'm being followed, or tracked by this tracker.

Right now, no one is in sight; I'm not being followed unless they're very good at it. There's no CCTV cameras anywhere that I can see, and they'd have to be well hidden for me to miss them – I'm used to spotting them, from years living with Cate. Most of the time it's second nature to avoid them without thinking about it.

Time for an experiment: I slip off the path, between some bushes. There's a tree stump. I sit on it, and I'm completely screened by hedge, trees, bushes.

I undo the strap of the tracker. Take it off.

It hadn't been annoying me – other than thinking what it might be doing in monitoring my whereabouts – but now that it is off it feels good to rub at my wrist underneath.

I'm still doing this when there are footsteps, getting closer then further away, then closer again, as if someone isn't quite sure where they are going.

Then Nadya peeks around a tree.

The look of worry on her face is quickly hidden. 'Hi, Tabby. That's a quiet place you've found.'

'Sometimes I like to be alone with my thoughts.'

'I can understand that. Me too. Is there a problem with your tracker?'

I shake my head. 'No, it was just a bit itchy underneath, so I took it off to scratch.'

'Maybe it was done up too tight? Let me see.'

I hold out my wrist and the tracker. She does it back up again. 'Is that better?'

'I think so.'

'You've not supposed to ever take it off, so leave it on, all right? You need to always keep it on so we know that you're safe. You seem to wander about and get lost regularly, don't you?'

I bend over my wrist and pretend to move my tracker to a more comfortable position to hide my face. Getting lost: the only time I ever said I was lost was the day I saw the Penrose Clinic door. Does she know I saw it? And wandering around – did she mean like last night? Malina said she wouldn't tell anybody, and I believed her – but if my location was being monitored, she didn't have to.

'If you're having any problems with your tracker, come over to CSME and we can adjust it for you.'

'Sure.'

'Aren't you supposed to change and head for the pools now?'

I glance at the time; there's still half an hour to go. 'I'll wander back.'

I walk back to the path, feeling her eyes on me still even when she's gone the other way back through the gate to the lane.

That's proof enough for me. They always know where I am. They know if I take off the tracker; they come fast if I do. And Nadya knew what I was doing, didn't she? Testing to see if someone would come. It was on her face, what she said, what she didn't. She didn't even pretend to be surprised when she found me.

Between the gates, high fences and this tracker, I've never felt more trapped.

It's like prison, Cate's voice whispers inside me. She said that about going to school, but this place has got to be more controlling than a school could ever be.

And I *chose* to come here.

They said no phones or internet to keep us focused on training, but what it's really done is make us completely cut off and isolated.

73

That afternoon when our group meets by the pool, Coach is there along with Malina.

'Hi, everyone,' Malina says. 'We're going to split you into two groups today, so half of you come with me for some tank training and the rest stay for extra swim training. We'll switch groups around tomorrow.' She looks at a tablet in her hand and calls out six names, including mine and Isha's.

'Follow me,' she says.

We cross the lane to CSME, and once through the front door we go down the first flight of stairs and along a corridor past the room I've been to before with Malina, and to another door.

She opens and holds the door for us to go in. We have to step down to do so; the floor is lower inside than out. In the room are three glass tanks, about thirty centimetres or so taller than me, and maybe a metre wide in diameter. They're full of water, with what looks like a metal lid on the top. Each has an inlet pipe, gutters for overflow, and a ladder. The taste of salt is in the air – it's seawater.

'OK, girls. Today we are doing oxygen apnoea training with a difference. You work in pairs. You take it in turns to be suspended in the tank, do the usual breathing technique and then your partner closes the tank. They watch you and open the tank if you point at the lid or if you start to breathe out – shown by any bubbles coming from you. Any questions?'

'Yes, I've got one,' Isha says. 'Why? What is the point to doing this in a tank and having a lid on it?'

'Being underwater should be as natural to you as being out of it. You should be able to control any alarm you may feel under conditions of reduced oxygen – this will help you compete in stressful situations.'

Isha's face: she's not happy with the idea of this at all. She shakes her head. 'I don't want to do this.'

'You can choose not to participate in any aspect of training at any time. But then you go home. Do you want to go ahead? It's up to you.'

I'm staring at Malina, shocked that they would send her home just for that. And Isha is right. What's the point of doing this at all?

Isha is biting her lip so hard I'm afraid she'll draw blood. 'I'll do it,' she finally says.

'Wonderful. Now, everyone, pick a partner, one you trust.'

'Isha?' I say. She nods, and there is a murmur of voices as the others arrange themselves in pairs.

'What's wrong?' I say to her in a low voice.

'I'm claustrophobic. I can't stand being shut inside something.'

'Tell her.'

She shakes her head. 'They'd send me home. I can do this.'

'Are you sure?'

'No. But I'm going to try.'

'Want me to go first?'

She nods.

She's scared – there's no way she should do this. But Malina is ignoring her and what she said.

'All right then,' Malina says. 'Whoever is going first, head up the ladder and open the lid by turning the wheel.'

I climb up the ladder to the top. There is a metal wheel as she said on the lid, but it's stiff, hard to turn and has to go around and around before the lid releases. I swing the lid open; it's heavy. I don't have a problem with small spaces or being held underwater and the whole idea is making even me uneasy.

'In a moment I will tell you when it is time to get into your tank. Once inside, relax fully as you've been taught. Your partner must now climb up the ladder. When you are ready, take in your breath and signal to them to close the lid. There are handles you can hold inside so the lid doesn't hit you in the head if you bob up. Once the lid is shut, relax completely once again. And as I said before, when you need to come out to breathe, point at the lid and your partner will open it for you. They will also open the lid if you emit any bubbles or appear in distress. There is an emergency release to empty the tank quickly that I can activate if necessary.

'OK, time to get in your tank.'

I swing my feet across from the ladder, ease myself in and as the cool seawater touches my skin, my nerves ease.

I close my eyes, suspended in the water with my head tilted back and out enough to breathe, letting my arms and legs go limp. Breathing from out to in, relaxing every muscle of my body. Gradually my breathing slows. Exhale completely; in completely. I open my eyes and signal to Isha, reaching down at the same time to hold the handles to keep myself underwater as the lid closes. The thud it makes above me is loud even through the water, and there is a flurry of nerves in my stomach.

Be calm. Relax. I close my eyes again but I'm not floating, drifting away, and I don't want to. It's not being in the tank – at least, I don't think so – it's everything else I've been thinking about.

And *why* are we doing this in a tank? I get that learning to hold your breath for longer – getting more used to both low oxygen and high carbon dioxide – makes sense for a competitive swimmer. But the extent to which this is taken doesn't, and now I just want to get out.

I open my eyes. Isha's anxious face is just through the glass. I point at the lid and she scrambles to twist it open. It takes ages and I'm struggling to not exhale. When it finally swings open I'm in such a hurry to get out that I hit my head on it before it is out of the way.

'Ouch,' I say, rubbing my head.

'Are you OK?'

'Fine, just a little bump.'

'What's it like? Being in there?'

'It's OK. But make sure you point before you need to breathe because it takes longer than you think to open it.'

'Tabby?' Malina says. 'That was four minutes eighteen seconds. You didn't drift, did you?'

I shake my head.

'None of you did.' There is a tinge of disappointment in her voice. 'All right, switch over. Easiest if you both come down the ladder and then swap.'

Isha goes down and I follow.

Malina comes over now and takes Isha's hands in hers. 'We're here, we'll look after you. All you have to do is try. You can do that, can't you?'

Isha nods and starts to go up the ladder. She reaches the top of the ladder and swings her feet into the tank: the look on her face as she does so – she's petrified.

It feels wrong to make her do something she is so afraid of.

'I have a question,' I say. 'What happens if I refuse to close the lid? Would I get sent home then?'

Malina tilts her head. 'No, but someone else will do it. It'll be easier for Isha if you don't delay.'

I go up the ladder, next to Isha. 'Listen. I'll just put the lid down and open it up again straight away. Right?'

Her eyes are dark with fear. I'm not sure she even heard what I said.

'Isha? You are not alone.'

This time my words seem to register. She nods, lets her body relax more, slips deeper into the tank.

Soon she signals for me to close the lid.

I don't think she's ready. 'Are you sure?'

She nods, and grabs the handles to pull herself down.

I swing the lid across, taking care to hold the weight so it doesn't make a loud thud.

'Close and lock it properly, Tabby,' Malina says.

I watch Isha through the glass sides of the tank. Her eyes are tightly closed as if she's pretending she's somewhere else.

I turn the locking wheel as fast as I can, pause, prepared to open it again straight away. But before I can, Isha's eyes are open, she's pounding on the glass, her mouth opening to scream.

I turn it back as hard as I can but it's jammed.

'Malina! It won't open!'

'Try again.'

I really put my shoulders behind it. Nothing. Isha is pounding and kicking at the glass, there is blood in the water.

Malina does something at the bottom of the tank. The water rushes out underneath. Isha can breathe now but is still pounding at the glass. I put everything I have into turning the wheel at the top and finally it gives a little, then more, and I turn and turn it until the lid is free and I swing it out of the way.

'Isha? Isha! It's open now, you can come out,' I say, but it's like she doesn't even hear me, just keeps pounding at the glass with her bloody hands. Two of the other girls come up the ladder. They hold my feet and I lower myself into the tank, grab Isha's shoulders. She struggles at first, then seems to realise who I am. I hook my arms under hers and they pull us both up.

She's crying. Bleeding – her hands, knuckles, forehead where she smashed it against the glass. We help her down the ladder.

There's a medical person here now, and another. A stretcher. They take her away. The other girls are out of their tanks now; some didn't see what happened and the others tell them.

I'm staring at Malina. '*Why* did you do that to her?'

'It's an important lesson for all of you,' she says.

'What is?'

'Fear. It can kill you if you are controlled by it. Never allow fear – or any other emotion – to take your reason. You must always stay in control.'

Malina keeps talking – tells us why Isha's failure to control her emotions was a flaw, one we can't share if we want to succeed.

Everything she says sounds completely just and reasonable as she says it, and it'd be easy to be lulled by her voice.

But I don't believe what she is saying. This was wrong and there is nothing she can ever say that will make me think any different.

74

I don't go to dinner. Instead I have a shower, get into bed. I need to be alone with my thoughts.

A while later there's a knock at the door. It's Nadya.

'I've brought your dinner.'

'Thanks.'

'Supplements, too.' She crosses the room, holds them out with a glass of water, watching me closely. I sit up, take them. Too late, I wonder: *Are they really just vitamins, like they say?* Thinking that, some of the water goes down wrong and then I'm coughing.

Pills from the Penrose Clinic; they said they'd change them here if they weren't right, but the Penrose Clinic is here, too. Who knows what they've been making us take, and why?

'Are you all right, Tabby?'

'Is Isha OK?' I ask.

'She just has some minor injuries from having a panic attack in the tank. How about you?'

'I don't know. She was so scared. Maybe I should have stopped it somehow, not let her do it.'

'It was Isha's decision to try it. A brave thing for her to do.'

'But why did she have to at all?'

'It's part of the recognised training programme. Now, have some dinner and try to get some sleep. All right?'

'I'll try,' I say, but it's a lie. I know I won't. *What is really going on in this place?*

'Bye,' she says, and closes the door behind her.

I half pick at the dinner she's left on my desk, but soon push it aside and get back into bed. Too much has happened in the last few days that I don't understand, don't feel comfortable with.

I need Cate. To explain things, yes, but I'm also missing her so much that it's like a wound that will never heal. When everything is going well I seem able to hold it back, but when it's not, I can't.

Sometime later there's a soft knock on my door. Ariel peeks in.

'Hi,' she says. 'Are you all right?'

'Depends what you mean by all right.'

'Can I come in?' She doesn't wait for an answer, comes through and closes the door behind her. 'Rumour has it that at tank training Isha nearly drowned because you couldn't get the hatch open.'

'What? That's not true!'

'So tell me what really happened.' She perches on my desk chair next to the bed and I tell her – how scared Isha was, her panic attack in the tank. The lid jamming.

'Why did they make her do it?' I say.

'Let me ask you a question first. *How* did they make her do it? Did they drag her up the ladder and force her into the tank?'

'Well, no – but Malina said she'd be sent home if she didn't try.'

'That's life. It's sport. Push yourself and push yourself

again, past fear and pain, and you just might have a chance of representing your country, even winning gold one day at the Olympics.'

I'm looking back at her, horrified.

'Isha *chose* to try it, didn't she? Even though she was scared.'

'Well, yes, but—'

'No buts. That's amazing. And she'll either run screaming from the building now, or be stronger than she was before. But either way, none of that is your fault.'

Now I'm confused, doubting myself – what I saw, how I reacted to it. 'It just felt so wrong.'

'That's because you're soft. Toughen up.'

I don't understand the difference between what I saw and felt, and how Ariel sees it. I want to talk to Denzi, ask what he thinks of it all, and that reminds me of everything else.

I sit up. 'Look, there's other stuff going on that doesn't feel right.'

'Tell me.'

'Well, Denzi vanished.'

'He went home, didn't he?'

'Without saying goodbye?'

'He's a loner, Tabby. I'm sorry if he hurt your feelings, but he's not the sort to tell anyone what he's doing or why.'

Part of what she says about him is true, I know it is, but she didn't know him like I did. Though maybe I'm the one who had him wrong. I thought we had this connection – maybe I imagined it.

'What about our trackers? I think they track where we are all the time.'

300

'Of course they do! It's part of the technology behind them. They measure time and distance travelled to get speed; they can only do that if they know where we are. Didn't you know that?'

I shake my head, feeling a bit thick, like I should have realised from the beginning what only came to me later.

'Though, there is a way around it, if you want to go places you don't want them to know about.'

'What's that?'

'Get someone to wear your tracker for you while you sneak out. Last year there was a girl going to a boy's room at night all the time and that's how she got away with it.'

I process that and sigh. 'I don't want to do anything like that, but knowing someone is always keeping track of where I am really bothers me.'

'You've had a tough day, huh.'

'You could say that.'

'I know what would make you feel better.'

'What's that?'

'Chocolate.'

I get up – find it inside my desk. 'That's why you're really here, isn't it?'

'Part of the reason.' She winks, accepts a piece of chocolate and touches it against mine. 'Cheers!'

As before, we sit in silence while the chocolate slowly melts on our tongues. Both sweet and bitter at the same time, I concentrate on the feel and taste of it, on making it last.

'Hmmmm. OK, maybe that does make me feel a *bit* better,' I say when it's gone.

'Honestly, Tabby. All this stuff that's freaked you out – it's just completely normal at this level of sport. Now try to get some sleep: free sea swim to look forward to tomorrow, right? But first, Isha is back in her room – I saw her coming back before I came across. I think she wants to talk to you.'

She gets up, waves at the door and closes it behind her.

75

Isha is sitting up in bed. I'm shocked. She's got bandages on both hands, colourful bruises on her forehead.

'Oh no, Isha. How are you feeling?'

'It's not as bad as it looks, honest. I'm glad you came,' she says. 'I wanted to say thank you.'

'What for? Getting you in that mess?'

'It wasn't your fault.'

'I can't help but feel guilty. I knew you were scared, and it was me that shut the lid. And then it wouldn't open.'

'Truly, it's not your fault. I know you tried to get me out, and you said to Malina about refusing to shut it and stuff. So thanks.'

'It was wrong to make you do that.'

She shrugs, uncertainty behind her eyes. 'Somehow Malina made it all seem reasonable. She talked to me after and convinced me to promise to try again. But once I was back in my room, I didn't want to do it any more. I just want to go home.'

'Are you sure?'

She nods.

'Tell them, then. Anyhow, they're probably bluffing about sending you home if you don't do it, aren't they?'

'I don't know. Maybe. Could try them on it and see, I guess.' She looks closer at me now. 'Is something wrong?'

I shrug, not sure if I should say anything. And what is the point even mentioning the trackers if everybody but me thinks being monitored like that is normal? But that's not the only thing.

'Something *is* wrong, I can see it on your face. I won't tell anyone. What is it?'

I hesitate. I almost told Ariel earlier but for some reason held back. But with Denzi gone, I need to talk to someone.

'Well, it was something I thought I saw. Though maybe I was mistaken.'

'What was it?'

'Have you ever heard of the Penrose Clinic?'

Her eyes open wider. 'I have. I was actually a test-tube baby – you know, IVF. At the Penrose Clinic.'

'No way. *Really?* I'm a Penrose baby, too.'

'Wow.' She shakes her head as if trying to put that thought into place, much like I am.

'That is a huge coincidence, that we're both from that clinic, and both here.'

'Yeah. But what was it that you think you saw?'

'I got lost in the CSME,' I say – a small untruth. 'And I saw the Penrose Clinic symbol on a door downstairs.'

'The four-leaf clover?'

'Yeah – exactly like they use.'

'That's weird if it is them. Why would they be here?'

'I don't know. But maybe I was wrong – I only saw it for a second.'

'Ask somebody?'

I shake my head, uneasy. 'No, and don't you do it either

– ask anybody about it, that is. I don't think I was meant to see it.'

She's frowning, concerned, and now I wish I hadn't mentioned it. 'I'm sorry, you're not feeling great, are you? Just forget about it.'

Back in my room a bit later, I sigh and curl up, arms around one of my pillows. My thoughts are disorganised, unsettled.

How can it be that both of us are Penrose babies?

Maybe this whole swim school is some kind of front for the clinic, but *why*? I can't think of any reason, but I'm going to ask around, see if we are the only ones. And find a way to check that door and see if I'm right about the symbol. And even if all of us here *are* Penrose babies, what would that even mean?

I'll find out, I will. But not yet. For now all I can think about is going swimming in the sea tomorrow morning, and I don't want to give them any reason to not let me go.

It's been a whole week. I tried not to think about it, but it's not like I could ever forget. This longing is always there, a background note to everything else I say and do, getting stronger by the day. All I want is the sea – the feel of it on my skin, the taste of salt on my lips. The joy of diving down, down, under the waves. Maybe once I'm there everything will make sense again.

There's a sound at my window: it's Dickens. I reach across to my desk drawer, to a piece of cheese I'd put there in case he came by. I break a bit off and hold it out. He jumps down to my bed, eats it. Then curls up next to me. It's too hot to want his warmth but it feels good to have another living creature here with me, between me and the door.

I close my eyes and wish for sleep to take me through the night to morning.

I swim, skimming the ocean floor far below the surface then back up to bask in the sun before diving down again, the kin all around. We've feasted and now it's time to play.

But then there is a call of distress. One of us is in trouble and we turn together to investigate – cautiously, as her calls become more urgent.

She's caught in a webbed thing under a ship, thrashing food all around her, all struggling for release, but it tightens and pulls them closer together, drags them through the water. Up, up, up.

We circle around her and search for a way out. There is none.

Her calls grow weaker as it is raised from the water and then we hear her no more.

76

I wait until the last possible moment to turn up for our morning run.

Becker glances at his tracker. 'Just made it,' he says, and we set off.

My longing for the sea is so strong that it's all I can do to not scream with impatience. At the same time the dream I had last night echoes inside me, and I don't want to think about it, not now. Instead, I push myself to hold it all away. I start at such a fast pace that Becker glances back and ups his to stay ahead.

Breathe – evenly – don't – gasp. Long, even strides. The CO_2 burn is starting but – ignore it – keep – going. Don't ease off – at all. Once I do, that'll be it. It's hard, so hard, but then . . . I'm relaxing into the pace, keeping it up but almost losing connection with how my body feels, where I am.

We go around the bend. In the periphery of my vision is the sea, but I don't turn my eyes. Instead I stare at Becker ahead of me, concentrate on trying to go that bit faster to catch him up.

I don't manage it, but still come in second after him.

'Where did that come from?' he says, while we wait for the others.

'I . . . don't . . . know,' I say, struggling to get my breathing under control. 'It all sort of . . . clicked.'

He whoops and holds up a hand for a high five, and that and the feeling in my body, my muscles, from having pushed myself as hard as I could, makes me feel giddy.

And I laugh, my hand against his. Is he actually OK, just wanting to push me to do the best I could at something I wasn't sure I could do at all? Is that the whole point of everything that happens here?

I don't know.

At the dining hall when I go to get my supplements I palm them into my hand, pretend to swallow them with the water and slip them instead into my pocket. I'm not taking them any more, not when I'm not sure what they are.

I take my usual seat across from Isha. Her bruises look even worse than they did last night, but she smiles to see me.

'How are you feeling? Are you coming with us?' I ask.

'Not too bad, and you couldn't keep me away. But I'm not allowed to swim for a few days.' She rolls her eyes. 'I'll sit on the sand and cheer you all on.'

I feel coiled, poised like a spring, and it's not just me. An unbelievable tension fills the small bus as it parks by the beach.

Clothes are left behind. A barely contained walk that wants to be a run crosses the hot sand.

Finally, it's time.

I walk more slowly now, wanting to draw it out. The kiss of cool salt water on my feet, legs, body.

I dive under and swim, going deeper, darker – and then, like flicking a switch I didn't even know was there, something *flips* inside of me. I'm still here but held apart – a passenger in my own body. I detach more and more until I'm not even that.

That is all I know.

Freedom! This is my world. It is right that I should be in control here, and I take it.

Her resistance is weak, feeble. Then she sleeps as I so often am forced to do.

The limits of her body are more than mine once was, and I'm soon weary.

This could be our end. The time and place are fitting; she is weakening, taking me with her.

We're dreaming together, at last.

77

Fear. Pain.

We're being attacked.

We?

We're too weak to fight back. Hands clutch at us, drag us up through the water, to the air. A hard surface. There are voices but it's as though they are far away, fading.

Our throat is opened, air forced into our lungs.

There is a rush of sounds and feelings and I'm pushing it away, breathing, gasping air in and out by myself.

I open my eyes. Coach is there, relief all through her face, and Ariel and a few of the others around us on the boat.

'Welcome back, Tabby,' Coach says.

When we get back to the school, Coach says I have to go to the CSME. She comes with me and helps me walk. I don't notice at first; when I do I shake her off, stand and walk on my own.

'I'm fine,' I say, but I'm scared. I don't understand what happened. One moment I was diving into the water . . . and then I was gone. It wasn't like sometimes when I seem to drift away, to sleep or some other state. It happened all in a rush. I didn't know anything else until I was lying on the boat with everyone freaking out.

'You scared the hell out of us for someone who is fine,' Coach says.

Malina meets us in the waiting area.

'Hi, Tabby,' she says. 'Follow me.'

We go down the stairs to her small room.

'Come. Sit.'

We sit cross-legged on the floor, across from each other.

'Tell me. What went wrong?'

'When?'

'So have things been going wrong for a while? I was thinking mostly about this morning.'

'I don't know. The last thing I remember is diving under the water.'

'And then?'

I shake my head, not wanting to think about it, not wanting to go back.

'Please, Tabby. It's important. If you can't work this out, you'll have to stop going to the sea. It's too dangerous.'

'No!' I'm horrified.

'Don't be afraid. We can sort this out together if you try. Can you do that?'

'I'll do anything.'

'All right. To begin, lie down. Empty your mind: focus on my voice, only my voice. There is nothing else.'

I lie down, *listen* with all of me.

'Close your eyes. Follow my words.

'Breathe in . . .

'Breathe out . . .

'In . . .

'Out . . .

'Relax your fingers, your toes. Your hands and feet.

'In . . .

'Out . . .

'Your forearms, arms, shoulders.

'In . . .

'Out . . .

'Calves, legs. Core.

'In . . .

'Out . . .

'Good. Keep at this rate of breathing.

'In . . .

'Out . . .

'This morning, you arrived at the beach. How did you feel?'

'Excited.' *Beyond anything that a word can hold inside of it.*

'And then you walked across the sand?'

'Yes.'

'And you walked into the water. How did that feel?'

'Amazing; like coming home.' *The only home I know that has always been there.*

'Did you rush in?'

'No. I walked in slowly, sand under my feet, until waves were reaching past my waist.'

'And then?'

'I dived under.' *I feel the rush again, as if the water is all around me now – like I'm reborn.*

'All right. Now take yourself back to the next thing you remember. You don't need to feel it or justify it, just let it wash over you. It's all right. You're safe here, I promise.'

And I'm listening to her words, her voice, trying to do as she says.

There's a rush of colours and feelings, an explosion of joy that I can't interpret now. I didn't know what was happening; I still don't. And then . . . and then . . .

Nothing.

Until fear. Panic. I'm being attacked. I strike out, but I'm too feeble and weak. I'm being moved. Forced to breathe. And then there is *pain* – not the physical sort, more, the essence of who and what I am . . .

Being wrenched away to die again.

I breathe in sharply and sit up.

'What is wrong with me?'

'What happened? Tell me.'

I try. In halting words, stops and starts. But how do you explain the inexplicable? It was all sensations and feelings, nothing like a memory normally would be.

'We talked before about the rope – the rope you must hold on to to get back to yourself if you begin to drift away. This is what you must do.'

'But that other time I let go of it. I only got it back because it twisted around my neck.'

'How about, instead, the rope is tied around your hand in a tight knot. You can't let go; you can't untie it. Can you visualise that?'

'I'll try.'

'Do it now.'

She has me lie down again, go through the steps to relax, to slow my breathing, and then . . . and then . . .

Hold.

I'm afraid to let go again; afraid what will happen if I do. But Malina is there. Her voice soothes, encourages . . .

I drift into the sea – the one in my mind. It's cool, safe, in the deep.

Joy! I swim faster and faster along the bottom of the sea.

But something is slowing me down. It's a rope – silver in the dim half-light – and it's tied to my hand. It's pulling me up to the light above?

I want to stay.

I want to go!

I'm torn, conflicted, confused – but it doesn't matter. The rope around my wrist pulls me up, up to the light.

I sit up and breathe in deeply.

'Well done, Tabby.' Malina is beaming. 'You did it!'

'What did I do?'

'You held your breath for nearly thirty minutes, and then, when you needed to breathe, you pulled yourself out and did it.'

'I still don't understand.'

'The rope is kind of like a safety net. This will make more sense to you in time, I promise. You're doing very well.'

She's so happy, her arms are around me in a hug, and I'm relieved that whatever it is, it's working. I won't be kept away from what I need.

Then I see it. There, on her shoulder, where her top has pulled to one side as her arms are around me. A tattoo.

Circles. Four circles, exactly like Cate's drawing.

Beware The Circle.

78

Somehow I say goodbye to Malina, and thank you, and get back to my room. It's almost dinner time but I can't face anyone yet.

The Circle. The symbol Cate drew – it was there, on Malina's shoulder.

How can this be? What does it mean? Does it have anything to do with what happened to me today, the Penrose Clinic being here, or any of the other weird coincidences?

I don't know, and everything is rushing around and around in my head, looking for connections and finding none.

I'm too exhausted to think straight. It's hot, humid, and I open my window wide and lean out. There's not a trace of a breeze.

Think. Focus.

That whole thing with going to the sea, what happened there – then Malina – distracted me from what I must do. I have to find out if any others here are Penrose babies. I have to find out if that door really does hide the Penrose Clinic in the CSME, and what, if anything, it has to do with The Circle.

None of these things I can do alone in my room.

I open my door just as Ariel comes out of hers.

'Hey, are you all right?' she says.

'I'm still breathing.' I hesitate. 'Come in for a sec.' I close the door once she does. 'What happened? I mean from what you saw?'

'Well, you disappeared down deep. Coach had us looking for you. We were really starting to panic; you were under for too long.' She hesitates. 'This is going to sound mad. But this dolphin came out of nowhere and pushed me in the right direction, and there you were, lying on the seabed, not moving, tangled in seaweed. When I tried to drag you up to the surface you struggled. I had to get Zara and a few of the others to help. You weren't breathing until Coach used the oxygen tank – it's under pressure and made you breathe, then you took over. So now you tell me: what happened? And why did this random dolphin show me where you were?'

A dolphin. Like the one that nudged me up to breathe after Cate died? I'd convinced myself I imagined that. Did it really happen?

'I honestly don't know,' I say. A random dolphin, or a friend? I shake my head. This does sound mad, like Ariel said.

She hesitates. 'Tabby, you'd tell me, wouldn't you, if you were trying to, well, end things?'

'*What?* Do you mean, like kill myself? I wouldn't do that.' I'm shocked but something of what she said echoes inside and there is a sense of panic. Is that what I was doing?

No. I could never do that. Never.

'It's like you weren't breathing *on purpose*. Coach had to make you.'

'It's not that – it's more like I was unconscious. Malina just showed me a way to come back to myself if it happens again.'

She is looking back at me, nodding. 'Is it like when you hold

316

your breath a long time – like I did the other day – and you're kind of . . . not there?'

'Yes. Just like that.'

Her eyes echo the fear in mine.

'What is going on with us?' I say.

But now she's shaking her head. 'Nothing. It's just training and stuff. Nothing.' Is she refusing to think about it? 'Anyhow. Are you coming to dinner or what?'

'Yes.'

She links her arm in mine, and we're heading down the stairs, across to the dining hall. We're a little late; no one else is around. And now I remember what I wanted to ask her before.

'Ariel, have you ever heard of the Penrose Clinic?'

'I don't think so. Why?'

'You're not by any chance an IVF baby?'

'As far as I know my parents did it the old-fashioned way, though even thinking about that makes my skin crawl.'

Well, there goes that theory.

After dinner I make excuses and head straight back.

'Tabby, wait.' I turn; it's Isha. 'You'll never guess.'

'What?'

'Zara – she's a Penrose baby, too.'

'No way. Really?'

Her eyes are wide. 'I don't understand what all of this is about.'

'Have you asked anyone else?'

'No. You?'

'Just Ariel. And she says she isn't.'

317

'Still, three of us – all here? Strange, isn't it? And there could be more.'

'Listen. Can you do me a favour?'

'Of course. What?'

'After lights out, can I come round and get you to wear my tracker? I want to check that door I saw, see if it really is the Penrose symbol.'

'What if you get caught? They'll send you home for sure.'

'I don't care. I have to know.'

79

I slip into Isha's room at midnight as agreed.

'Still good to do this?' I whisper.

'Yes. I just wish I could come with you.'

I undo my tracker and quickly slip it over Isha's other wrist and do it up.

'Try to sleep, I'm not sure how long I'll be.'

'Be careful.'

I walk silently down the dark hall, then the stairs. Open the door a crack and look out into the night, listening; it's quiet.

I step outside and walk. I feel light, almost carefree; I wasn't aware how heavy wearing a tracker weighed on me once I knew what it did.

When I get to the CSME I try the front door; I'm not surprised to find that it's locked. My real hope is that, as it's been so very hot, there will be a window someone has forgotten to close.

I check all around the front of the building; no luck. Down one side of the building likewise, and I'm feeling increasingly despondent that they're too careful with security for me to get in this easily. But when I head around the back of the building, there – at last! – is an open window.

It's a bit too high to reach. What can I stand on?

There are some potted plants around the front.

I go back, find one that looks big enough and drag it along to the back, sweating in this airless heat.

Once it is in place under the open window I step up on the pot. It's a sash window. I hope it isn't locked part open. I push; it doesn't give. I try again, harder and harder still. Finally it goes up. I open it as far as I can and then pull myself up and through the space.

There's a loud crash as I knock into something on a desk under the window, and I freeze. Is anyone here at night to hear that? Heart beating fast, I count down a few minutes, listening, but no one comes.

I'm in an office; it was a vase of flowers I knocked over. I hope whoever returns to this desk tomorrow will think Dickens or some other animal knocked them over.

I'm disoriented as to where I am. The ground slopes down to the back and it's a big building, so I think the level I've come in must be down a flight of stairs from the front entrance on the main floor.

I go down the hall. Past more offices. To another door, that leads to stairs up and down. I think this is the landing that leads to Malina's rooms. If so, what I'm looking for must be down these stairs.

It's dark with not even moonlight in the windowless stairwell, and I'm wishing Simone had thought to put a torch in my case full of endless things I might need. I'm feeling my way down, listening for anything at all. It's quiet.

At the bottom of the stairs I keep one hand on the wall and walk down the hall.

It's still quiet, dark. I keep opening my eyes wider as if that will help me see better.

My hand feels the frame of a door. If I'm where I think I am, it will be the locker room.

I listen carefully at the door; no sound. It's pitch black inside and I feel for a light switch, risk turning it on. It's so bright I blink and blink again.

There are the white coats on hooks, the row of lockers. What looks like a laundry bin. I search the coats, one after another. Surely someone has left their pass on the front – but no. I go through the laundry bin; it's a no again. Next, the lockers. I go through them quickly, finding only photos, snacks, spare shoes and umbrellas, despairing more and more, but in the second-to-last locker there is a small handbag. Inside, under a bunch of junk, is a pass.

I turn out the lights and wait a moment to let my eyes get used to the dark again.

I freeze, heart racing. Did I hear something?

I listen, not breathing. All is quiet. And then – *thud thud*. Very faint, so faint I could have imagined it.

I'm about to dismiss it when I hear it again.

I stand there, caught in indecision; part of me wants to run, but I can't turn back now, not when I'm so close.

I open the door, step back into the dark hall. The next door is the one that was locked; the woman I saw held her pass up to the plate thing and it opened.

I feel for the plate in the dark, hold the pass against it: nothing.

Try again; still nothing.

No. After all this I *am* getting through this door. Was it more a swipe across than touching it to the plate?

I try that, and this time there is a soft *click*. I push the door open and go in. There's a small window so there is enough moonlight to vaguely see the shape of a door across the room. I walk up to it, but it's too dark to see what is on the glass panel.

Thud, thud: louder again and my instinct is to run – I'm getting closer to whatever is making that sound. But I'm not leaving without doing what I came to do, and for that, I need light.

I feel all along the walls for switches; nothing. OK, maybe there are switches on the other side of this door?

It's locked. Will the pass work here, too? I swipe it; another soft *click*. I push the door open; there are switches I can feel on the wall. I flick them down and lights on both sides of the door come on.

Thud, thud: a little louder again.

I hold the door open, step back through it to look at the glass. Even though I felt pretty sure what I saw, it's still a shock: it *is* the Penrose Clinic four-leaf clover.

Thud, thud.

Time to get out of here. I hold the door and reach back through for the light switches. As I do, I glance once again at the four-leaf clover on the glass, seeing it now from the reverse. There's something about it, and I look and look again, then come back around to look at it from the front.

Thud, thud.

Dread twists my stomach. Now that I see it I can't believe I didn't see it before.

Inside the four-leaf clover, hidden in plain sight within the image – it's the four circles, the way Cate drew them, one in each leaf of the clover. Exactly like the one I saw on Malina's shoulder.

It's more obvious from the back, with the foreground and background reversed, but easy enough to see from the front as well once I'm aware of it.

What does this mean?

Is the Penrose Clinic a front for The Circle?

Is this the reason I was hunting for – the *why* Cate took me away from my parents? Was it to get me away from the Penrose Clinic and therefore The Circle?

Thud, thud.

I don't know what they're doing here, or at the clinic at home for that matter. I could turn around, go back to Isha's room, get my tracker back and pretend nothing has happened. Bide my time until I can either call home or get away on the next sea day.

But what is the Penrose Clinic doing here? Does it have anything to do with me?

This is the moment: decide. Go back, or go on.

Heart racing and fear twisting my gut – of being caught, or what I might I find? – I step all the way through the door and let it shut behind me.

Thud, thud.

80

I turn out the lights and wait a moment for my eyes to adjust. It's not as dark on this side even though there are no windows; there are little lights on computers, printers, other equipment. I walk along until I reach another door; it leads to more stairs.

I go down. The next level is some sort of aquarium – there are tanks covering walls on both sides. Fish glide silently, eerie with only dim lights in the tanks to light the room.

There are also several empty tanks that look a lot like the ones we used for training with Malina, except instead of glass walls these ones have bars.

There is another door at the back. *Thud, thud*. Louder again, and my hands are shaking as I open it.

Rough stone steps down. The air is cooler, and damp; it tastes of the sea.

The *thud, thud* comes from below. It repeats again and again but doesn't sound like a machine. It's not regular enough.

The further I go the more there is a feeling of dread inside me, dank and deep. A panic that has nothing to do with where I am or anything I've seen. It's *fear* and *pain* and it's as if I've been here before, but of course I never have. Everything inside me is screaming to get away, but it's like I'm caught in someone else's will and have to go on.

At the bottom of the steps is another locked door. Hands

shaking, I swipe the pass on the plate. The door clicks open, darkness beyond.

Thud, thud: it's louder again.

I make myself step through. Now the walls feel like uneven rock, and there are steps down into water – water I can sense rather than see. The air tastes of salt: this must be the old caves Denzi told me about, flooded now with the rising seas. But even though it's the sea – and every part of me longs for it all the time – that isn't true, not now. Instead of attracted, I'm repelled.

Thud, thud.

I've never been here before. What is it I'm afraid of?

It isn't just the strange noises, the unknown in the dark. My body is reacting in a way I don't understand.

I have to know what is here.

I feel my way down the steps, forcing myself to go on until the water is almost up to my shoulders. I overbreathe a moment. Hold air within – and swim under.

After a moment my eyes adjust enough to see vague shapes. They resolve into tanks, like the empty ones with bars upstairs.

Some have fish within that shimmer and seem to catch what little light there is. They swim in circles, looking at me as if they know who I am.

Thud, thud.

I'm pulled on by the sound.

Thud, thud.

As I go down, deeper underwater, there are more fish in tanks. If that is what they are. Something about them is . . . *unnatural*. They don't swim. Some sit on the bottom of their tank, with almost-limbs that hold the bars.

325

Thud, thud.

Another tank. A fish as big as me. She turns — it is a she — and looks at me. There's a rock in her hand, one she's been using to strike at the bars — the sounds that I could hear echoing in the water.

Her face . . . is *human*. It's . . . it's *Ariel's* face? But the eyes aren't human the way they look at me. And locked in a tank like this she must be able to breathe underwater? Her body, her almost-arms, are shorter than human. Her almost-hands hold the rock, but the rest of her is more like a fish. She looks at me and I look at her, but I don't understand what my eyes are seeing.

She rushes at the bars, reaches through and grabs at my neck, slamming me into the bars.

I can't stop myself from screaming and then I'm taking in water, choking, kicking against the tank. I push at the tank with my feet until finally her grip loosens and I get away. I swim in a rush along the cave to where I came in and surface into darkness, to cough and breathe and cough some more.

The *thud, thud* begins again.

Who or what was *that*? What is this place? Have they been doing some crazy experiments with people and fish? This *has* to be illegal. Is that why this branch of the clinic is hidden the way that it is?

What does it have to do with me? There is *something* there; I can almost reach out and grasp understanding, but I'm horrified and back away from it instead.

Thud, thud.

What now?

If I go back, there's no way I'll be able to pretend everything is normal. And if they work out what I've seen, what are the chances of them ever letting me leave?

No. I'm getting out of here, and I'm doing it *now*. The only way I can think to do so means going back past *she* or *it* or whatever it is, underwater, and finding the way to the sea. I'm shaking with dread to even think of it.

But there's no other choice.

I force my body to relax, to give myself as much time underwater as I can.

Overbreathe; hold. Go under. Swim.

I'm swimming as quickly as I can without wasting energy, down through the cave, past all the tanks. Past the one with almost-Ariel in it. Something in her eyes holds me and makes me want to stop again, but I don't know how long I'll have to hold my breath, with no idea how far or how long it will take me to get out of this place – or even if the way out exists. I go past her, wondering now why it seems I can see so much better in this dark water than I can above it.

After a while I reach a larger cave.

I search the edges of the space, feeling the pressure to breathe so strong it's hard to keep going.

A rock juts out – there is space behind it. It's too dark to see anything, but I search blindly with my hands, my feet, but it's rock, rock, more rock. Has the way out been blocked by a fall?

There are spots in my vision. I'm *desperate* to breathe.

It's tempting to make this stop. To give up. Stop struggling, take in water, and it'll all be over soon. Lost in the water and the darkness.

I relax, stop fighting. *Switch.*

Why did she bring us here?

I'm full of desperate fury and rage, and strike at the rock but the way out is blocked.

This could be it: it could end, if I let it. Like I tried to do in the sea, but they dragged us out.

But not here. NEVER HERE. I will not die in this place again!

We swim back. Past the cave with the she-fish with the strange face and eyes. Up the flooded steps.

She forgot her feeble rope, but no matter. This time, I let her win to get us out of here.

Wake up!

My eyes open and air slams into my chest. I cough and breathe and cough again, coming back slowly to here and now.

I'm back by the way in – where I first went underwater. What happened?

No time for that. Get out of here. NOW.

I half run back out through the labs and offices, through doors and up stairs, not even trying to be quiet any more. When I get to the office window I came in through, I force myself to calm down, to breathe easier. To move with stealth.

I climb out on to the plant pot and jump down. I want to run, to leave it there, but I don't want to leave a trail. I heave it bit by bit back around to the front of the building, finding it harder now as I'm so tired.

All is quiet as I walk across the dark lane, then the school grounds. My mind is reeling both with what I saw, and what happened to me afterwards. I was out of oxygen and there was no way I could swim back to save myself, and then – like at the sea day – something *switched* inside of me, and whatever it was took over. Just thinking about it makes me panic so much that it's hard to walk.

Go careful; be quiet.

I calm myself again. I've made it to our building, up the stairs and to Isha's door.

I open the door, carefully, quietly.

The lights come on.

81

'Hi, Tabby.'

I'm blinking at the bright lights after so long in the dark.

It's Nadya. In Isha's room? Where's Isha?

Nadya is looking calmly back at me. 'I see your tendency to wander is still there, and this time you had an accomplice.'

'Where is she?'

'Don't worry about Isha. Let's focus on you. Where have you been?'

'I . . . I couldn't sleep, so I went for a walk. And then a swim – it's so hot,' I add quickly, realising I need to explain why my clothes and hair are wet. That's when I remember the door pass. It's still in my pocket. I should have put it back where I found it and I'm panicking she'll see the outline of it in my wet shorts, ask me what it is.

'I see.' She's looking back at me with eyes that don't believe. She sighs. 'You've broken so many rules, Tabby.'

'So send me home.'

'We'll meet with Director Lang tomorrow to discuss just that. Go to her office at nine a.m. For now, put this back on.' She hands me my tracker. 'Go to your room. It's late; try to get some sleep.'

Back in my room, I take out the pass. What do I do with it? I look around my room but anywhere I can think of putting it

– under the mattress, in a drawer, in my case – would be easily found if anyone comes looking for it.

I lean out the window. I noticed the gutters rattling when Dickens was running along them that first time. I hoist myself up to sit on the window ledge, reach as far as I can along and jam the pass under the gutter, then pull leaf litter around it – it's out of sight.

I lie on top of my bed. What I saw hidden under the CSME tonight – it has to be *so illegal*. That girl-fish. She looked like Ariel?

Ariel didn't know about the Penrose Clinic so I don't see how she can be a Penrose baby, but even if she were: what would it mean?

I feel like there is something I'm close to understanding, but it's like looking over the edge of a cliff and not wanting to jump. I can't even think about it without a sick feeling of dread.

I push it away for now, to focus on one thing I do know: I have to get out of here.

There isn't much chance they won't work out what I've done. I was in such a panic I easily could have knocked things over or left doors open and not even realised. If they find things amiss and put that together with me being AWOL . . . will they work out what I know? If they do, they won't let me go. They won't want me to tell anyone what I saw.

Maybe the director will send me home, but somehow, I'm sure it won't be that easy.

I need rest, desperately, but can't still my thoughts. Images flit through my mind, like watching a jumbled-up movie on fast forward:

The tattoo on Malina's shoulder.

The Penrose Clinic's four-leaf clover.

Denzi. Where are you? And Isha, too.

Cate's desperate face, the last time I saw her. *Beware The Circle*, she said.

The drawing in my notebook.

The tattoo on Malina's shoulder . . .

'Now?'

Laughter. 'Go on, then.'

The sandcastle is almost as tall as me. I stand, one hand on Cate to steady myself and then launch myself at it, pushing, kicking until it falls and sand flies everywhere.

I'm laughing now, too – we're laughing together.

Cate is sitting on the sand. She puts an arm around me, pulls me close, kisses my forehead.

'Again!' I say.

'You want to build another one?'

I clap my hands.

'OK.'

The bucket, the spade. Another castle is soon built to be knocked over, but I'm sleepy now and snuggle into Cate. She strokes my hair.

I run my finger around and around on her ankle, tracing the circles drawn there. They don't wash off, not like when I found a pen once and scribbled on my knees and hands.

Around and around and around . . .

82

I wake slowly, wanting to stay in the warmth of Cate's arms, but the more I wake up the more I know it was just a dream. Cate will never hold me again. My tears are there before I remember how the dream ended.

There was a tattoo, of four circles. On Cate's ankle?

This doesn't make *sense*. She didn't have that or any other tattoo – I'd have seen it all the time if she did.

Oh. She had a scar, though, on that same place on her ankle. Maybe she did have a tattoo there, but it was removed?

If that's true, did Cate belong to The Circle?

It was a dream, but it felt so *real*. Did it come from a real memory, maybe triggered by seeing Malina's tattoo?

I don't know. But I *do* know this: Cate said to beware The Circle. She drew four circles in a particular way; Malina's tattoo was just the same as Cate drew it.

Did coming here bring me exactly to what Cate warned me against?

At nine a.m. I stand in front of Director Lang's desk. Malina pushes a chair towards me, sits on the other one.

'You have been busy,' Director Lang says. She's looking at some notes on a tablet. 'Were you meeting someone last night? Is there someone else for us to track down and punish?'

She means a boy. I feel colour rising in my cheeks.

She misinterprets. 'I thought so.' She shakes her head. 'I don't suppose you'll save us some trouble and tell us who it was and what you were up to?'

I stay silent.

'We did work out that this was done sometimes last summer – a tracker put on someone else to stop detection. We added a program that flagged it up if the readings from two trackers were too similar. Now, Tabby: what are we going to do with you?'

I find my voice. 'Send me home.' *Please*.

'That would be the easy option. We never like our swimmers to take the easy way, though, do we, Malina?'

Malina shakes her head.

'No. You'll stay, but you're in isolation this week. Separate training and meals.' Malina hands me some sheets of paper, and I'm looking at her, then at Director Lang. 'Also, you've lost your privileges. No more trips to the sea or phone calls until further notice. We may lift these restrictions if you tell us where you were last night.'

This isn't it. Is it? They're still deciding what I know, what to do. Until they do, they're making sure I can't talk to anyone inside or outside of the school.

What about Isha – what has happened to her?

'Where is Isha?' I ask.

'Given her unfortunate accident in the apnoea tank, she decided to go home.' I'm staring at Director Lang. Isha said as much earlier – that she wanted to go home rather than try that again. But in the middle of the night? Without saying goodbye?

Like Denzi. The two people I confided in are both gone. I can't involve anyone else in case the same thing happens to them.

83

'Where've you been all morning?' Ariel asks.

'Long story,' I say.

Nadya is at my shoulder now. 'I'm afraid Tabby has broken a few rules and will be eating and training in isolation.' Ariel's eyes open wider and everyone is watching as Nadya leads me to a small table set for one next to the staff table.

I sit down and my food is even brought to me, so I don't go to get it with everyone else. My mouth is dry; it tastes like dust. I feel as if I'm naked – everyone is looking at me, their eyes trying to pry inside.

Block it out. Think.

I have to get out of here. I can't see a way to get over the fences; the sea caves are blocked. The only other way is down the cliffs to the sea.

The gate is locked but would be easy enough to climb – right over the danger sign. Denzi said there were rock falls, that you'd have to have a death wish to try it. Heights don't bother me, but when a slip or fall could mean crashing on to rocks below, can I do it? Do I dare?

Assuming I can even get away from everyone to get to the locked gate, as soon as I go over it someone will come running because of my tracker. I'd have to climb down the cliff *fast* – not a good idea when taking time and care are essential. So I have to get rid of my tracker.

Even though they worked out that Isha was wearing both of our trackers, it couldn't have been instantaneous. I got away before Nadya came. But there's no way I can ask anyone else to take that risk for me, not when I don't know what happened to Isha and Denzi.

Lunch is over. People are getting up and starting to leave. What am I doing?

I grab my sheets and my stomach sinks. I've got one-to-one training with Malina.

84

'Hi.' I keep my eyes on Malina's, resolutely away from her shoulder. The tattoo is hidden by her top, but I know it's there. *Beware The Circle; beware Malina.*

'Hi, Tabby.' She smiles, the same as always. 'Come in. How are you feeling?'

I shrug, say nothing. Sit down.

'Ah, a difficult day perhaps, away from your peers? Look, just tell me what you were doing last night, and I'll see if I can convince Director Lang to return things to normal for you.'

'I just went for a walk.' *To CSME.* 'And a swim.' *In secret, deep places, behind the Penrose Clinic door.*

'I wish you'd trust me. Ah well, perhaps in time. Now today, we're going to reinforce the training from last time.'

Again and again she gets me to close my eyes, relax myself in stages, and hold my breath. But again and again I fail to let go and disconnect. I can't relax enough, not when I'm alone with Malina. Not any more.

'This isn't working today,' she says, finally. 'Why don't you go back to your room until dinner?'

I get up, turn for the door. Look back. 'Would it be OK if I go for a run around the perimeter? I missed it this morning.'

She tilts her head. 'All right, if you answer one question.'

'What is it?'

'Did you meet anyone last night?'

I pause. Does it matter? 'No,' I say. At least this way they won't be looking for someone else to blame.

Her eyes on mine are considering, then she nods. 'Go have your run. We'll try again tomorrow.'

The first time around the perimeter I don't stop by the gate; I slow a little, thinking about what I have to do. Looking at the land around and seeing where it is higher and lower and the best way to move to the fence unseen.

The second time around I stop by the gate, hoping if anyone notices they'll think I'm out of breath and need a break. Quickly I study the way down that I thought I saw before.

I still think it can be done. If it isn't wet. If rocks I cling to don't come loose and fall down, to crash below. If that doesn't cause a rock fall that takes me with it.

I head off to do the rest of the lap. As I run, the problem of my tracker goes around in my mind, but I can't see a solution.

I head for my room. Dickens is sitting in my window, licking his paws.

'Did you come for your treat?' I say, and get out a bit of cheese from my desk drawer. He jumps down next to me on the bed. His warm, rough tongue licks my fingers to get every last crumb, then he rubs his head against my hand until I stroke him.

'They can't keep me away from all my friends. I've still got you,' I say. Purrs rumble through him; he half lies on my knees, head back so I can stroke his chin and throat and rub his tummy. His heart beats fast under my hand.

His head perks up – he hears something. He jumps back up to the window and runs along the roof.

Must be nice to go wherever you like and not have to wear a tracker. And I smile to think of Dickens putting up with that.

Then I smile some more. I think I've got a plan.

85

It's almost two a.m. I'm alert and full of nervous energy, bits of cheese taken from dinner all over the window ledge and leading a trail to my bed. *Dickens, where are you?*

Finally there's the sudden thud of him jumping into my room.

'What took you so long?' I ask as he follows the cheesy trail. 'Secret cat business, I guess.'

I give Dickens another small piece. He flops down next to me, and I rub under his chin and can feel his fast heartbeat again.

Will this work? I don't know, but I'm going to try.

'Dickens, would it be OK if I give you this – my tracker – for a while? It'd really help me out.'

He stares at me as if he is thinking about it very carefully. I hold out another piece of cheese on the palm of my hand and he takes it. I'll take that as a yes.

First I undo his collar, and give him a good scratch where it was. I put it aside and undo the tracker strap, careful to keep it in contact with my wrist until the last second. I stroke him again and quickly transfer the tracker from me to him. I just hold it against his neck for a moment while he eats another piece of cheese.

I do it up around his neck – he's a small cat, and on the loosest setting it's just the right size to be a collar.

'Thank you,' I say, and scratch all around his ears. There is a deep rumbling purr inside him: I wonder what the tracker will make of that?

He curls up on my bed, watching through slitted eyes as I change to a dark T-shirt and shorts.

I apologise for leaving him in my room. Tell him it's all right to go out the window if he wants to leave, but it'd be great if he could wait a while. He seems to say that is OK, and I walk down the dark hall.

I head down the stairs, listening for any noises at all. If Dicken's heart rate is too different to mine they might come running to check it out, but as long as I'm out of sight by then I'll have a good head start.

I open the door and set out at a run. The moon is bright tonight and I thank the sky for this gift.

When I reach the gate I stop, regain control of my breathing. It's so hot and still, and I'm sweating. I dry my hands on my T-shirt before climbing over the fence.

The edge is three metres or so from the gate. When I get nearer I see something I couldn't from behind it: the grassy slope on this side reaches out and then it looks like the rock cuts in underneath. Will it hold my weight?

Dark water churns below – that means rocks, just under the surface.

I'm crazy, that's it. Aren't I? This is *insane*. I should go back, hope nobody has noticed what I tried to do.

Caught in indecision, I look back the way I came.

A light flickers, goes out, flickers again. Someone with a torch is on the path. Have they found Dickens with my tracker; are they looking for me?

Fear and adrenalin surge through me. I drop to the ground on my stomach and edge backwards to the drop. Asking sun, sea, earth and sky for their care, I swing my feet, legs, over the edge. Committed now, gripping tight to grass and moss-covered rocks, easing further over the edge, questing with my toes. Further and I'm slipping. I can't hold on—

My feet touch solid rock.

I slide down with a bump, careful not to cry out – somehow managing to scramble back in instead of falling. I'm under the overhang. I'm panting, struggling for the nerve to go on. Not that there is much choice now; having half fallen to this ledge I can't get back up the way I came.

I start to pick out the path I want to follow with my eyes, when light shines from above. I freeze.

There are low voices. A scrambling noise – is someone climbing the fence?

'Don't go too near the edge. It's dangerous.'

'Just need to make sure.' The torch is swinging back and forth above and I'm hoping I'm tucked in enough that I can't be seen.

'She wouldn't be stupid enough to try this. Let's go.'

Steps retreating. The light is gone.

The breath I was holding comes out in a rush.

Just stupid enough is all it takes, I guess. I give it a few more minutes – minutes that seem so long – before clinging on with my hands, backing out and reaching down tentatively with my feet. Inching along and then down to the most likely place to climb a step down, and then another. Move one hand, then a foot, then the other hand, the other foot. A foot slips once but I hold with the other three points of contact until I find a better toehold.

It's working; I'm actually doing this! Before long I'm more than halfway down and over most of what looks the worst of it. There's just this next long reach across to the left and then down. I can feel the ocean spray now and I'm so hot, it's a relief. I reach across with my left hand, feel for a good grip, then move my foot – almost too far to reach but should just—

The rock gives way under my left hand. Splayed across the rockface like I am, my weight is too far to the left and now I'm falling. My hands are scrabbling uselessly against rock, trying to find something to hold and finding nothing.

A scream is building inside me, but I have just enough control to choke it off.

Then the back of my head smacks against rock and that is all I know.

Pain, yes, but I've had worse. She retreats from it as we hit the water; control is now mine. I judge the current, the waves, the rocks, and am more careful than I would have once been; she is so fragile and that means I am, too.

We swim underwater, out, out. I break the surface to breathe and look back; there are lights on the cliff so we dive down deep.

I know her plan: to swim along the coast, to find that beach with the bench. But what I should do now is not straightforward.

That place: why did she take us there last night? I never wanted to see it again.

A place of torture and death.

I could keep swimming out as far as we can go until it is all over, like I tried to do the last time we were in the sea.

But now I see how I need her – how we need each other.

We will *be avenged.*

So I swim along the coast, head for her meeting place. The sea is warm – oddly so.

Soon the kin are alongside me, going slow and circling to keep me safe. It's good to feel their concern.

They're worried, anxious. Something unseen further out to sea has acted on the surface water, warming it, they say. Some fish without the sense to get away from the place have died.

Why? What will happen?

None of us know, but dread runs through the kin.

86

I'm bathed in the early light of sunrise when I open my eyes. I'm floating on my back in the sea – the water is still, warm. Warmer than it should be.

Where am I? I tread water and look around. Land is near; the curve of the coast is familiar. It's the bay, the one with the café and bench.

I don't remember swimming here; the last thing I remember is that handhold I had on the cliff breaking away, the fear, falling. Hitting my head. And now I'm here?

I feel the back of my head and wince. There's a good bump; that must be why I can't remember.

I swim for the shore.

Is Simone the sort of person who keeps her phone next to her while she sleeps and checks it as soon as she wakes up? I'm imagining her in bed, waking and checking the beach webcam as part of her morning ritual, using positive visualisation to convince myself that she *will*. If not, what do I do? I haven't got anything but the clothes I went out in so many hours ago.

I'm nearly at the beach now. The water is shallow, but I stumble when I try to stand. I take a moment to get used to being upright, then walk the rest of the way to the water's edge.

Exhausted and without water to support my weight any more, the bench seems far away. I force one step forwards, another.

Finally I reach it, and sink on to it, *willing* Simone to be up early and see me here.

The sun is coming up slowly, red in the sea as if born in fire deep inside. With it comes the warmth it has too much of lately.

I stretch out on the bench, keeping my face towards the camera so there'll be no doubt who is here if she looks.

Please, Simone. I'm counting on you.

The sun is too bright and I close my eyes.

87

'Excuse me?'

Awake in an instant I spring up on the bench, full of panic and poised to run. A man stands nearby; I don't know who he is.

'Are you Holly? I'm Brian from the café. Your mother Simone called, asked if we could get you some breakfast. And to tell you that she is on her way.'

Relief is so strong I almost cry. 'Thank you,' is all I manage to say.

He's looking at me curiously as I stand up.

'Come out of the sun,' he says. I follow him to the café but don't want to go in: if anyone comes looking for me, I'm cornered. There's a table against the back of the café with an umbrella to hold the sun at bay; the building will block anyone looking for me unless they come all the way around. He brings me water and tea to start. I have a long drink of water and savour the tea – it's the best tea, *ever*.

The sun has moved up the sky; I've been asleep on the bench at least a few hours. My shorts and T-shirt are pretty much dry, but I'm covered in sand, sticky from salt and sweat. It's so hot and there isn't even a trace of a breeze. It feels how things are just before a spectacular thunderstorm. Even though I'm not in the sea any more, it's like I can't get enough oxygen into my lungs in this heat; thinking about breathing and how to breathe just makes it feel worse.

What's happening back at the swim school? Are they still looking for me there, or have they worked out I left by sea?

I'm thinking about everything but what scares me the most. That girl-fish with Ariel's face. Her eyes looked like Ariel's, but they were weirdly blank without her personality to go with them. Just thinking about her and when she grabbed me, tried to strangle me through the bars – the fear and the horror are back.

And all the while my mind is veering towards what, if anything, this all has to do with me, and the other swimmers there – the ones who hadn't trained for years, who just had a knack for swimming, like I do. But I can't focus on that too closely, not now.

Footsteps pull me back to where I am: it's Brian.

'Our best breakfast,' he says and puts a plate in front of me – but it's eggs on toast with what looks like some sort of creamy sauce and salmon. Definitely not vegan; I'd been in too much of a state about everything to think to say, and after him helping me like this I'm not sending it back.

'Thank you.'

After he's gone, I take the fork and knife, and gingerly cut into the egg. Yolk runs out, rich yellow.

The salmon is pink – smoked, I think. I'm gripped by a desire to try it. I cut a small piece of it, then hesitate. Leaving it will not make it swim in the sea again, will it? It'd just waste what it was.

I sniff – it's salty, smoky – and then, I taste. And the smell and the taste and the feel of it in my mouth are *amazing*. And the eggs are good, too, and I've eaten it all – almost inhaled it – before

I've even thought about what I'm doing, not sure if I've even chewed properly.

That's so *weird*. I've never been the least bit bothered by not eating this kind of stuff before, and now all I can think is that I want more. That, and a nap.

I lean against the brick of the building, trying and failing to keep my eyes open.

88

Footsteps come close. I open my eyes – ready to run if I have to – but Simone appears around the back of the café.

'Holly?'

I'm out of my seat and running into a hug.

Simone pulls away, brushes my hair from my face. 'Are you all right? How did you get here? You're covered in sand.'

'I'm OK, really I am. Now.'

'What's happened, what's wrong?'

'Can we just go? Please. And I'll tell you on the way home.'

'Of course. Do you want to stop by the school on the way to get your stuff?'

'No!' I say, and must say it too sharply; Simone's concern shows on her face. 'Can we get it sent later instead?'

'All right.'

As we leave, Brian is putting boards over the windows, and a closed sign on the door. 'Head for the hills; a storm is on the way,' he says when Simone goes to pay for my breakfast. And I notice now the darkening sky.

'There wasn't anything forecast, was there?' Simone says.

He taps the side of his nose. 'I can smell it and I trust my nose over the BBC.'

The wind picks up as we walk to the car. We get inside it just as the first fat raindrops begin to fall.

'Looks like he was right,' I say.

'Made it into the car just in time. Before we go, I brought something for you,' Simone says. She holds up her wrist: the bracelet is there.

'Thank you,' I say.

She takes it off, hands it to me and I put it on my own wrist.

We start up the road and I'm trying to work out what to say, how to explain what happened without sounding crazy, but my thoughts are taken away by the storm. The rain is so heavy now that Simone is slowing right down to see the road. It's hitting with such fury that it's bouncing off the front of the car. Lightning flashes across the sky; there is a deafening boom of thunder at almost the same instant. The wind is going crazy, too – the rain being blown around so much it seems to be hitting us from all sides.

It's wild, free; it's not just weather. Somehow the storm is alive and I feel the way I feel when I dive into the sea, but we're driving down the road.

'This looks fierce,' Simone says.

She tries the radio; it's crackling but then starts to come clear: '. . . and batten down the hatches on the south coast. A storm . . . hiss, hiss . . . storm surge . . . hiss hiss.'

'Should we stop and wait it out?' I say.

'I think we should keep going and get away from it instead,' she answers. 'Anyhow, Ali is coming from London to meet us at home; he'll worry if we're late.'

We go around a corner and follow the road as it dips down along the coast. The rain is thunderous and the wind seems to catch the car, swaying us to one side then another. Simone slows down again but the car still lurches.

I know the sea is there below us, that we're getting closer to it; but I can feel it more than see it. Salt water seems to rise to meet the rain and the line between the two is blurred.

A massive streak of forked lightning crosses the sky; a tremendous crash of thunder follows, and goes on and on. The lightning dazzles and shows what was hidden before — waves like I have never seen.

'We should turn back!' I shout to be heard over the storm, and see the uncertainty on Simone's face, and then the fear.

It's too late.

The sea rises up and rushes towards us. Simone screams and hits the accelerator as if we can outrun this, and I'm full of panic and the angry joy of the wild storm at once. And then the water is over us and around us and the car is spinning, tumbling, and there are screams in my throat and Simone's, too.

The sea is drawing back again, but this time, it takes us with it. Drags us out, out. When it rises again we are tumbling down.

Simone is saying, open a window so that water comes and then we can open the door, and we both try but nothing works.

Water starts coming into the car.

The car is dropping. We're down deep and then deeper; the light is faint. It's rocking, settling, filling with water.

Simone is gripping my hand, hard. 'I love you, Holly.'

This time there *is* a second chance: to say what should have been said before, words that shouldn't be so hard yet somehow are.

'I love you, too, Mum.' I finally say the words she has been desperate to hear.

The car is swaying, not tumbling, now; water is coming in

faster, as if it has found new ways in. The level is rising and we undo our seat belts to stay up in the air space.

'Hold your breath while the car fills up,' Simone says. 'Then we can open the doors.'

The water is up to my chest now. My neck. My chin. I tilt my head to breathe as long as I can, then overbreathe, hold.

The air pocket is gone. We try our doors – nothing. Neither of them will open. Simone has her feet up against the window, kicking at the glass.

It holds.

No. *No.* This can't happen.

And Simone is choking on the water. She's striking her fists against the window. Her head is tilted back as if trying to find an air pocket that is no longer there.

Pain is swelling inside of me, bigger than the storm that did this to us. *Mummy. I love you.* Even if it is mostly three-year-old me that felt that way, it *is* real and all there is inside of me now.

And then she's still. Her eyes are open, but they're not seeing mine, or anything else. They never will again.

I close my eyes and switch off, shut down. There is no silver rope – what would be the point of it? I collapse inside, and everything *changes.*

I call the kin. It's not a net that has caught me, it's something else. Can they help?

They come.

They rock the metal cage, slam it against rocks. Again, and then again.

The back window breaks – glass fragments swirl in the water.

I'm at the end of what I can do without breathing. It's too late, isn't it?

Then there's intense pressure inside of me, pushing, making me move when all I want to do is stop. It makes me crawl through the car to the broken window, kick more of it out.

I crawl out. My last energy is gone.

Supported, gently. Taken up, up, to the surface. My head cradled when the air touches my skin. A shake and a slap when I don't breathe.

If I breathe, I can't stay with the kin – I'll die again. If I don't breathe, then I die for the last time.

I'm so weary.

There is pressure inside me again: the kin tell me to fight, to live, but is that enough?

Then a glimmer inside me remembers what I need more than peace:

Vengeance.

I cough, gasp in air again and again.

Both alive and dead.

89

I'm somewhere quiet, soft, floating, and don't want to leave it behind. Something plucks at my consciousness. Pulls me towards wakefulness.

Someone is holding my hand.

My eyelids flutter.

There is a sound – a sharp intake of breath? A movement and a distant bell.

Swift footsteps.

'I think she's waking up,' a voice says.

Is that what I'm doing? I don't want to.

'Tabby?'

I open my eyes. It's Elodie who is holding my hand. It's her, but it doesn't look like her at the same time. She looks old enough to be a grandmother now, something she never did before. There are tears in her eyes.

A doctor is here, a nurse. There are soft voices, talking to me and then about me, but I can't concentrate enough to make out the words. I'm sliding back to black.

90

The next time I wake up it is more of a certain thing. I feel myself in my own body again, anchored by gravity in this bed.

Elodie is in a chair next to me, asleep. It's night.

I sit up; my head spins. OK, this is a hospital. What happened? Why am I here?

Elodie is here, not Simone. What does that mean?

There's a flash of a car, the two of us in a car.

Simone came and got me.

Why?

Then water – water filling up the car. And then?

I don't know.

There's a flood of panic inside me that doesn't understand what has happened or what to attach these images to. There are machines next to me; there is an increased *beep-beep-beep*. A moment later the door opens, and a nurse is looking in.

'Hi, Tabby,' she says. And Elodie stirs now, wakes up. She smiles at me, but there is so much else behind her smile that is wrong.

'Where am I?'

'You're in the Bristol Royal Hospital for Children,' the nurse says.

'Bristol? How? Why? What's happened?' With each question my voice is raised further.

There's more beeping from machines. 'Hush. Everything is OK,' she says, in that soothing sort of voice that makes me even more certain that everything is the exact opposite of anything even approaching OK.

Another nurse — or is it a doctor? — comes in and something is done to a bag hanging on a stand next to me, and then there is a flood of calm inside me. My breathing slows.

'There now, Tabby, everything is all right,' the nurse says. 'Sleep is what you need now.'

But everything isn't all right, is it?

'Where's Simone?' I say, and I'm looking at Elodie and see the sadness there, and I *know*.

However I came back from what happened to us, she didn't follow.

Tears slide out of my eyes as my eyelids close.

The kin, my kind. We were together again, and then I was taken away. A sadness runs through me, as deep as the darkest trench in the sea.

I've been alone for too long.

91

An almost unimaginable ache of loss runs through me before I'm even awake. It holds me to the bed, keeps my eyes shut even when sleep is gone. It's somehow a separate thing, a weight on every part of me.

Someone strokes my hand.

'Tabby? Are you awake?' It's Elodie.

My eyelids flicker open.

'There you are. It's breakfast time.'

Hunger stirs inside me and I wake further, sit up.

'They've just brought it for you.' There's a tray that swings in front of me, but what is there isn't what I want – though what I want, I don't know.

'I'm not sure I can eat right now.'

'Try a little?'

I have a sip of juice. A few bites of toast.

'At least take your vitamins.' She shakes out a few tablets and gives me a glass of water, and I swallow them.

Soon I close my eyes and go back to sleep.

Sometime later I hear the door open and I stir, look up. A man in a white coat stands there.

He looks exhausted, but smiles. 'Good afternoon, Tabby. I'm Dr Evans. How are you feeling?'

I don't answer. Even if I wanted to, somehow putting words together in a sentence seems beyond what I can manage just now.

He exchanges a look with Elodie.

I settle back again and close my eyes, wishing for sleep.

They're talking in low voices. Something about trauma, memory.

Memory? Mine is fuzzy. There are things on the edges of my thoughts but if I try to focus on them, they slide away.

Trauma?

I open my eyes again. I try to *think* for a moment, turn my thought into words.

'What happened to me?' I say, with a frown. 'Why am I here?' I look between the two of them.

Elodie strokes my hand.

'Everything is going to be OK, Tabby,' she says. 'Go back to sleep.'

92

I wake up later, head full of troubling dreams that vanish as I open my eyes. I'm alone.

My thoughts are confused, and I try to focus.

So, I'm in a hospital – got that much. Private room.

Is the door locked?

Somehow, this is important. I check I'm not still connected to any beeping machines or have things in my veins; all clear. I get up; my head spins a little and I wait a moment then cross the room to try the door.

The handle turns. I open the door a little, look up the hall. There are doors in both directions; a desk with a nurse sitting there, but she is facing the other way and hasn't noticed me.

OK, the door isn't locked. I push it closed.

I feel dizzy, a bit sick, and cross back to the bed. I sit on the edge of it, legs hanging off the side.

Think, Tabby.

Something happened. Something bad.

Elodie has been here.

Simone. Something happened to her – to my mum. But then where is Ali?

There's a tap on the door – a nurse is there. 'Ah, I see you're awake. What would you like for dinner? We've got—'

'Is there any fish?'

'Yes.'

I'm still sitting there when she brings it later. My head doesn't feel as fuzzy but all I'm thinking about is fish, fresh fish. *Hunger.*

The tray is barely put in front of me before I start to eat. White fish. It's cooked – overcooked? – but I don't care.

She seems startled by how I'm eating it, with my hands. And I look down at them, wipe them with a napkin, and pick up a fork.

Dr Evans and Elodie are both back after dinner, along with another nurse.

'Hi, Tabby. Is it OK if I ask you a few questions?' Dr Evans says.

'Can I ask some, too?'

'Seems fair. You go first.'

'What happened? Why am I here?'

'What is the last thing you remember?'

'I . . . I don't know. Since when do you mean?'

'You were away, weren't you? For the summer, doing swimming training?'

Denzi. Ariel. Winning the relay! Sea swimming? The sea, from the gate. Denzi was gone. And . . . and . . .

A cat.

'There was a cat there. Dickens. He came to my room; I was feeding him bits of cheese.'

'And then?'

I shake my head. 'I don't have *and then*. Something happened, and then I was here. Where's my mum?'

'When was the last time you saw her?' he says, the sort of

thing you ask somebody when they can't find their keys. 'It might help if you close your eyes, and picture her in your mind.'

I don't close my eyes, but there is a flash of Simone. Her hair a halo, floating around her, eyes wide, staring.

I gasp and shake my head, trying to push it away.

'What is it, Tabby?'

'In the water,' I whisper. 'The last time I saw her. But how . . .'

My words trail away.

Rain, pounding and so full of fury that it bounced off the front of the car, the road. The sea, pulling back, back . . . then rushing for us – a *wall* of water?

'Tabby?'

'There was something . . . a wave? I don't know. It's like images flash in my mind, but if I try to focus on them, nothing is there.'

'It may take a little time. That's OK.'

'What about my mum? Is she' – I swallow – 'gone?'

'I'm afraid so, Tabby.'

He's confirming what I already guessed, but *knowing* it is worse than fearing it. I try to hold away the pain, to focus on here and now, and what is missing.

'Where's Ali? My dad. Why isn't he here?'

Dr Evans exchanges a look with Elodie. He nods, and she takes my hand.

'We don't know,' Elodie says. 'He's missing.'

'Missing? Was he caught in the water, too?'

'We think so.'

How can this be? What made it happen? My brain fumbles around for the words, and fails.

'What was that storm? I've never seen anything like it.'

'None of us have, not in England. It was a hurricane. It brought the storm surge.'

'And it got us. Because Simone came to get me? We were in the wrong place at just that moment.'

'A great deal of the coast was affected.'

'Did other people die?'

'I'm afraid so.'

My hand is at my wrist – it's bare, and I panic. 'Where's my bracelet? I was wearing it, wasn't I? Simone – my mum – gave it back to me. When she . . .' I shake my head. 'Please. Can I have my bracelet?'

'See if it is here, in patient property,' he says, and the nurse leaves the room. 'We'll get it for you if we can.'

The nurse brings it to me a little later and I hold it in my hands. Simone's bracelet. Mine now. Is it all that is left of her?

I was only just beginning to understand what my parents could mean to me – *meant* to me. And now she's gone, and he may be, too.

Elodie comes back later. She's got a bag.

'I've brought some clothes for you,' she says. 'They said you'll be able to go home soon.' She tucks it in the cupboard next to my bed. 'Time to get some sleep?'

'I'll try.'

'Don't forget your vitamins.' She gets me a glass of water, a few pills, and I swallow them down.

I lie down. 'Will you stay? Until I'm asleep?'

'Always.'

I close my eyes. Her hand is stroking my hair. Go home soon? I think of my room with the stupidly big bed and the amazing view. My notebook and phone tucked away in the wardrobe. But how can it be home without Simone and Ali there?

I'm sure there is no way I'll fall asleep, but even as I'm thinking that, my thoughts start to do that weird thing that means sleep is on its way – random images that don't go together flit through my mind.

The cat, licking my fingers with his rough, warm tongue.

What's that on his neck?

Walking in the dark.

A door: a door with a symbol.

Swimming in the sea . . .

93

The next morning Dr Evans comes back to see me again.

'Did you sleep OK?'

I nod. It surprised me, but I did. 'Can you explain what's wrong with me? Why I can't remember things the way I should?'

'Well, we've checked you over physically. Although you've had a bump to your head, it's unlikely to be responsible for any memory loss.'

'So it's all in my mind.'

'I wouldn't put it that way. It's most likely a form of psychogenic amnesia, which means something happened that you don't want to remember. Like you're protecting yourself from it.'

'Oh. Is that because if I remembered, it'd be so bad I wouldn't be able to cope?'

He tilts his head to one side, thinking. 'Something like that, but not being able to cope doesn't necessarily follow.'

'Will my memories come back?'

'Usually they do. Sometimes it takes hours, days, occasionally months, but usually the memory comes back. If – when – it does, you might need someone like me to talk to, to sort it out and deal with it.'

'Someone like you? Does that mean I'm leaving the hospital?'

'Soon. We just need to make sure you're OK. Maybe in a day

or two. How do you feel about checking out, going home with your grandmother?'

'I don't know.'

We talk about it a while longer, and somewhere along the way I realise: I'm being honest with him. Unlike how I was with Dr Rasheed or Dr Chang. Maybe it's because I have nothing left to hide.

Nothing I can remember, at least.

'If you're feeling up to it, there is someone who wants to talk to you this afternoon. He's from the police. His name is DCI Palmer. I'm told you've met him before.'

'What's the point when I can't remember anything properly?'

'He is aware that your memory has been affected by recent events, but he still wants to talk to you.'

Dr Evans and Elodie are with me when DCI Palmer comes in.

'Hi,' he says. And I do remember him; he's the one who told me Cate had died. More death.

'I know you've had a hard time, Tabby. I'm so sorry. But I need to ask you a few questions.'

'OK,' I say.

'It's about something we talked about before: The Circle.'

I'm surprised.

'You'd said that Cate said to beware of it — you thought it was something she was afraid of, but you didn't know what it was. Is that right?'

'Yes, but why are you asking me about this now?'

He glances at Dr Evans.

'We haven't had the news on or papers here,' Dr Evans says.

367

'We thought it might be too distressing. But if you need to explain, then do so.'

He nods. 'I understand. Well, Tabby, it's like this. There were a number of letters sent to news agencies and governments around the world, all postmarked the day before the hurricane hit England. There was another even more devastating hurricane in the US, also at around the same time. These letters spelled out the disasters that were about to happen, and said they were caused deliberately. The scientific community is split on whether that is possible, but the fact remains that the letters were written before the events happened, and both hurricanes were so quick to form and unusual that they escaped usual storm-watch protocols. The letters said that it was a warning of what would happen if climate change is allowed to continue unchecked, and that if certain measures to assure carbon neutrality aren't met within a few months, more would follow. And they were all signed by an organisation calling itself The Circle.'

I'm staring back at him, trying to make sense of what he said. Ali told us a while ago that they thought something was being planned against oil and gas interests. What happened wasn't against companies – it was against *everyone* who was in the wrong place when the hurricanes hit – but was it the big thing they were worried about?

And The Circle did this.

'Do you think The Circle killed Cate, too?'

'We don't know, but it is a possibility we are considering. Is there anything else you know about The Circle?'

There's a flash in my mind – an image – of four circles. I concentrate, trying to remember.

A note. In Cate's handwriting.

'There was a note I found that Cate hid in my notebook. It just said, beware The Circle. But there was a symbol drawn on it. I could get it from my bedroom – it was in the top of the wardrobe.'

Elodie shakes her head. 'Tabby, I'm sorry. The house was too close to the coast; it slipped into the sea.'

'What?'

'This is too much,' Dr Evans says.

'No, I want to know.' Another thought crashes into me: Ariel and all the others. 'What about the swim school? What happened there?'

Elodie and Dr Evans exchange a glance and I see it in the way they look at each other before they decide what to say.

'Did the hurricane go there, too? Tell me!'

'I'm afraid so,' Elodie says. 'That part of the coast was badly hit.'

'And Ariel, and all the others at the school? Did they get away?'

'I'm sorry, Tabby. There were no survivors found from the school.'

I stare back at Elodie, trying to take this in. Ariel, Zara and the rest of them – gone? I never knew most of them, not even their names. I didn't even *try* to remember all their names; it seems so wrong now that they're gone.

'I think that's enough for today,' Dr Evans says in a voice that no one sensible would argue with.

'One last thing,' Palmer says. 'Can you describe this symbol that Cate left you on a note?'

I swallow, trying to keep myself rational, under control, when all I want to do is howl. 'I could draw it if you want.'

A pen, a piece of paper, are found. At first my hand is too shaky, but I breathe in deeply and steady it.

Four circles, in two rows of two, the edges just touching.

'There,' I say, but there's something about it as I look at what I've drawn, some other connection to . . . something. I shake my head in frustration at these gaps in my memory.

'Thank you, Tabby. The letters sent by The Circle had a symbol very like that. If there is anything else at all that you remember about The Circle or things Cate may have said, you'll let us know, won't you? Even if it doesn't seem relevant.'

'Of course,' I say.

'I'll leave a card,' Palmer says, and he gives one to Elodie, one to me.

He and Dr Evans say goodbye. As the door closes behind them Elodie comes closer, sits in the chair Palmer had been in.

She takes my hand. 'I'm sorry, Tabby. I hope that wasn't too much at once,' she says.

'What else has happened that I don't know about?'

'I think that pretty much covers it. We haven't been keeping secrets from you, Tabby. We just didn't want to overload your ability to cope.'

'Our house is gone?'

'Afraid so. But you have a home still, Tabby: with me. Always.'

'When?'

'Dr Evans said he'll talk to you in the morning, and if everything is all right, I can take you home then.'

Another new place to live. Another adult – however lovely she may have been to me so far – that I don't really know to live with. Someone else I might grow to care for and then have taken away.

'I'll keep this safe for you,' she says, and takes Palmer's card, puts it in her pocket with the one he gave her.

'Now here are your vitamins.' She pours a glass of water, shakes them out into my hand. I swallow them. 'Try to get some sleep; we'll get you home soon.'

She kisses my forehead, then waves to me from the door. As she does, her sleeve falls back and I see – there on the inside of her arm above her wrist – she has a tattoo. I hadn't noticed it before. It's a four-leaf clover.

There's something about that that niggles in my mind, but my thoughts feel thick, sluggish, and I slip into sleep.

Images, sensations, feelings *flash through my kaleidoscope mind and mix in with each other almost too fast to follow.*

Circles. Four circles: hidden in a pattern.

Thud thud. *A rock against bars. An almost human nightmare with Ariel's face, but not her eyes.*

Circles, in green.

A four-leaf clover?

Thud thud.

Circles hidden in green flash in and out of focus.

I want to be free of these things, to slip to black, but they won't go away.

Underwater?

Eyes open, wide and staring.

94

I breathe in in a rush. My heart is pounding.

Four-leaf clover – circles – circles hidden in a four-leaf clover?

The symbol of the Penrose Clinic. On Elodie's arm.

What does this mean?

My brain . . . *urgggh!* It's maddening: so sluggish, I can't think right. They are going to release me tomorrow so they don't think anything is medically wrong or they wouldn't do that. I don't believe this is all from trauma; it's like something is stopping me from thinking and working out my memories about what happened.

Almost like I've been . . . drugged.

My door opens and the night nurse peers in.

'Hi, Tabby,' she says. 'I saw you sitting up. Is everything OK?'

'I had a bad dream.'

'Oh dear. Do you want to talk about it?'

I shake my head.

'If you're having trouble sleeping, I can ask the duty doctor if you can take something?'

'I think I'll be OK. Thanks. I haven't been taking anything like that before, have I? To help me sleep?'

'Just that first night. You've been sleeping a lot without anything since then.'

Then there's only one other thing it could be.

'Sure. Oh, I think I forgot to take my vitamins.'

'What vitamins?'

'The ones my grandmother gives me.'

She half frowns. 'You shouldn't be taking anything here we don't know about; I'll ask her about that tomorrow. Try to get back to sleep. You can push the call button if you need anything, all right?'

'Yes. Thank you.'

I obediently lie down and close my eyes – best to fake being asleep, in case she comes back to check on me.

There is so much mess in my head that I can't think through, but as if there are red flags inside me, that tattoo on Elodie's arm made me remember. The Circle symbol; the Penrose Clinic four-leaf clover that hides the circles. They're one and the same.

Palmer said The Circle were claiming responsibility for the hurricanes here and in the US, that they were blackmailing the world to stop climate change. It's like Simone had said might happen: they've given up talking to governments who won't listen. While I can't argue with their aim, what they've done, what they're threatening to do? They're terrorists.

Elodie has the Penrose tattoo on her arm; Malina had the circles on her shoulder – the symbol Cate drew.

The nurse didn't know about the so-called vitamins Elodie has been giving me. Has she been drugging me, to stop me thinking clearly?

She is taking me home tomorrow, and sooner or later she's bound to take me to the Penrose Clinic. Would I ever get out of there again if they find out what I know?

I have to get out of here before that can happen.

It has to be tonight.

95

I keep still, eyes half open, waiting for the nurse to go past on her rounds, struggling to stay awake the whole time.

When she goes by what feels like an age later, I count down a minute, then get up. Hoping to fool a casual glance through the door, I bundle pillows under the blankets.

I open the cupboard next to my bed and see the bag Elodie left for tomorrow. I take it out. Inside are jeans, a T-shirt, trainers.

I get dressed quickly in the dark; as quickly as I can, that is, when I still feel thick, clumsy.

It'd be so easy to just get back into bed . . .

No.

Where am I going? What am I going to do?

I don't know. One thing at a time. Concentrate on getting away first.

I open my door a crack, look out into the hallway. I don't know the best way to go to get out – I don't remember coming here – but the nurse went right, so I go left.

There are stairs at the end of the hall. I go down a few flights to the bottom level and peek out the door. Another ward? It's quiet. I go down the hall, afraid someone will come and demand to know what I'm doing, but I reach the door at the end undisturbed. It leads to what must be a main hall; there are signs everywhere to different departments.

I follow the signs to Emergency. Cate always said the best place to go unnoticed is in a crowd, and that's where it'll be busy at night.

There are people in chairs, staff bustling about, and people lying on gurneys, waiting, in various stages of distress. I see the exit across on the other side and want to get out of here as soon as I can, but there is BBC news up on TV. When I see what is on the screen I find myself slipping into a seat to watch.

'And now the latest reports on the hurricane, devastating storm surge and floods that hit the southern coast of England. The confirmed death toll has risen to over two thousand with many more still missing and feared dead. Emergency shelters are stretched. Churches are opening doors again tonight as more fleeing the southern coast reach nearby centres. Those displaced by the hurricane are estimated in the region of two hundred thousand.'

It's *real*. Not that I thought it wasn't, but with my memory being such a mess and these images flashing in my mind, it felt more like a dream, like a waking nightmare. But it isn't; it really happened. And not just to me and my parents.

There's a map; it shows which parts of the coast were affected. I study it; northern Cornwall looks clear, so Jago should be OK.

The reports continue, going beyond the UK now. The eastern coast of the US has been badly hit. The sheer scale of it all and the numbers of people killed, displaced, are too big to get my mind around.

And The Circle say they did this?

The horror I'm feeling has me immobilised, staring at the news and unable to look away. But I give myself a mental shake.

I don't know how much time I've got before they start looking for me.

Get up, get out of here.

I start to cross the room to the exit, but stop short when I glance back at the TV screen.

'And this just in. There have been reports of dolphins rescuing a girl off the coast of Exmouth. Images recovered from a water-damaged phone seem to show a girl being supported in the water by a group of dolphins, swimming side by side. The photos were taken by a local fisherman who'd been caught in the storm and was heading back to shore when the dolphins appeared. Once the girl was safely on board his vessel, the dolphins circled the boat until it was almost to shore. Experts were divided on whether any of this was possible, but here are the photographs.'

They start interviewing the fisherman but I'm standing there, staring, at the images still shown on the side of the screen. A girl, face not clear, with dark hair like mine across it. Wearing dark shorts and T-shirt. The same as I wore that day. Dolphins, as the newsreader said, supporting her.

I don't have to see the face clearly to know: it's me.

Dolphins saved me?

Those other times, too. Ariel said a dolphin led her to me when they pulled me up from the bottom of the sea. The day I found out Cate had died, when I thought a dolphin had nudged me up to breathe. A strong sense of unreality is weirdly mixed inside me with a feeling of, *Yes, that is as it should be.*

'Excuse me,' someone says, trying to get around me to an empty chair.

Startled back to where I am, what I need to do, I turn and

walk to the exit. I keep my head turned away from the CCTV, all the time wanting to go back to see the images again, as if this will all make more sense if I do.

Don't think about this now. Focus on what must be done.

Outside, I pause. Which way should I go?

It looks busier to the right so I go that way. I'm tired; I go past a bench and have to make myself keep going. Concentrate: one foot in front of the other, and again and again.

What will happen when they realise I'm gone? *When* will that happen?

It depends how thoroughly the night nurse is checking on me. At latest it'll be in the morning, but it could be sooner.

Once they notice I'm gone, then what? A missing patient who is underage with possible amnesia and mental health issues – the police will be involved. But there is a lot going on at the moment for them to focus resources on finding me; I'm more worried about Elodie.

I need to find somewhere I can wait out these drugs in my system, then work out what to do. She gave me her so-called vitamins twice a day, so I'm hoping they will start wearing off tomorrow morning.

For now, just keep walking.

I go past houses, businesses – buildings that blur into each other. Walking without falling over is taking most of my attention. After a while I go past a green area and wonder if I should stop, find a hidden corner to sleep.

But then I hear voices: are they singing? I walk on a bit further.

Yes, people are singing, holding candles. Is this a candlelit vigil for those lost in the hurricane? They are standing in front of a huge, grand church – Bristol Cathedral, a sign says.

On the news it said that churches were opening their doors. Is this one of them?

I stay at the back of those with candles. Someone leads a prayer; many are crying.

Are they praying for people they know personally, or just everyone who was hurt or killed?

Like my parents. Ariel, maybe Isha and all the others, too.

I've never had anything to do with religion, not in the way most people mean it – Cate never took me to church or anything like that – but there was a spiritual relationship we had with the natural world, and the promises we made to protect sun, sea, earth, sky.

Yet the thought that these people might be praying for Simone, Ali and my friends? Somehow it both makes me want to cry and soothes me inside, just a little.

After a while I make my way around the crowd of people, into the open doors of the church. There's a man by the door – is he a vicar? He's got one of those collar things on.

There are people lying down on the floor of the church, scattered all over this grand building, under stained glass.

'Do you have room for one more?' I say.

'Always.' He smiles. 'We've been asked to take names, in case people are being looked for.'

'Of course,' I say. I need to answer fast and haven't prepared: I put my friend's and doctor's names together. 'I'm Ariel. Ariel Evans.'

'Age?'

'Eighteen,' I lie, guessing if they know I'm a minor there'll be more trouble.

'Welcome, Ariel. Are you hungry or thirsty? There are sandwiches and bottles of water.'

'Just tired.'

He hands me a blanket. 'Sadly, we're out of pillows.'

'No problem.'

He gestures towards the far end where there are women and children.

I look around until I spot a bit of empty floor that isn't in direct view of the doors. I wrap the blanket around me, curl up with my head on my arm, and close my eyes.

96

I must sleep later than most. When I wake there aren't many people left around me. I get up, trying to unkink my neck and fold my blanket. There are some other people by the door now. The sandwiches are gone; my stomach is growling.

'Good morning,' a woman says. 'Hope you slept OK.'

'I did, thanks.' I hand over the blanket.

'There are some government agencies sorting places to sleep where it isn't on the floor. They just need some details.'

'Could I find a bathroom first?'

She tells me where it is. I do the usual, wash my hands, and splash water on my face. Drink from the tap.

I stare at myself in the mirror. OK, I look like me and feel more like me than I have in days: whatever drugs were in my system are gone or nearly gone at least. I shy away from trying to think about what I can and can't remember. First, I need a plan.

I smooth my hair with my hands and as I do, I see the bracelet on my wrist.

I sigh. There isn't any other option, is there? I slip out the back way.

The sun is shining relentlessly. My stomach is growling and I'm thirsty. I don't know Bristol; I don't know where to find pawnshops, but I do know it has to be soon so I can get something to eat, something else to wear — since what I have on will be known by at least Elodie, and she may also tell the police — and get away from here.

Shops are starting to open. I ask in a second–hand shop where to find pawnshops; the woman there doesn't seem surprised. Is this the sort of question that is being asked a lot lately? I follow her directions and think about what to say on the way, trying to remember how Cate did it in Manchester.

In the first shop, I browse. They don't seem to have high value stuff so probably not a good choice, but I'll use it as a practice run.

'Can I help you?' a woman says, but her tone says she doubts it.

'I have a bracelet I want to sell.' I take it off my wrist and hold it in my hands.

She raises an eyebrow. 'Pretty, but not worth very much. I'd give you . . . twenty pounds.'

'You're kidding.'

'I don't kid.'

I walk out, shocked.

A few more pawnshops, with not much better results. The most I'm offered is fifty pounds.

I'm getting hungrier, thirstier, hotter and more frustrated. Can they see my desperation, is that the problem? Maybe I should I walk back to that church and see if they will give me something to eat, and try again later.

Undecided, I keep walking and come across another pawnshop. OK, I'll give it one more try.

I go in, look around.

'Can I help you with anything?' a man says, a sceptical look on his face. And I'm getting so close to losing it that I just think *stuff it*, and veer to the truth.

'Look. My mum died in the hurricane and my dad is missing. I'm hungry and thirsty and need money. All I have is my mum's bracelet to sell, but I need a good price for it so don't even try to offer something ridiculous or I'll go away and starve.'

He stares at me a moment, face unreadable, then his expression softens and he sighs.

'Sit,' he says, and pushes me into a chair. He goes behind the counter and through a door behind, and comes back a moment later holding out a bottle of water, a wrapped sandwich. 'Eat my lunch. I'll get by without, and then we'll talk.'

Now my eyes are filling with tears. He puts them on the counter next to me.

'Go on, eat it before I change my mind. It's my favourite – tuna with little bits of cut-up celery and mustard mayonnaise that my wife makes special for me.'

It's good. And I'm eating it too fast.

He takes the lid off the bottle of water. 'Now drink that.'

I take it, have a long drink. 'Thank you,' I say.

'Now show me the bracelet.'

I take it off, hand it to him.

He whistles. Takes out an eyepiece thing and studies it. 'It's a beaut. Emeralds and sapphires, solid 14-carat gold. Are you sure it's not stolen? That it is yours?'

'I promise you, it's mine.'

'This isn't a charity. I need to keep my family in tuna sandwiches.' He's thinking. 'Tell you what. Value is hard to estimate in a piece like this. If I base it on the stones and the gold . . . Hang on.' He's got a calculator, scales. 'OK. I'll give you six hundred and forty pounds for it.'

My jaw drops.

He scowls. 'OK, six eighty, but that's it.'

'Thank you! Yes.'

'You got any ID?'

I shake my head.

'Name?'

'Ariel Evans.'

He writes it out – my fake name, his, a description of the bracelet, the price. Then he signs it and points to the place for me to sign.

'I'll get the money.' He disappears through the door at the back, then reappears a bit later with an envelope. 'Last chance,' he says. 'Are you sure?'

'Can I hold it?' I say, and he hands it back to me.

The bracelet that Cate gave me, that she stole from Simone. That I remembered as a baby on Simone's knee. And I have to let it go. I know there is no real choice, but it hurts so much. I hand it back to him, tears in my eyes.

'If you come back with the money and interest – OK, just the money – within six months, you can have it back. I'll put it away until then, all right? In my safe. So if you come and don't see it, don't panic. It'll be locked up in there. Have you got a place to go?'

I nod. It was unformed in the back of my mind, but I do.

There is really only one place I can go. 'I'm going to use this money to get there. To go to a friend.'

'OK.' He gives me a copy of the contract along with the envelope of money. 'Stay safe.'

When I look afterwards, he's actually given me seven hundred pounds.

Wow.

97

The train station in Bristol is chaos, full of people trying to get places they can't get trains to any more – all stations south of Taunton are closed because of floods, wind damage, storm surge or all three. Extra information desks have been set up, with harried staff and long queues while they try to sort everyone out, and I hope no one notices me enough to remember my face. I'm careful to turn away from CCTV, to avoid eye contact, and have different clothes and a scarf I bought from a second-hand shop on the way, wrapped around my hair.

There is no way to avoid talking to someone, though, to work out how to get where I want to go. My head still feels muddled from being drugged, and I'm exhausted by the time I get through the queue to information; even more so when I find out it is going to take a train and three buses. Can I even manage this?

One step at a time.

I buy a ticket to Taunton from a machine and work out which platform I need. The train isn't for twenty minutes and I start to make my way through the crowds to the ticket barriers. There's a ripple of annoyed sounds somewhere behind and I glance back. Two women are pushing through the queues, not waiting their turn.

One of them looks towards me just as I turn towards her.

It's Malina. She sees me but there is no surprise, just

determination, and despite the resistant crowd they're getting closer.

Panic rips through me and my fuzzy head is gone. I can't run, caught up in all these people moving forwards to the ticket gates – I'm trapped.

Now I'm at the gate. People are pushing behind me, impatient, and I don't know what to do . . .

I put my ticket in and go through. My train isn't for ages; they're getting closer. What now?

There's a whistle being blown a few platforms down – another train is about to leave.

Run.

I dodge around people and get there just as the doors are closing and throw myself at the gap. I'm caught – they close on me then open again. I go through fully and they close again.

I look back the way I came through the door window. Malina and whoever is with her are running towards the train, saying something to the guard on the platform but the doors stay closed. They reach my door just as the train begins to pull away, leaving them behind.

I lean back on the door, heart pounding. That was so close. They nearly caught me – what would have happened if they did?

'Is everything OK, love?' a man says, and now I notice his and other eyes, all looking at me.

I nod. 'Thanks, I'm fine,' I say, and remember to school my face to calm, to look down and away.

What next?

The announcements tell me this is a London train. They'll think I'm going there, won't they?

I get off at the next stop. Go to the ladies, change my top, take off the scarf and tie up my hair, hoping that it makes me look different enough to not be easily spotted in a crowd.

What I need to do is get on the next train going the other way. Transfer in Bristol. Stick to my plan.

But I'm scared. What if they're still watching for me in Bristol?

Why would they? They think I've gone the other way. They're probably on the next train to London.

I get on the next train back. At Bristol I stay behind the barriers, find the platform for Taunton. I want to both keep my head down and look all around at the same time, and struggle to maintain a semblance of calm when inside all I want to do is run and hide.

My train pulls in at last and I get on. No one follows that I can see.

Later I'm staring out the window, heart rate nearing normal. Thinking.

It's tempting to go to ground, just disappear; to keep out of whatever The Circle has done or may yet attempt to do. I could do this. All my years with Cate were like training for this exact moment.

But how can I? The Circle has caused so many deaths, such suffering. They could do it again – they've threatened as much. What if there is something I could do to stop them?

My thoughts are clearer now. The details of what happened with Simone – in the water – are still uncertain, and trying to think about it makes me flinch away. But what came before that has fallen back into place. The reason I ran, the horrors hidden under the clinic.

Penrose babies like me, Isha and Zara – maybe there were more of us – were brought together at the swim school. That *can't* be coincidence. Not when the Penrose Clinic was also hidden at the school. Did they do something to change us in their test tubes? Not as drastic as the girl-fish, but did they do something else?

Isha told me she felt like a freak. Ariel said as much also, and that she fakes it all the time. At some level I've always known I'm different. From things Cate said and didn't say, she did, too.

How am I different?

I can hold my breath longer than is reasonable.

This anomaly in my blood that everyone else was so interested in was dismissed as unimportant by the Penrose Clinic. But they said my blood was better at carrying oxygen; that would help hold my breath for longer.

Dolphins seem to come out of nowhere to help me.

Anything else? My broken arm healed faster than it should. So did that cut on my knee.

I can get by with very little sleep, so long as I'm near the sea.

What do all of these things have in common as an objective? Is it all about swimming – and staying underwater – for longer and longer?

And then there is the something else hidden inside me, the *other* that appears sometimes in the sea, and sometimes in my dreams. Somehow I feel my dreams must hold a key to working this all out – dreams that Dr Chang at the Penrose Clinic was all too interested in.

Overall, if I accept I am different, that something was done to make me this way, *why*?

And what about the others? Ariel said she wasn't a Penrose baby, which made me doubt it all. I'd been so sure she must be. But then how about that lookalike fish with her face?

Then I realise something else. Whatever happened at the swim school when the hurricane hit, Malina survived. How about all the others? Not just the staff, but the students?

Whatever the Penrose Clinic and The Circle were doing at the swim school, if The Circle caused the hurricane, they knew what was coming. They could have decided who lived or died by taking them away before it hit.

There are too many unknowns to process. I need help to find the answers; I need someone who understands how the world works and knows how to find things out better than I do.

We're nearly at Taunton now, and still I'm questioning: am I doing the right thing?

I hope so.

I could only come up with two options. I don't have his card — Elodie made sure of that — but I could call Scotland Yard, ask for DCI Palmer. But what could I tell him? That something feels very wrong about the Penrose Clinic — that they are a front for The Circle — based only on intuition and the use of circles inside their four-leaf clover. And Elodie is a part of it, based on a tattoo I saw across a room on her arm. I think I'd be locked up straight away and face a lifetime of doctors who want to get into my head. Or even worse: I could be handed over to Elodie.

The only other option is Jago. My friend.

I've tried and tried, but can't remember his number. I

probably shouldn't call him, anyhow – the police might think of it and monitor his phone, since I called him that time from Manchester. I'll find him at the beach where we met if I watch and wait long enough, I'm sure of it.

Will he help me? I hope so.

Jago, I'll be there soon. Please be all that I think you can be.

If not, I will find another way.

Acknowledgements

No matter where I find myself in the world, nothing makes me happier than being on or near the sea. The wilder the seas the better – I've memories of being out in a storm so violent even the crew were ill, and loving every minute of it. With global warming our seas and planet are under threat in a way they never have been before. This is something I had to write about.

Thanks to Dr Melanie Thornton for her insights into emergency medicine. Thanks to George Kirk and her understanding cat, Ember, for Fitbit experiments. And Anita Loughrey: thank you for spending a day of your holidays exhaustively photographing Bossiney Cove and surrounds in Cornwall.

Thank you to Megan Larkin and everyone at Orchard Books for launching and sustaining my career, and also for first excitement with Tabby's story. Thank you to Tig Wallace and everyone at Hodder Children's Books for taking it from there, and to Michelle Brackenborough for a cover of extreme awesomeness!

And finally, to Graham and Scooby, my yin and yang – calm and chaos. Thank you. I couldn't do it without you.

TABBY'S SEARCH FOR
ANSWERS CONTINUES IN

COMING JULY 2021
AVAILABLE TO PRE-ORDER NOW!